THE TADA
CONVENTION

A Jordan Kline Thriller

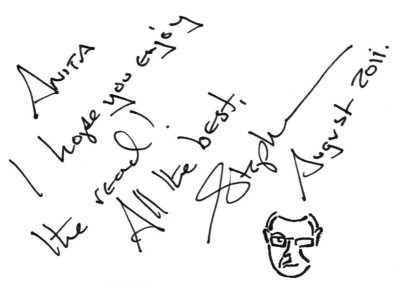

Anita
I hope you enjoy
the read.
All the best.
Stephen
August 2011.

STEPHEN W. AYERS

For Zen, a handsome, true and faithful companion and part of our family.

ACKNOWLEDGMENTS

Although I very much enjoyed the adventure of writing my first book in the Jordan Kline Series, and my first book ever, it would not have seen the light of day without the help of many people to whom I owe a lot of thanks.

Firstly my wife Mali and my children Natalie and Nimrod who encouraged me to continue writing and showed so much patience along the way. The book would not have been published without their help and creativity in all areas of the "Taba" project.

I also would like to thank all our friends who agreed readily to read the draft manuscript and who pushed me to publish and continue writing the Jordan Kline series: Neil Rabinovitch, Dunnzy Kaufman, Laura Stadler, Eva Fodor, Mimi Gottfried, Bonnie Loubert and Ido Rosen.

A special thanks to Aaron Milrad and Brenda Coleman for their invaluable help and encouragement to continue writing.

And finally a special thanks to all those I have encountered and worked with on the long and winding road of my international career in the hotel industry, guests and colleagues alike. I could not have written The Taba Convention without experiencing all those colorful years.

THE TABA CONVENTION

CONVENTION

A Jordan Kline Thriller

PROLOGUE

Peace in the Middle East had always seemed impossible, a dream that could never approach reality. Another war was always just around the corner, inevitable. Deep-rooted hatred of the other side lay embedded within both the Arab and Israeli national souls. Politicians gave speeches about the need to negotiate, but no one broke the status quo. Talking of peace was always in fashion, and all politicians were doing their best to look as if it were possible all along.

The President of the United States had finally run out of patience with both the Israelis and the Palestinians. He instructed the Secretary of State to announce unilaterally that agreement had been reached, and that a peace convention would be held in September.

The Israelis woke up to headlines in both the *Yediot Ahronoth* and *Maariv* newspapers that screamed up at them from the newsstands: "Peace convention to be held in Taba. U.S President forces hand of Prime Minister and Palestinians. Agreement to be signed at Taba."

The Israeli left rejoiced. The right was enraged. The Palestinian leadership was taken by surprise. Most people were happy at the chance that peace was perhaps near. The world waited. Would it be possible? With so many against peace at any cost, could the President pull off the biggest foreign policy coup of generations?

Was the Taba Convention about to make peace in the Middle East a reality?

CHAPTER ONE

ALP GRUM, CANTON GRAUBUNDEN, SWITZERLAND. FRIDAY, AUGUST 10TH.

A crisp, high-altitude summer breeze took the heat out of the relentless sunshine. The crystal clear visibility and views were breathtaking. Two thousand meters up, Alp Grum was the highest point reached by the open tourist trains that left St. Moritz. The train climbed the mountains before making its laborious way down into Tirano in Italy. The view was picture-perfect, a Swiss postcard—even down to the cows with bells grazing in the lush green pastures on the mountainsides.

The morning had been excruciatingly boring for Yuval Eisenstadt of the Mossad. He had followed the Palestinian activist since leaving Israel, catching the same flight two days earlier out of Ben Gurion International to Kloten Airport. Since arriving in Zurich, the Palestinian had done nothing to arouse suspicion.

The Mossad always dispatched two agents when tailing people abroad, but this mission seemed so routine that only Yuval had been assigned. It was a break with agency protocol. Yuval had tried to argue the decision with no success. He did not like being alone. He felt naked, exposed.

Mohammed Iyad from Gaza had been the model tourist;

he strolled the Limmat-Quai and window-shopped on the famous Zurich shopping street, the Bahnhofstrasse. It would be extremely difficult to lose Iyad in Zurich. Shunning modern suits, Iyad wore the traditional Thoub one-piece gown with a brown belt holding in his considerable girth. The Keffiyeh Arab headdress figured prominently on his large round head. He stood out like a sore thumb among the colorful summer crowds of tourists and the exquisitely suited Swiss bankers going about their business.

Yuval knew from the briefing in Jerusalem that his quarry Iyad was involved in furniture imports and supplies to shops and hotels in Israel. He had expected to follow Iyad on a tour of Swiss factories that made the wooden country-style furniture that he imported. He had been wrong. Apart from a brief stop at a large shop on Niederdorfstrasse where he had seen Iyad in earnest conversation with another Arab for about ten minutes, the two days had been spent endlessly walking the beautiful, clean streets of Zurich.

Getting up early on the third day, Yuval idled near the front desk after a hurried coffee. Iyad appeared and he followed him as he left the hotel. He caught the same train that arrived at St. Moritz at ten-thirty in the morning. Iyad then bought a ticket for the five past eleven mountain train to Alp Grum from platform twelve. Arriving just in time before departure, Yuval had been fortunate to find a seat on the open wagon three rows behind the Palestinian. Yuval thought there must be a good reason for the trip, perhaps a clandestine meeting that he would witness high up on the mountains. A momentary surge of fear washed over him. The train pulled into Alp Grum with typical Swiss precision at twelve noon.

Climbing up a winding track to a cafe perched on a ridge above the train station, Yuval sipped on a double espresso. He saw Iyad converse with a blue-coated railway worker down below. The feeling of unease crept back. They looked like they knew each other.

Iyad started on a short hike along one of the many trails that led past mountain streams and meadows and the ever-present views of the deep valleys and the Italian landscape far down below.

The Palestinian joined a group of three hikers, and it took Yuval a second before he realized that they all knew each other. He knew in that instant that Iyad had lured him here, that he must have been made some time ago in Zurich.

He pulled out his cell phone. He looked at the screen and another wave of panic hit him. No wireless reception. Goddamn it, they must have been too high up there. There had to be a landline in the restaurant; he would make the call from there.

He hurried back to the station and entered the restaurant to place a call.

Yuval brushed against another railway man in the narrow corridor on the way to the telephone. It was wall-mounted in the corner, and Yuval was relieved to see that it took coins and not a phone card. He lifted the receiver with one hand and searched in his pocket for some Swiss francs with his other hand.

He put the receiver up to his ear. Dead. The damn line was dead. They had gotten there before him. Following the wire from the phone, he traced it along the wall. It was cut in two places, a gap of five centimeters cut to make sure that no new connection was possible. The trap was closing in on him. Like a fly trapped in a spider's web. This was not supposed to be the way it happened. He had been trained to hunt, not to be the hunted.

He heard the train pull in after the loudspeaker announcement.

He walked briskly along the platform toward the train. Fresh air washed over his face, but the foul stench of fear clung to him.

He chose the open car, and sat at the very back of the last one. Other passengers got on and took their seats in the middle of the car.

He spotted a group of dirty and disheveled looking railway workers dressed in stained blue overalls and muddy black work boots who were taking the opportunity to catch a lift down the mountain. He watched as they clambered into the last car behind the open one, a freight wagon.

From where he sat, Yuval could see Iyad still talking to the hikers. For a brief, terrifying moment their eyes met and the man let a small smile of satisfaction creep into his face. Iyad looked over his shoulder and acknowledged the group of workers. It was clearly done with the intention that Yuval see it, and he did. The execution had been given the green light.

The train started its descent to St. Moritz and briefly stopped at Bernina Diavolezza to pick up some hikers before continuing. As the train entered an avalanche tunnel, two of the railway workers left the freight car. Under the cover of darkness and the thunderous noise of the train reverberating in the tunnel, they came up swiftly behind Yuval. The young agent could not have realized how fast his death came. They crossed from the freight car behind him and stood on the links that held the cars together. It was as if he had chosen the ideal seat for them to carry out his execution.

They moved fast. It was quick and quiet. The heavily built Arab pinned him firmly against the side of the car. Yuval tried to scream for help, but his screams were drowned by the noise in the tunnel. The other Palestinian crushed his windpipe and broke his neck in one short, violent movement. It was over before the train pulled out of the tunnel, coming out once more into the clear, serene mountain air.

Iyad climbed into the freight car, bent down, and grabbed hold of the body by the pullover, lifting it up into a sitting position. He smiled as he arranged the hair above the lifeless eyes staring back at him. He pulled out a camera and took a few shots of the corpse. Then he lifted his arm and waved to the men with a gesture of dismissal. Two of the Palestinians opened the freight door and dragged the body to the edge of the car. They waited until the train was running parallel with a precipice and dumped the body overboard into a ravine. They watched it bounce off outcrops of rock until it disappeared below far from sight. It would not be found for a very long time, and then probably by wild animals.

BOLOGNA, ITALY.
SUNDAY, AUGUST 12TH.

Gilad Dolev was pleased when he received his assignment. The telephone had rung in his small Tel Aviv apartment on Weisel Street, a small side street off Ben Gurion Boulevard not far from City Hall. His boss had ordered him to the control office the following morning.

Taking the usual precautions, Gilad made sure that no one had followed him before entering the old building at 126 Hayarkon Street opposite the Sheraton and Ramada hotels. The salty humid smell of the nearby sea was heavy in the air, and Gilad noticed the damage that the salt had made on the exterior of the building. Rust was showing on the balcony rails, and the paint was peeling off the façade in many places. Still, it was a good location—just a two-minute walk from the great beaches of Tel Aviv. Below the hotels there was a wide stretch of golden sandy beach and the deep blue inviting and cooling waters of the shimmering Mediterranean. What a waste of prime real estate, Gilad thought, as he mounted the narrow staircase leading to the safe apartment. He would have been happy to live here.

David Applebach, his controller, was approaching retirement and it showed in the disinterested approach to his work. A short, chubby Cockney with a shock of white hair and a weather-beaten face, he motioned Gilad into the office and gave him his orders. Follow a contractor named Hofstein who worked with marble, was all he offered. "Follow him and tell me what he does."

By seven a.m. the next day he had passed all airport security checks and sat at the "Green Spot" refreshment counter in the departure lounge at Ben Gurion International Airport. He sipped on an espresso while waiting.

The flight to Milan was announced. Gilad waited for most of the passengers to go through before paying, showing his boarding card at the gate, and descending to the transit bus.

Once landed, Gilad was the first to receive his bag and clear passport formalities.

The girl from Hertz was waiting for him with the keys, and by the time Hofstein appeared, Gilad already had the keys to the nondescript grey Opel Vectra. It was parked outside the arrivals hall.

A black Ford Sierra pulled up as Hofstein exited the terminal. He climbed into the front passenger side and the car pulled away. Gilad guided his car out into the traffic a safe distance away and followed. The traffic was light on the outskirts of Milan, and the Sierra soon eased on to the autostrada to Bologna. It stopped briefly to pay for the toll at the highway entrance.

Arriving in Bologna, Gilad enjoyed the winding one-way streets and the old ocher-colored buildings with columns, so typical of this historic city. He kept the Sierra in his sights as best he could as he followed down the winding cobbled streets.

Hofstein headed out towards Modena driving parallel to the autostrada on a secondary feeder road and took the turn to Castelfranco.

Driving into town, the Sierra turned into a large yard filled with stacks of marble of every size and color. Gilad pulled the car to a stop outside the perimeter fence. Careful not to be made, he found a spot shielded from the yard by a rusty shipping container. He saw Hofstein enter the offices of the "Castelfranco Marble Co." He decided that he had the time to call in his daily report to Tel Aviv control so as to be free later. He fished his cell phone out of his pocket. As it would be a recorded message, he spoke clearly and precisely, stating everything that he had seen since arriving in Italy. Not wanting to leave out any details he included the Sierra number plates and reported his present stakeout at the marble factory.

Hofstein reappeared and climbed back into the Ford. The car pulled out of the yard and onto the main road kicking up a cloud of dry summer dust behind it. It headed back towards Bologna taking what seemed to be a country route. The road became narrower and rough as it ran through the farmland. He followed from a distance. The road began to wind through the fields, but he had no trouble keeping the Sierra in sight ahead of him. He could see the cloud of sand and dust it kicked up behind it. On both sides of the road were cornfields, golden and swaying in the summer breeze. It reminded him of an impressionist painting by Van Gogh.

Hofstein turned into what appeared to be a field and hit the brakes. Gilad slowed the car. A large, rusty red tractor turned out of the field and onto the narrow road in his direction. Suddenly Gilad's heart started to pound in his chest. He could almost hear it. He realized now why Hofstein had taken the scenic route. He slammed on the brakes and skidded to a halt in a cloud of dust and gravel. He felt weak and numb. The sun reflecting off the tractor windscreen blinded him. Through the dust he thought he saw Hofstein drive out of the field and back onto the road.

As he turned his head he saw a rusty, battered old Fiat Regatta round the corner and skid to a halt behind him. The cloud of dust kicked up by the car obscured his vision. Through the haze he saw three men get out of the Fiat carrying machine guns. They approached the Vectra. His body tensed, as if it could deflect the bullets he knew were coming.

The men opened fire, spraying the Vectra indiscriminately. Caught in the first hail of bullets, Gilad died instantly. His body was held upright as the bullets jerked him from side to side. It only slumped down over the passenger seat once the shooting stopped. The dust settled. A bearded man got out of the car and approached. Bending slightly, he looked at the bloodied, bullet-riddled body inside. He pulled the corpse up into a sitting position and cleaned what was left of the blood-covered face with a piece of cloth. Then he pulled out a digital camera, leaned down, and calmly snapped a few shots of the dead agent. He was careful to get the best angle.

TEL AVIV.
MONDAY, AUGUST 13TH.

David Applebach was thinking about his sailboat and how much he would use it when he retired this coming fall. It seemed like a lifetime ago that he and Dvora, his Israeli wife, had decided to leave London and immigrate to Israel. The years had gone by so fast.

He alighted from the bus on Ben Yehuda Street and walked down Mapu Street toward the seafront and the office. He did not notice the tall man following him from a discreet distance.

He turned into Hayarkon Street and headed toward the old building at number 126 and the security of the safe house. Turning on the lights in the dimly lit stairwell, he started to climb the three flights to the office. I'm getting too old for this, he thought. Perhaps one day they would install elevators in these old buildings, but it would be too late for him. Arriving at the wooden entrance door to the control apartment out of breath as usual, he fumbled in his pocket for the keys. He found them and was inserting the key into the lock when he heard a shuffling noise behind him.

He barely saw the outline of a tall man before the automatically timed stairwell lights went out.

"Mr. Applebach?" inquired the stranger softly in the darkness.

"None of your fuckin' business," retorted Applebach, turning around. He pushed the light switch again, eager now to get into the apartment.

The tall stranger did not speak. He took out a small automatic pistol with an attached silencer and calmly shot

Applebach three times, twice in the chest and once through the head.

Applebach was thrown back violently against the wooden door, smearing it with blood and spattering it with brain matter as he slid down slowly and slumped over. His upper body fell awkwardly over the first three stairs. Blood started to well up under the body and flow onto the stairs.

The stranger pocketed the gun and calmly took out a small camera with a built-in flash unit. He turned Applebach over and took three shots of the gruesome scene. He was careful not to step into the pooling blood. It was still possible to make out the face, even though half the skull was blown away. The man put the camera into his top pocket and rubbed his hands together. He opened the door to the safe house with Applebach's key and pulled the corpse into the apartment. He closed the door behind him. Then he turned around silently and calmly descended the stairs. He walked briskly out into the seafront sunshine.

ISRAEL.
TUESDAY, AUGUST 14TH.

Jordan Kline was one of those few people who looked peculiarly Israeli when talking Hebrew and unmistakably North American when conversing in English. Of average height, he had dark brown, short-cropped hair above a round face and pointed chin. Unusually long eyelashes accented his dark green eyes.

Leaving Tel Aviv after the meeting with the hotel interior designer about the new lobby furniture, Jordan drove out of town on his way back to Eilat. The traffic had been pretty heavy past Rishon Lezion. Located just south of Tel Aviv it was known chiefly for the Carmel Mizrahi winery founded by the Baron De Rothschild almost a century earlier. The rest of the going was pretty easy. He reached Beer Sheba the capital of the Negev desert within one hour in his Audi Eighty and bought a bottle of iced mineral water at the gas station snack bar in Dimona.

The town of Dimona was mostly a very poor and run-down immigrant town with ugly low-rise poorly maintained buildings and a high crime rate. Unemployment was rampant. Its dubious claim to fame was that the main road to Eilat ran just outside the main town and so a lot of traffic passed this way. This was the reason for the brisk business at the gas station. The snack bar was a very popular rest spot for many of the travelers passing this way on their travels. It was a good place to take a break with plenty of parking spaces and a good selection of refreshments.

When driving to Eilat, Jordan loved to stop and look at the Arava desert stretched out below him. He was about halfway down the Dead Sea heights and was stretching his legs at a viewpoint popular with tourists. This was one of the most beautiful sights in Israel, and he always felt exhilarated. Each time was a new experience for him. He marveled at how the desert changed color depending on the time of day. These were soft colors with hues of peach, orange, and delicate blue.

The beginning of the Arava valley lay below him like a biblical scene from a Roberts print, inviting him to start the drive that led one hundred and seventy kilometers through the dusty, windblown desert to Eilat. It was hard to imagine that the Arava desert had once been seabed thousands of years ago. This place sat right on the Syrian-African rift. Earthquakes were commonplace here. Thankfully there had been no large ones recently, just small trembles. Over in the distance he could see the trucks and cars winding their way up and down the Jordanian side of the Arava. They would either be on their way to the port city of Aqaba opposite Eilat or about to take on the steep, dusty, and laborious climb up the mountains of Edom to Amman, the Jordanian capital.

The noise of heavy traffic coming around the corner behind him and the sound of a heavy rig blowing its horn brought him back to the present with a jolt. Large supply trucks were on their way down to Eilat. The line of cars was building up behind the slowly descending rigs. Down below, Jordan could see the army checkpoint positioned just after the turning into the Arava desert. Soldiers were questioning some passengers in a car, and a small queue was waiting to pass inspection.

Jordan sensed the real heat of the desert as he opened the car door and climbed in behind the wheel. The inside of the car was like an oven. Turning right out of the car park area, he eased in behind a rig. He turned the air conditioning on high and continued his descent towards the checkpoint.

Accelerating onto the desert road with the checkpoint behind him, he punched the hotel number into his cell phone.

"Hi, Rache," he greeted the switchboard operator. "Put me through to the office. Linda, if she's there, please."

"Nice to hear you, Jordan, we've missed you this past couple of days. Putting you through now."

The canned hotel music came on the line followed by two short rings, and Linda, his secretary, picked up the phone.

"Jord, hi," Linda said cheerfully in her high-pitched voice. "Where are you?"

"I'm at the entrance to the Arava and should be there in about an hour and a half. Everything good?"

"Everything's fine. Jord, listen, the boss has been looking for you since yesterday. What do I tell him?"

"I'll give him a call this evening, see what's bothering him. Thanks, Linda. See you in a bit. Bye." He cut the connection.

He snapped in a disc of Enigma, turned on the stereo, and accelerated, feeling the surge of power as the engine responded. He liked the three-and-a-half-hour drive from Tel Aviv; it gave him the chance to be alone with his thoughts and his music, something he rarely had the time for. He had a box of discs in the Audi for every mood. Right now it was Enigma, but it could easily have been classical, jazz, or rock.

The car sped down the Arava, flashing past the Kibbutzim and co-operative farms that dotted both sides of the road. He wondered out loud how anyone in their right senses could live in such a God-forsaken part of the world, stifling hot and right above the rift. If they didn't die of the scorching heat, then one day an earthquake would probably get them.

The Arava desert, stretching all the way from Eilat to the Dead Sea and further North, was a dusty, windswept, and unimaginably hot place in summer. Yet these diehard farmers had managed to grow all sorts of crops using agricultural techniques that made the desert bloom under huge, white plastic tents. They had been incredibly successful, and their produce was in high demand all over Europe. Still, what an existence, Jordan thought as he drove by.

The Audi entered a long straight stretch and from afar Jordan could make out the flashing lights of a police cruiser. There were a few cars clustered on the shoulder of the road. What the hell was going on, he wondered, had another poor guy driven into a camel crossing the road and gotten himself killed? It was a quite common occurrence, but usually at night, not in broad daylight. The Bedouin were known to let their camels roam free in the desert.

Slowing down, he approached the scene and hoped that he was not going to witness yet another of the many deadly accidents on Israeli roads. We kill more of each other on the roads than the Arabs ever do, he thought to himself. He got out and walked towards the police car. Beyond the police cruiser he could see a red car that had left the road and rolled and smashed into a large outcrop of rocks.

An unwanted feeling welled up within him, a feeling of revulsion and fear of what he worried he was about to see. The red Alfetta was barely recognizable, a mess of twisted metal. Worst of all, he feared that the battered car belonged to Josh, an old Mossad colleague. He could make out the white sport stripe that Josh had had painted right down the middle of the car, like it was a Shelby Mustang. Josh had been so proud of the car, as if he owned a famous car right out of NASCAR. Jordan hoped desperately that he was wrong but deep down he was dreading what he would see. Oh God, not again, not another friend dead! It was bad enough getting killed on a mission, but going through all that only to die in a road accident?

Jordan broke into a run. It was Josh. He lay on the ground by his mangled wreck of a car. The police were afraid to move him due to his extensive injuries. He was semi-conscious, his chest crushed by the steering wheel. Blood trickled out of his mouth and dripped down onto the sand. Experience told Jordan that the injuries were fatal.

Jordan was surprised by the faint whisper, the flash of recognition. He saw Josh beckon him with his remaining strength. Jordan knelt down and put his ear just above Josh's mouth, cradling his friend's head in his hand.

"Jordan, they got me...Arabs...ran me off road. Many dead already...The dying man rambled, not making much sense. "Apple..." Josh's head fell to one side; he was finally out of pain.

Death had once again entered the life of Jordan Kline without invitation. He instinctively knew that he was once again about to get involved with something from which he so desperately wanted to get away.

He closed Josh's eyes gently with the palm of his hand and straightened up. He had to get away from the accident. The killers were sure to be around to make sure Josh was dead. He did not recognize anyone around him, but he sure as hell knew that they were there. They could have been among the Bedouins and local Arabs that had gathered out of curiosity. As he passed the others on the way to his car, he noticed a man filming with a large video camera and was amazed at the way newsmen always found out about accidents so soon. They listened on the police radio band and were always first at the scene of accidents and terror attacks. But this instance was remarkably fast.

He got back into the Audi and pulled out into the Eilat-bound traffic, trying to convince himself that this was just another accident. But it wasn't. He knew that.

Josh had told him that Arabs had run him off the road. Had they known that Josh was in the Mossad, or had it been a random killing that was happening all over the country these days? The Arabs were getting bolder, and drive-by shootings were commonplace, but usually in the captured territories, not in the Arava. That Josh had died was a tragedy.

Jordan had left the Security Service such a long time ago, so finally, so completely. Such a sense of calm had come to him that he knew he had been right. He was finally a man at peace, repelled by war, with no going back. Josh, with whom he had faced death a hundred times, was dead. Suddenly Jordan knew that he was cured, different. He felt a tremendous sadness where once he would not have given it a second thought. Many comrades in arms had fallen, but that was the business that they were in. It was something that they clinically put behind them. This was the way doctors confronted the death of patients—a method of coping that allowed them to remain above it all. It allowed them to continue treating others and saving lives. Emotion was not part of the equation in this business.

So it was all the way to Eilat, the self-convincing that he knew would not work. Josh had died. It looked for all intents and purposes like another nationalistic killing. And yet maybe it wasn't. He knew that he had to try to find out if there was another reason behind the killing. Josh's dying words repeated themselves over and over in his mind as he continued to drive.

Josh had uttered the word "Apple." What the hell did that mean? Josh had been in his final moments when he spoke those words. Were they the ramblings of a dying man no longer in control of his thoughts? And yet he had recognized Jordan. Why had he died before he finished that sentence?

"Goddamn it, Josh, what were you trying to tell me?" Jordan shouted out loud in frustration as he punched the steering wheel with his fist. Josh's death pulled him unwillingly back to his last days in the Mossad.

It was on a mission in Beirut that he had finally decided that peace perhaps was a goal that was justified after all. He had led a commando team sent in to wipe out a group of high-ranking PLO officers. Intelligence had informed them that the officers were concentrated in a downtown apartment and were alone. Jordan and his team, dressed as Arabs—some of them as Arab women, had nonchalantly driven into town in a battered Mercedes. They had stolen it after the navy had dropped them off in a Zodiac rubber craft near Beirut harbor. They'd parked the car directly below the apartment, ready for their escape.

The team burst into the apartment to find the officers in the company of three young scantily-dressed women. Realizing the danger they were in, the PLO officers shielded themselves quickly with the women. The women's faces were frozen with fear and dread. The Israelis had no choice but to shoot both the Palestinians and the women in cold blood. It was not something that Jordan was proud of.

He wished that they could have had the time to throw the women out of the apartment before the hit, but he knew that that would have been impossible. The hit had to be over as soon as possible if they were to make good their escape. Surprise was imperative. It was another scene of carnage backed by blind faith. Another horror etched in his memory. Another justified killing, or was it? The PLO officers, yes, but the women? It was not the Israeli way. The dead faces of the women wore the look of utter surprise and frozen fear that had caught them in death. The PLO officers had the mixed look of surprise and paralyzing fear, as if they had not believed that the Israelis would really go ahead and kill the women.

That was when Jordan realized with sickening certainty that he had become an automatic killer, carrying out executions, asking no questions. He was suddenly tired of it all. It was enough. Back in Tel Aviv after the mission, he had lain awake for most of the night picturing the bloody scene in Beirut. Like a horror film, it played in his mind through the night, rewinding automatically to replay again and again. He just could not delete the scene from his mind as he had always been able to; it kept appearing in his mind's eye, the colors vivid, and the blood and horror all too real. He kept seeing the women trying desperately to break free from the PLO officers, to get out of the way of the hail of bullets. He saw the bullets tear into them, the look of surprise and horror and pain on their faces. They did not scream out in pain. They'd had no time. They were dead by the time they hit the floor, their lifeless eyes staring up at Jordan accusingly.

By early the next morning he had come to a decision that he would not go back on. He would and could not repeat this again. It was not that he did not understand the need to carry out these missions, to eliminate their enemies. It was just that he was tired, he had become too disillusioned. He was done with the killing. He wanted desperately to pass the torch to someone else.

The morning after he handed in his resignation from the Mossad.

He then studied hotel business at Tadmor Hotel School in Herzliya, and following promotions in the Sands Hotel group he transferred to Eilat to manage the Sands Hotel on the Red Sea.

Irit, his girlfriend of almost five years, joined him after six months. She was now Public Relations Officer at the Neptune Hotel, a five-star hotel on the seashore and only a couple of minutes' drive from the Sands.

Jordan did not know if it was plain dumb luck or if he really deserved it, but he knew that the day he met Irit was the best and luckiest day of his life. He could hardly remember their first meeting. He had downed numerous beers summoning up the courage to approach her. It was at one of the Friday night parties a friend had thrown. They had exchanged more than a few glances across the room. Her eyes seemed to challenge him to come over and introduce himself, taunting him.

Irit Modell was a beauty. Long brown hair cascaded around an oval face. Large green eyes looked out from below thick brown eyebrows, and a sensuous mouth gave her the face of a model. She was olive-skinned and had a long, slim body with long legs and generous, firm, pointed breasts. Slim but not anorexic. A fashion designer would have loved to hang his creations on her frame and see her walk them down the catwalk.

She came from a very large and extended family with four sisters and two brothers. She was the youngest in the clan and spoiled by the family. Her parents proudly touted her as their child for their old age, their "bat zkoonim." She was soft-spoken and almost seemed embarrassed by her own beauty. As intelligent as she was beautiful, she had graduated in International Relations from Bar Ilan University near Tel Aviv.

Irit had not known the poverty that greeted her parents' arrival in Israel. She knew of their early life and loved them deeply for the way they had succeeded in bringing up six children while fighting to get ahead. Sure, she had had her fair share of hand-me-downs but loved to wear the clothes of the sisters she adored. The family shared a small house with only two bedrooms but with her arrival they had celebrated the enlargement to a four-bedroom property. Irit's mother, Luisa, never tired of telling her that Irit had brought the family luck when she was born. Frail and sickly as a child, Irit was given special care and attention by the family who often went without if she needed special medical attention not included in the national health insurance. She grew stronger over the years and became the beautiful, vivacious, and intelligent woman that Jordan loved. He knew that she was not a strong person health-wise and always made sure that she did not over-exert herself.

When they'd lived in Tel Aviv, Jordan and Irit visited with her parents nearly every Friday evening for the Sabbath meal. He loved going there. Her parents had come from Syria when they were very young and had worked hard to make a good life for their family. Her father had worked his way up in a plastics factory and was now the plant manager. He earned a decent salary and had spared nothing in giving his children the best education he could afford. Her mother had supplemented the family income during the early years by sewing clothes and selling fresh eggs from the many chickens that ran freely in their front yard. With the passing years came promotion and better pay, allowing her father to realize his dream for his children: a good education and a better start in life than he'd had. He was a man intensely proud of his family.

It had taken Irit a good few months to invite him into her family; she had wanted to be sure of his intentions and was anxious about the possible implications.

Almost all the family would gather together for a Friday meal filled with delicious Syrian food; the table was overloaded with Kubbe Hamda, Lachmajin, Sofrito, Queysat, and a host of other typical Syrian dishes. How Mrs. Modell managed to prepare so much food during the few days that separated each Friday Jordan always wondered in amazement. The small grandchildren that had come along over the years did not miss out either. On the table were chicken schnitzels, fries, and food that all small kids love.

It was a chance for Irit to catch up with family. Jordan could see how much she loved to be with them. He soon became the "third son," adopted by her parents as one of their own. That was just the type of people they were, and he could see a lot of them in Irit, in her joie de vivre, in the love she showed to those around her. He figured, being an only child himself, that he had the luck to now have two sets of parents and quite a few more siblings. They all got on together famously; there was nothing he wouldn't do for them.

He remembered what a friend had told him about the difference between optimists and pessimists: that all humans belong to one category or the other. Irit had her feet firmly planted in the first camp, and he could understand through her why optimists always got up in the morning and declared, "Ah, this is the first day of the rest of my life." The pessimists sullenly woke up and thought, "Well, we're one day closer to death." Each morning she greeted the new day with a smile, excitement, and renewed optimism.

So much love and laughter was present in the house on those Fridays. He realized that this was where she had gained her self-confidence. While she was gentle and courteous with everyone, she could be fierce when crossed. Jordan had experienced this on the very few occasions that they had quarreled, and he was careful not to cross the line too often. If he did, he knew that punishment would come his way, and inevitably it did, with a deafening silence between them until she decided to forgive him. He felt depressed on the days after they argued and it affected his mood at work. He may be Jordan Kline, ex-Mossad agent and hotel general manager outside the house, but at home Irit ruled.

Irit did not yet know much of his past. He was pleased that he could look forward to a life with her and the real possibility of marriage. She knew that he had been in the Mossad but assumed that the work had been in intelligence, maybe monitoring foreign language broadcasts, studying satellite images, or perhaps just a desk job. He was grateful that she did not ask prying questions. There would be time to tell her. It was an unspoken pact between them that he did not want or feel ready yet to elaborate on. Just something that was there, something that stood between them that only time and the right occasion would bring out.

Irit had come to understand Jordan well over the five years they had known each other. But he knew that she sensed that something from his past still troubled him and that she wondered what it was and why he had not shared it with her. He still could not bring himself to tell her of the past that stood between them. He was grateful for her never-ending patience and her understanding when his past came back to haunt him.

Now that past had come roaring back into his life with the death of Josh back on the road behind him. Why did death seem to follow him? He had left that life behind five years ago. He had done more than his part for the state, so why this disruption to the life he had chosen?

Jordan thought again about Irit and her ignorance of his violent past. He knew that Josh's death was pushing him towards that inevitable conversation he wished he could get away from.

CHAPTER TWO

EAST JERUSALEM.
WEDNESDAY, AUGUST 15TH.

Four men sat in a darkened room in an old Arab house in East Jerusalem. The four were bound by one single determination. All were prepared to kill for their beliefs.

The group had already ordered the deaths of the Mossad agents that had dared to investigate their organization. They had, they agreed as one, been destined to work together to destroy this perceived threat of peace.

Not one of the men wanted peace, or even considered it a viable alternative to the status quo. Each one in his own way considered peace a threat to his whole existence and way of life.

The Palestinians were divided into two main camps, the PLO and the violent Hamas faction. While the PLO proclaimed peace for land, the Hamas declared that only total annihilation of the State of Israel was their goal. Neither side was prepared to accept and recognize Israel as a sovereign state, the Jewish homeland. To add to this, the Palestinians also declared that Jerusalem was their eternal capital. They would accept nothing less.

Successive Israeli governments had backed the settlements that sprang up around Gaza. They created a buffer zone between

Gaza and Israel, and they had become successful agricultural farms. Generations had grown up in these settlements and had known no other life. Surely they must disappear, or at the very least most of them, in any peace agreement?

Now the President of the United States was forcing the Israelis and Palestinians to sign an agreement in Taba. Why had the Prime Minister and the Palestinian leadership gone along with it? This was just not right, and they had decided to act against it as a group. Of the four men, only Hassan Fawzi was from East Jerusalem.

They had gathered here to follow events of the last few days. The events had worried them, events that, if allowed to continue, would undermine their organization and the plan they had so carefully conceived.

Three of the four were men of considerable wealth. It had been natural for them to come together, to form this alliance against peace. It was their beliefs that had drawn them together.

They had to move fast. They saw the peace writing on the wall and had built a strong organization with money and the help of people that believed as they did. Their followers were fanatical believers and included government officials and PLO officers alike. They were all working towards their common goal: the undermining of the Taba convention, a peace convention they knew would come one day.

They had ordered the deaths of the Mossad agents and demanded factual recording of the executions. This was a prerequisite in the orders handed down to the hit teams selected for the missions. They had to be sure.

The tallest man sat at the head of the table, signaling his undisputed position as head of the organization. In his fifties now, you could read his life by looking at the man. A weather-beaten and deeply lined face was proof of the days, weeks, months, and years that he had spent on construction sites. Sun-bleached light brown hair grew above honey brown eyes creased at the edges from squinting against the sun. Ever-present stubble on his face could not cover the damage that the elements had wrought. Neither tall nor short, he dressed in expensive clothes that bore witness to the success of the corporation he had built. He wore Cole Haan pumps and light brown denims held up by a fine leather belt and a white cotton shirt opened two buttons below his neck. The expensive clothes were there, but he didn't really look as if he fit in them comfortably. He had made the upgrade to executive but looked like he should have stayed on the construction sites. He was used to being called "Rais," meaning "President," by all the employees—Arabs and Jews alike—at the construction sites. He loved that; it made him feel good, played to his ego. He had sold thousands of apartments and now owned many construction developments. He felt most comfortable when he was on the development sites.

"The death of agent Eisenstadt was unavoidable due to the chance meddling in our affairs by the Mossad," he stated by way of opening the meeting. "Iyad is well known to the authorities as an active member of the PLO in Israel and we maybe should have sent someone else. But agent Gilad was an unacceptable oversight!" His voice was very matter of fact and showed annoyance with the man to his left as if this event had been completely superfluous to the cause.

The man thought for a minute and decided not to argue. "All those on our fucking case are now taken care of," the man said. "The operation is well on target again. There are no loose strings left that could jeopardize our Goddamn operation."

"First things first. Not so fast, not so fast, my good friend," the tall man said. "The evidence please, Hassan, if you would be so kind." He steered the meeting back to the first point on the agenda, ignoring the reply. He disliked the man, the way he spoke, his boorish attitude, and even the way he looked. He had to tolerate him at least until this was over. Politics, he thought, really did make strange bedfellows.

Hassan opened a large brown envelope lying on the desk in front of him with his fat dirty fingers and took out some photographs. These he slid across the table.

The tall man looked at the photographs spread out on the table before him. The first was of a blond, freckle-faced young man propped up in the corner of what seemed to be a freight car. The next ones were of the same body snapped from a different angle. In one picture the open, lifeless eyes seemed to be accusing him. He quickly turned it over to avoid the dead man's gaze. He felt nauseated.

The next set showed the bullet-riddled, blood-soaked body of Gilad Dolev, framed by the window of his car. The same chilling scene repeated itself in the following photographs until he came to the picture of Applebach propped up against the door to an apartment. God, the man's head been almost totally blown off! He looked again at the pictures. He counted only three. He looked up at Fawzi.

"There's one missing, I agree. You know how to count, my friend!" Hassan Fawzi broke the silence, wheezy laughter rising from his rippling stomach, his fat face breaking into a smile. Hassan Fawzi, the influential owner and publisher of the *Voice of Jerusalem* newspaper, was amused. He was a fat, almost bloated Arab, with a large round, unshaven face. Beady eyes and tobacco-stained yellow teeth showed when he laughed. He wore the Jellabiya, the traditional Arab dress, held together by a wide leather belt that separated his ample girth into two parts: his upper and lower folds of fat. He wore leather sandals over white ankle-length socks. A Keffiya covered his bald, shiny head. He sweated incessantly, and looked like he had not washed in days—his clothes not cleaned for even longer.

Hassan was an outspoken PLO member. His editorials had on more than one occasion gotten him arrested and detained by the authorities. Luckily he had managed to avoid being named to the Palestinian delegation due to the objection of the Israeli Prime Minister. Did the PLO comrades in Palestine really think that the "Leadership" wanted peace, the fools? Peace would mean the dissolution of the organization as it existed and would leave the great leadership as legitimate governors of a very poor land. Their luxurious lifestyle would be a thing of the past, and they would be as beggars among the community of nations. No, not at all, thought Hassan, we cannot allow it to come to this, we cannot!

On more than one occasion he had been summoned to PLO headquarters in Tunis. He had not only witnessed but enjoyed the fabulous lifestyle that the leadership enjoyed in exile. The very best and celebrated chefs cooked up magnificent meals, and the most beautiful European girls were ever-present to be enjoyed whenever the urge took him. Even young boys were available for those so inclined. Luxury housing compounds with swimming pools were where the leadership lived. Shopping trips to Paris and London were frequent for the wives and mistresses. How would this be able to continue in Gaza? Once they lived in the impoverished Gaza strip they would have to live by example, be humble before their people. What kind of a life was that? This would all come to an end with peace, and beautiful Tunis would be traded for the dusty, run-down, overpopulated city of Gaza.

From their center in Tunis the PLO could continue to harass the Jewish state and appeal to the world for a motherland, a country that Palestinians could be proud of and bring up their children in. They could continue to amass personal fortunes from the donations that came in from the countries supporting the cause. They cared little for the poverty in Gaza, for the miserable conditions in the refugee camps and the worthless lives of their people. It was in their interest to keep the status quo as it was.

The free world looked on in pity and sympathy on the plight of the poor Palestinians in Gaza while the Israelis lived a contrasting life full of luxury. The Arabs were the victims, always the victims. It was vital to keep it that way on the international stage. The contrast was a superb backdrop to the Palestinian public relations effort. If they returned to Gaza they would have to deal with the Hamas faction and their ever-increasing popularity. They would actually have to govern an impoverished people to improve their lot. They would have to work rather than live the lives they enjoyed now. Trade all this for a bunch of losers in a dusty run-down piece of real estate worth nothing, situated next to the despicable Jews? No way! Hassan could not let his leaders down. This was why that he was sitting in his own home with these three men.

"The one missing is right here, my brothers," he added, getting up and shuffling towards the television in the corner of the room, laughing and coughing with delight.

"This one they recorded for our personal viewing pleasure. Pictures are so boring, don't you agree? Our people spoil us today, yes?" Hassan wheezed, inserted the disc into the video, and pressed the play button.

The Arava road jumped up on the screen. The filming was done on a home video judging by quality and taken from the inside of a moving car. Suddenly a bright red Alfetta roared past and someone shouted in Arabic, "That's him, let's do it!"

At first the Alfa had pulled away from them but soon the distance shortened. The noise from the engine competed with the oncoming wind.

Then the car was level with the Alfa. In a flash it was over. The cameraman was jolted as the car bumped the Alfa, forcing it off the asphalt. Desperate fear could be seen on the driver's face in a brief, jumpy, zoomed-in close-up.

The red car left the road, rolled, and smashed into the rocks at high speed. The next footage came from the side of the road near the wreck. The driver had crawled out of the wreckage and was lying beside the red car. He was obviously mortally wounded and close to death. A police cruiser was there, people milling around to see if something could be done to help. A youngish man bent down above the dying man for a few seconds.

The shot was taken from behind, but for a split second one of the men in the room thought he recognized the man, although reason said it couldn't be him. The odds against it being the man he thought it was were incredible. He didn't want to blurt out something that would sound stupid. He didn't need any more scorn.

A policeman covered the upper torso of the dead man with a blanket. The film went blank and then reverted to a video of Arab songs. Hassan turned off the television, took the disc out of the deck, and broke it with his hands. He threw it into the bin, poured some lighter fluid on it, and set it alight. Black smoke and the acrid smell of burning plastic filled the room.

Hassan would have liked to keep the disc as a souvenir. It wasn't everyday that you could see the live filming of the death of a Zionist pig. He knew this was impossible with the other men in his house looking at him; they would think him bloodthirsty. He gathered up the photographs and then fed them into a paper shredder on his desk in the corner of the room.

"Keep it to stills next time. That was disgusting. You fucking sonsabitches are turning this into a real road show! Kill them, yes, but making a show of their executions, that's disgusting!" The smallest among them was almost shouting. "Any more of this stuff going down and we will not be able to stop the Israeli committee from declaring a general alert. We need to keep it quiet or they will be all over us!"

"Now, are you sure, that all traces that could lead to us are gone? After all, four people have been eliminated, both here and in Europe. The slightest slip could get someone on our tracks again." The tall man turned his gaze towards the man to his left again.

"There are no longer any 'them' to get on our tracks, and I already told you guys that this bloody thing is over. No more fucking bodies. Break Peace is back on track and running," the small man stated, looking annoyed.

"Better fucking believe it, all of you!" The tall man took back control of the meeting, mimicking the man. "Back to business. The Italians have promised delivery of the marble in four containers due into Ashdod by today. They have already been sent from Castelfranco. Customs clearance should take a couple of days tops, and the containers should be in Taba by the seventeenth. Some is already there, sent a month ago. That's plenty of time to lay the floor in the lobby of the casino and still give the interior people the time to arrange the Swiss furniture. The container will arrive in Taba by the twentieth," he continued.

"From the construction side we will be ready well before the requested time of the sixth of September. You said you needed twenty-four hours, right?" he inquired looking over.

"Damn right, as long as all the electrical stuff is there with the containers," the small man answered.

"Allah be blessed, you worry too much my friend," Hassan interrupted, pointing his fat finger in the air. "The goods have already entered the country. Iyad arranged this after taking care of the foolish Zionist agent in Switzerland."

The tall man ignored Fawzi, and turned to the small man. "How are we placed for security on site on the eighth? I will have all my construction people there but they do not have security clearance and can only carry out the preparatory work as we planned."

"The Egyptians are so cooperative. I have already placed at least fifty of my recruits on top security clearance on the list for the opening ceremony, all bloody carefully screened. All are to my personal satisfaction. All of them are believers. All are experts in their field of operations. I will issue a chosen few with an identity badge so we know who is with us and can be trusted in an emergency. We have close ties with the Egyptian security apparatus. We can't bloody miss!" He smiled at the thought of victory over fools that would sell him cheap. "The bastards will never know what hit them!"

"Very well. Good. We shall meet here once more on the fifth in order to co-ordinate the final phase of operations. With the help of God and Allah, we shall prevail. The traitors will be liquidated. For once and for all, the peacemakers will be dead. They deserve nothing less. No one will suspect us, and when the investigation is opened, we will make sure that the finger

points to Baghdad. Brilliant!" The tall man was so pleased
with himself that he scarcely noticed the others as he talked.
He was swept up in his vision of conspiracy and the victory
ahead.

Samira, Hassan's plump wife, came waddling into the room
with a tray of strong Turkish coffee. She placed the tray on
the edge of the table, picked up the Arabic "finjan" coffeepot,
and poured the steaming coffee into small glass Turkish coffee
cups decorated in gold. All four men drank the aromatic coffee
that was strong with the distinctive taste of the added chicory.
Hassan followed this with an Arak. The others politely refused,
anxious to get the hell out of the Arab's home.

Darkness had fallen as they got up to disperse. Hassan went
to the door, opened it a crack, and spoke a few words to the man
on the other side. He closed the door and waited. In less than a
minute there was a knock followed by two quick knocks.

"May Allah bless and protect you my brothers! You may go
now, the way is clear. I will report on progress to my people in
Tunis, and we shall meet once again on the fifth, Allah willing,"
Hassan said. "We will all one day be made heroes of Palestine
by our leader when we take back our land," he laughed shrilly,
showing his yellow teeth. The smell of stale tobacco hung in
the air around him.

The three men filed out past him, each waiting a minute
before stepping out through the door into the shiny cobbled
streets of east Jerusalem. They disappeared into the darkness of
the narrow alleys lit by the full moon.

CHAPTER THREE

TEL AVIV.
THURSDAY, AUGUST 16TH.

Ariel Einhorn, Deputy Chief of the Mossad, eased his car into a slot not far from the entrance to the apartment building in which he lived. It was a nondescript square apartment block located in North Tel Aviv just south of the old port. He was on a high enough floor to have a clear view of the Mediterranean and the tall chimney of the Reading Electric power station to the north, belching clouds of white smoke up into the air. On a clear day he loved to watch the flurry of activity down on the marina below the Hilton Hotel and catch the windsurfers far out to sea. Below him he could see people young and old working out on the golden sand below the promenade. In the distance he could make out the Voice of Peace radio station ship anchored just outside Israeli territorial waters, transmitting peace messages and pop songs. The radio had been set up and financed by Eddy Lustig, a peace fanatic who had also flown his private airplane to Egypt. He had done it without clearance in an idiotic attempt to broker talks between the Israelis and the Egyptians. Of course he had not succeeded, but he was certainly ahead of the times and a hero to some. He had brought a great deal of international attention to bear on the Middle East. Lustig was almost as fanatical for peace as he, Einhorn, was against it.

Einhorn unlocked the front door and hung his keys on a hook by the door. As always, he took off his watch, placed it on a shelf under the hook, and walked into the kitchen.

"Hi, my dear," he acknowledged his wife Rina. "How was your day?"

"Okay, I suppose. Cup of coffee?" Rina filled the kettle without waiting for the answer. It was the daily homecoming ritual. It meant nothing. It was an exchange that signaled his return.

Einhorn pecked her on the cheek and continued out onto the small balcony. He sat down on an easy chair where he could enjoy the panoramic view. He looked at the peeling paintwork on the balcony walls and made a mental note to buy some paint and touch it up on the weekend. There was a gentle breeze coming in off the sea, helping him feel cooler in the high humidity of the Tel Aviv summers. The humidity was never far below ninety percent during summer. It felt much higher nearer the sea. As always, nearly all the lights were on in the Hilton hotel rooms, and he knew that the hotel was enjoying high occupancy as usual. A four-prop Arkia De Havilland Dash 7 curved in from the sea and flew past. He could just make out the blue and orange colors as it came in to land at Dov Airport just beyond the power station.

Rina came out onto the balcony and set down a tray with two mugs of steaming coffee on the small metal table beside him. She had aged a lot over the past few years, he thought. She had kept her youthful looks right up into her early fifties but was now looking decidedly middle-aged. Her hair, which she adamantly refused to color, was much whiter now. She was not a believer in anti-aging creams and treatments, declaring that everyone should accept growing old naturally. Her face was still attractive but time had done its work; it looked tired now. She had the plump midriff that was all too common in women her age. A good wife and partner, she had stood by him through all the years he had been in the agency, never questioning his absences or prying into his work.

Above the noise of the traffic below, he could hear the neighbors chatting on the balcony below. He could not hear them clearly, but above the sound of their muffled voices he heard the signature tune that always preceded "Mabat," the main Israel TV news broadcast.

He reached over, picked up the remote control, and pressed the on button. The small TV, hanging in the corner of the balcony, came to life just as the newscaster was announcing the days' headlines.

The upcoming peace convention in Taba was, as usual, the headline story. Reactions from the world capitals were reported. The optimism for success could be felt as presidents, prime ministers, and various dignitaries were interviewed one after the other. Reports on the convention were also screened from foreign news channels including CNN, the BBC, Royal Jordanian TV, and others.

This was followed by a report from Taba, showcasing the Taba Hilton and reporting on the nearly finished casino and grand hall. The Egyptians were already starting to put up the grandstand in the square between the hotel entrance and the casino. In the background massive palm trees were being planted, and side lawns were being laid with square carpets of ready-grown grass that were unloaded off a truck.

The camera somehow captured the already dramatic importance of the place, with the magnificent views of the Red Sea on the one side and the stark, dramatic mountains on the other. Through the shimmering waters and the haze one could vaguely make out the Saudi Arabian shoreline in the far background.

The news then reported on the start of the new school year and the shortage of classrooms brought about by the massive influx of new immigrants from Russia and Ethiopia.

There were some uninteresting reports about settlement activity, something about rioting in South Africa, and a piece about the UN monitoring operations in Iraq.

The final report was about road accidents in Israel. Einhorn's attention was suddenly focused on the wreckage of the red Alfetta that had been run off the road in the Arava. It had been in the daily papers.

The newsman was reporting on the effects of speeding and the consequences in human lives cut short. Einhorn knew that Israelis were atrocious drivers, but he also knew this accident had nothing to do with poor driving.

The picture shifted to the funeral procession for Josh. Einhorn recognized quite a few of the Mossad people who had gone to pay respects and recognized Josh's wife and children at the front leading the coffin. Strange, he thought, how only accident victims and soldiers killed in combat or army accidents were buried in coffins. All others were buried in shrouds. He hated the Jewish custom of burying the dead in shrouds and not coffins. You could see the dead bounce about on the carts used to transport them to the graves over the uneven surfaces of the cemetery. At funerals he always stayed a safe distance from the head of the procession so as not to see the body lowered into the grave and the dirt being shoveled onto the bodies.

Suddenly Einhorn's eyes narrowed and focused on one man in the crowd. His training had taught him to look for the odd man out, and here he was. Not that he was an odd man out in this crowd, but he had left the agency a very long time ago.

It was probably a coincidence that the man had been at the scene of the accident caught on the news. He suddenly remembered the name, Kline, Jordan Kline. That was it. Everyone had been amazed when such a successful control had suddenly decided to leave the agency, especially a top combat operative with a brilliant future. He wondered to himself how long he would have lasted if he too had been in the killing fields. He fully understood Kline's resignation. He also vaguely recalled that the agent had gone into the hotel business. Probably the reason he had come across the accident in the Arava, he thought. The guy probably worked in Eilat. Yes, that was probably it. But was it a coincidence? The police had confirmed that it was a nationalistic killing. Was Kline doing more than stopping at the accident scene?

"Son of a bitch," Einhorn said under his breath.

"Say something, Ariel?" asked Rina, sipping her coffee, looking at him over her bifocals.

"Nothing, nothing at all, dear."

The first thing he would do in the morning would be to put a tail on Kline for forty-eight hours. He would see if there was anything to worry about that would require further action. Forty-eight hours was the accepted time during which a followed man would act, and the maximum time for an ex-agent to be followed. Any more time and Kline would probably make the tail.

It was probably nothing, but, just in case, Einhorn would order the tail. He would pull it after a couple of days. Just for his peace of mind, just to cover all angles.

EILAT.
THURSDAY AUGUST 16th.

The Arkia flight from Dov airport touched down in Eilat at three-thirty in the afternoon. As Jordan got off the plane he felt the intense heat of the afternoon sun hit him as he exited the cabin and stepped onto the small metal stairs. The stewardess had said that it would be forty-three degrees, but somehow you were never ready for the blast of hot dry air that greeted you on exiting the plane. Not that it hadn't been humid inside the cramped cabin on the flight down. Jordan always became uncomfortable when he felt damp sweat building up under his trousers and between the leather seats. He'd had to get up a couple of times to alleviate the feeling and then try to get comfortable again in the narrow seats. Thank God it was only a fifty-five-minute flight. Any longer and it would have driven him mad.

It had been difficult to get a flight to Tel Aviv and back because it was Thursday. He felt that he had to pay his last respects to Josh, to be there at his funeral. He had been through so much with Josh. So many missions, so many comrades killed in action, and yet he had always taken it as part of the job. No emotions—just the insistence to get on with it and never look back.

Yet emotions did well up within him at the cemetery, and he choked up when offering condolences to the widow. Funny, he thought, he never used to feel emotional, but that was before he'd left the agency, and definitely before he'd met Irit. His shared life with her had made a difference in him, had mellowed him, and made him more human. He had placed a stone on the fresh grave, and had turned away with a heavy heart. He was eager to get back to normal life in Eilat. There he could sit down quietly and calmly think over the events. He could decide what his next step should be. He needed time to think.

He met many of the old crowd at the funeral and was glad that the solemn occasion protected him from the inevitable small talk of long buried memories. He did not want those memories now; they were starting to invade his new life, threatening all the progress he was making in his new profession and his life with Irit. He thought for a second about his life with Irit. Where would that be when he told her of his past? He had no doubt that she would not take it well. He had to tell her, but how and when?

He saw that here too the news cameras were recording another "newsworthy" event for the interested viewers, another victim in the road death statistics of Israel. He remembered the joke that said that the Arabs didn't need to make war on Israel— just give each Israeli a car and they would take care of the rest. Nowadays you couldn't die in peace or even be buried in peace. There was always money to be made from someone else's tragedies, always a story to be told.

Jordan felt much better once he was back on the plane. He had pretended to be asleep in order to avoid conversing with a colleague from a neighboring hotel sitting next to him.

The taxi from the airport pulled up in front of the entrance to the White Sands. Jordan got out, thanked and paid the driver, and went through the revolving door into the cool air-conditioned hotel.

The main lobby was overflowing with guests. Suitcases, shoulder bags, and plastic bags were strewn everywhere. Some guests had even started picnicking on the lobby tables, splitting open watermelons and unpacking sandwiches brought from home with them.

Jordan approached the front desk, annoyed by what he saw. "Get me security, and tell them they better be here now," he snapped at the receptionist and then added gently, "I'm sorry, Yael. Didn't mean to bite your head off, just a tough day."

"Damn right, a tough day, Jord. It's okay. You should have seen the place a little earlier," Yael said. "I'll ask switchboard to get them on the Motorola. It shouldn't take too long for them to get here."

Jordan liked the way the staff called him "Jord"; he felt that it was a positive sign of closeness and far from disrespect. If it weren't fun to work together, then what fun would it be for the guests? The hotel was known for the feeling of a fun place that the staff passed on to the visitors. He knew that there was a fine line between getting too close to the staff and keeping their respect, but he still believed in a democratic way of running things. He believed that if you trusted the staff to do their jobs and supported them then they would deliver. Of course there would be those that took advantage of his style but they were the odd ones out. He did not believe in managing by fear or dictatorship. He figured that this led to factionalism and inter-departmental feuding. That could ruin a hotel. Anyway, he felt that so far his management style had been the key to his success.

A security guard approached him in the lobby.

"Yehuda, take a look at this! I've told you guys a thousand times that this is not a protected nature area. There are parks all around the country for that. The Goddamn Rabbinate could have my balls for this. There are people having a picnic here and others in wet bathing suits ruining the furniture. We've got people sleeping on the sofas, and where the fuck are you guys? Call the others and get this place organized, and get the suitcases in the luggage room please. Get to it before I get to you." Jordan turned and strode away towards his office before the guard could come up with excuses.

"Hi, Linda. Missed you." He went over to his secretary and kissed her on the cheek as he passed on the way to the food and beverage manager's office.

Sammy Baron sat behind the desk adjusting prices on a new menu for the lobby.

"How's it going, Sammy? How many dinners we serving today?" Jordan asked as he shook hands with his food and beverage manager.

"About two-fifty, but that's not the point. The ice cream machine in the snack bar is on the blink, the vegetable truck from Tel Aviv broke down in Beer Sheba, I have two cooks sick, and my car is in the garage. Apart from that it's Thursday and its August. Could you want more?" Sammy smiled. "The only good thing about today is you're back in town, a shoulder to cry on."

Jordan liked Sammy. He came from a Druze clan near Haifa up north. His parents had brought him up well, and he was the most polite and level-headed department manager on his staff. Everyone, guests and staff alike, really liked him. A short, thin man, he had piercing greenish blue eyes and a curly head of black hair. Sammy was clever, professional, and a hard-worker. His department ran well, and Jordan was glad the experienced Sammy was on board.

43

The phone on Sammy's desk rang, and Jordan instinctively picked it up.

"For you, Jord," Linda called from her desk. "The boss."

"Where in hell's name have you been, Jordan?" The question sounded more like an accusation. Why did Rami Benatan always make questions sound like accusations? Jordan disliked him and tried to talk as little as possible to him. Always preaching good relations with staff, Rami was the last one to practice it himself. He was invariably rough on the managers and staff alike when he was down on visits from the Tel Aviv head office.

"Death in the family—you probably saw it on the news last night. Had to go up for the funeral and got back just now. Got some stuff to go over with you, but since you're in town Sunday I'll go over it then. I'm in the middle of a problem right now so I can't talk. See you Sunday." He just didn't have the patience for another round with the man right now.

Just as he was finishing his call with Rami, a guest came into Sammy's office and sat down without being invited. Jordan kept the receiver to his ear and listened with the other. The man was middle-aged, shortish, with a beard that framed a square face.

"I wanna complain," he stated.

"Shoot, go ahead. I'm listening," said Sammy.

"Listen, I'm not getting any younger, and the kids are growing up. At home, I don't get the chance to fuck the wife very often since the kids are up at all hours. Here at the hotel it's a different story. You see, I know I can't keep the room hostage every day for twenty-four hours, so I didn't mind the girls coming in to clean in the morning, even though the 'Do Not Disturb' sign was on the door. A while back I had a heart attack, and underwent open-heart surgery. Let me tell you, with the medicine they give me, it takes me a good couple of hours to get it up for the wife."

"Today we had a nice lunch poolside, with a bottle of wine, no kids, and the chance was there. Real romantic, we felt. We worked hard back in the room, me and the wife, and after a while I had me a great little Eiffel tower. Pure steel." The guest gestured excitedly with both hands to show quite graphically what he meant.

"Suddenly I hear the room maid approaching from outside, and I said to myself, please, no, don't enter the room, not bloody again. It'll all fall down like a bloody house of cards. But sure enough, she came in, even with the 'Do Not Disturb' sign hanging out again, and it all fell down. Down like a pack of cards. Down like a high-rise in an earthquake. No hardened steel left, just limp rubber. So I told the wife, I said to her, if I'm not going to fuck you, they are going to invite us to dinner."

Sammy looked shocked but acted quickly. "You got it, Sir, and a bottle of wine on the house, too, to go with your meal. I apologize on behalf of the housekeeper." He quickly signed a meal invitation voucher and gave it to the guest who took it and left as quickly as he came, satisfied with his invitation to a free dinner for two, a victorious smile on his face. Job well done, he had gotten his planned compensation, and without a fight.

"Did you believe that? Either a bloody story or for real. If it's a story then he should get an Oscar for that performance. Either way the guy deserves dinner," Sammy laughed.

"Bet you forgot about your own troubles listening to this guy, huh, Sam?" Jordan said smiling as he replaced the receiver and left Sammy's office.

He walked out of the offices and went up on the floors. He liked to do this when time permitted so that he could raise morale among the room maids. They worked ceaselessly on these high room turnover days. He spent more than an hour checking some ready rooms, chatting briefly to some of the maids. He knew it meant a lot to them and showed them they were not alone, that they were valued by him and valued by the hotel.

He rode the elevator down to the pool level. He checked his watch. It was already almost half past six and yet there were still quite a lot of people lounging around the pool. The main heat of the day was gone now and a gentle breeze was coming in off the sea. This was the favorite hour for the fitness swimmers to do their lengths in the lower, half-Olympic-sized pool. He could see half a dozen of them bobbing up and down as they swam in the lanes. Their caps and goggles made them look serious, almost Olympian.

There were some beautiful girls sitting at the snack bar in skimpy bikinis, and they smiled invitingly at him as he passed. His thoughts went back to Irit, how much he had missed her during the past couple of days. He stood silently in thought for a while and then came to a decision. Tonight he would tell her about his past. Perhaps it was Josh's death. Perhaps it was the way that the funeral had affected him emotionally. He knew that he couldn't leave this bottled up in him anymore. It was eating him up.

He wiped the sweat off his face with the back of his hand and noticed that he was shaking slightly. Jordan Kline, Mossad agent, shaking! He had to do this, he must confide in her. She deserved to know. He could no longer hold back the truth of his past, keeping from her the fact that he had murdered in cold blood. It was time. He had to know if Irit would forgive him, would tell him it was war, and would understand his pain. God, he was frightened of her possible reaction. He was terrified of losing this beautiful woman. He had put it off for too long. He knew that she was expecting him to share with her the burden that he was keeping from her. Today he would do it, he would tell her. Would she have ever invited him into her family in the first place if she had known?

On the way out of the hotel a little later, he looked in on the switchboard and told them he'd be at home if they needed him during the evening. Then he walked out into the hot evening air towards his car.

EILAT.
THURSDAY AUGUST 16th.

Jordan and Irit settled down on the floor of their living room and relaxed on the thick throw cushions. Each nursed a glass of Gamla Cabernet Sauvignon, their favorite wine. They had eaten a light dinner and somehow Irit sensed that tonight he wanted to talk. She sensed his mood, and had been gentle and caring, careful not to upset him, waiting patiently for the right moment for him to unload what had been bottled up inside of him all these years. She looked over at him and realized the pain he was in. She saw the apprehension in his eyes and realized the courage he had summoned to finally tell her. She felt a sense of dread building in her and yet was eager to hear about his life before her, eager for no barriers to stand between them anymore. What could his story be that he had kept it hidden from her all this time?

Jordan was nervous and apprehensive. It was as if he had already decided that Irit would not be able to accept the man he was. How would she be able to comprehend that the man she had been living with for the past years had been a cold, calculating, trained killer for the state? Still, she had to know and know the whole truth, even if it meant that she would leave him. He would not leave anything out; he needed to get it all out so that there would be no more secrets, nothing that she would not know about him. He was at a loss as to how to begin, though. He sat silently on the sofa unable able to look at her for a while. For one of the few times in his life Jordan was afraid. It was worse than the feeling before his first mission for the agency. This was, he knew, the most important mission that he would ever undertake, and he did not know where to begin.

He breathed in deeply and relaxed his shoulders as he looked up at her and directly into her eyes. They were full of questions, expectancy.

Jordan at first asked her for her forgiveness, for not telling her of his past sooner. As his story slowly unfolded, he saw that she felt the very real pain inside of him. She relived with him his proud youth as he entered the army, the rigorous training for the Golani brigade, the stories of war and carnage on the battlefield. She heard him tell of his crowning achievement of acceptance into the Mossad. She saw how proud he was of the service he had given to the country.

He could see her horror as he recounted the missions, as he recounted all his kills. He felt the hot tears well up and run down his cheeks as he recounted that final mission to Beirut and the killing of the young women together with the terrorists. He was a man tormented by his once proud past, a past he was running from towards a future with her.

"Irit," he sobbed gently. "How could I tell you? How could you have fallen in love with the monster I had become? I couldn't have taken that. I needed, I need you to love me. I need that support to carry on, to be happy, and to have a future with you. Do you see that?"

She saw that his life with her, the love her family had given him had made Jordan a changed man. Jordan was more open, more capable of showing emotion. She saw terrible doubt and fear in his eyes. She realized that he feared losing her love, that he had feared this for the five tormented years that he had kept this from her.

Irit kept her silence, not wanting to disturb this story unfolding before her. She was both fascinated and horrified by the life Jordan had lived before they met. She felt a new, deeper love for this man. She was proud that his real character had finally been revealed. He had done the right thing, had walked away from it all to a new life. And yet there was no denying that he had killed in cold blood. It had stained him. He had been able to pull the trigger on those innocent women. How would she be able to accept that?

Jordan left nothing out. No detail was too small to recount. He chose his words carefully and told Irit the bare and utter truth. He knew she was hurting as much as he. He needed her complete understanding; he needed her to know him entirely, to love him knowing that he had killed in cold blood. He needed her complete acceptance. It was his ugly truth, his last hurdle, and he had to jump it for a future with her.

"Irit, you know that all the while I was growing up in Toronto all I dreamed of was coming over to serve in the IDF. I was very young and very idealistic. I came alone. My parents only made Aliya after they saw how serious I was, after I was accepted into the Golani brigade. They gave up a great life in Canada to be with me, to be here for me, and I am the stronger for their love. I loved the army life and I excelled; I was contributing to the safety and security of the state. So I welcomed the chance to continue active duty when the Mossad came knocking."

"The months and years passed and I turned into a hardened killer and didn't even notice it. I saw many of my friends killed on missions, but that made me even more determined to exact revenge. Kill as many bad Arabs as I can. I became good at what I did, one of the best, Irit, and yet all the while it was taking an invisible toll on me. I carried on excelling in the art of killing for my country. I can't say that I enjoyed it, but accepted that it had to be done by someone, and that someone happened to be me. I was on automatic pilot, going with the flow, running towards a brick wall, the wall I hit in Beirut."

"Irit, our people rose from the ashes of the Holocaust—we cannot let the Arabs complete what the Nazis started. Don't forget that I grew up on stories of the Holocaust around the Friday night table in Willowdale. I was just a kid but had already decided that I would serve in the IDF. So I continued with the agency. I honestly thought that I would spend all my life that way."

And so, deep into the night he told Irit about the darker side of his life, of his search for the meaning to the senseless slaughter, to the ever-continuing war. At times he cried openly, sobbing deeply as he told her again of the horror in Beirut. How, as he had pulled the trigger on the women, he'd felt revulsion and self-hatred for the first time as an agent. How he had turned and walked away from that life that seemed so far from him today.

It was early morning when he finally completed his story. He was exhausted, completely spent and drained by the effort. He sat silently, his chest heaving with emotion. Jordan looked deeply into Irit's eyes, looking for some sign, searching for acknowledgment and understanding.

Irit looked back into his eyes, knowing what he had gone through these past hours, knowing now how much he must trust and love her to tell her of his deep and inner feelings of his past. He had done unspeakable things. He had done them for the state but he had still done them. There was no refuting that fact.

Minutes drifted by. She sat thinking about the story that had unfolded. The tears slowly welled up in her eyes and rolled down her cheeks. She held his face in her hands and looked deeply into his eyes. She wanted to scream out in the agony of the moment, to pretend that she had not heard everything that he had told her. She was caught up in the moment, mixed emotions welling up inside her. Then she pulled him to her, her mouth crushing his in a sudden, violent and passionate kiss that they had not known before.

Their tears mixed as they kissed, over and over again. He had torn down a final wall keeping them apart, but would it heal the last wound or open it up forever?

Suddenly she pushed Jordan from her and once again looked into his eyes.

The tears were streaming freely now down her face. He returned her gaze. He waited apprehensively for her to speak.

Slowly she got up and stood in front of him and looked directly into his eyes. He was speechless and taken aback by her quick separation, kept spellbound by her intense gaze. Then she started to undress slowly, taking off her clothes piece by piece. Finally she stood before him naked and utterly beautiful. Jordan was still held captive by her eyes.

"I want to tell you, Jordan, that it is not for me to forgive you your past, but to share it with you. It is for me to help you with this incredible burden you carry. I hate what you did, the killing in cold blood, but the man I love is with me. His past is a part of him, something not even God can undo. It is also now a part of me. I know how incredibly difficult it has been for you to tell me all this, but do not ever question my faith. It is with you and will always be. You are my love. You are the one I have chosen. I am the one who is lucky. It is me who is lucky, Jordan." Irit cried openly, sobs wracking her perfect, naked body, her breasts quivering.

"I love you, Jordan Kline. I love you more now than you will ever know, more than you can ever imagine. I want you now. I want you more now than I have ever wanted you. I need to feel you with me. We need to be as one. Please," Irit almost pleaded as she bent down, took his hand, and pulled him up. She undressed him violently on their way into the bedroom, tossing his clothes on the floor along the way.

She threw herself on the bed. They made love, passionate love, in their search to know each other even better, to satisfy their new deeper love. It had never been this way for either of them; it was as if it were the first and the last time. They explored each other with their hands and tongues, and for a long time after they climaxed they looked into each other's eyes silently. Then they drifted off into a deep sleep in each other's arms. Through the windows the first rays of dawn appeared over the mountains of Edom.

EILAT.
FRIDAY, AUGUST 17TH.

Irit was the first to wake up. She looked at the alarm clock and saw with shock that it was nearly ten o'clock. She shook Jordan awake, quickly threw on some clothes, and went to brew some fresh coffee.

Jordan dressed hurriedly and followed her into the kitchen, thankfully taking the mug of hot coffee she held out to him.

"You really screwed me this time, Jordan Kline. No pun intended," she said mischievously. "I'll probably get fired for being late on a Friday in August. Still, it will have been worth getting fired for." She smiled teasingly and kissed him on the forehead, adding simply in her gentle voice, "Thank you for last night, Jordan."

"No, I thank you for last night, Irit. I should have told you sooner, my love. I should not ever have doubted your love. I was afraid. Enough said. We're outta here," he said cheerfully, picking up his jacket and pulling Irit along with him.

Driving to the hotels, Jordan Kline felt really good, good with himself, good with life, and good with the world. He had done the unthinkable, he had confessed to Irit. She still loved him, maybe even more. He had half expected her to walk away from him. He felt pure again. The burden was gone.

All he had to do now was to think of what to do about Josh's ramblings. He glanced over at Irit and saw and felt her happiness, too.

"I know, Jordan, I know," she said, looking back at him.

God, he should have done it sooner.

As he dropped Irit off at the Neptune she turned to look at him in the car. Her large eyes gazed into his and she said, "Jordan, I don't know how you went through what you did and stay sane, but you did and came out the other side a better man. Not many can say that. I am so very proud of you, proud to love you and say that you are mine." She leaned over to kiss him, angled her long legs, and climbed out.

Jordan pulled out of the car park and headed toward the White Sands. He felt elated after last night and after what she had just told him in the car. Almost like a new beginning. He arrived and could see that there was no space free in front of the hotel so he drove straight around to the back of the hotel. He parked the car by the hotel delivery ramp.

Jordan left the car keys with the goods receiver in case it needed to be moved for deliveries and rode the service elevator up the entrance floor. He walked to his office through the lobby and noticed that today nearly all the guests were by the pool or on the beach. There were only a few sitting in the lobby, probably getting away from the stifling heat in the cool air conditioning.

For no reason at all, Jordan suddenly felt slightly uneasy as he approached the front desk. He put it down to fatigue. After all, he hadn't gotten much sleep last night, almost none at all. He bypassed the desk and went into the office.

"Linda, please ask Yoel from maintenance and Martine from housekeeping to meet me in the lobby in ten minutes to get going on the public areas inspection. Anything of interest in the mail?" he added as an afterthought.

"Yes. We're being sued by the fat guy who complained about the air conditioning in his room a couple of weeks ago," Linda said while opening envelopes.

"We changed the guy's room four times didn't we? Also I remember that we gave him a fan. He also complained about the length of the beds, right?"

"Right. The guy says the temperature in the room was not low enough to stop him from sweating profusely. They want the whole holiday again. The case comes up in a couple of months."

Linda read the lawyers' letter and the summons.

"Send a faxed copy to our lawyers and we'll see what they say," Jordan said, "After all, if the asshole comes again, we still don't have longer beds or even colder air conditioning. Can I help it that the fat guy sweats a lot during summer in Eilat? Hell, even I sweat a lot in summer. And no, don't look at me that way. I am not fat. Okay, okay, I'll workout more often, I promise. Anyway, big guys sweat all the time, that's what they do isn't it? Do you believe these guys? I'll be on the floors if you need me urgently."

Yoel and Martine were already waiting for him by the front desk. They joined him in the walk toward the dining room. Once again that feeling came over him, a feeling he couldn't explain, something he knew was familiar but that he couldn't quite identify. He put it out of his mind to concentrate as they started the maintenance tour.

While Yoel wrote down the points to be looked after, the three of them did a thorough check of the public areas. They crossed off the list items taken care of and added were new maintenance jobs to be done: chipped paintwork, torn carpets, woodwork that needed attention, and broken electrical sockets. The tour took them a good couple of hours as they inspected all the corridors, the lobbies, and restaurants. Jordan always enjoyed these maintenance tours. It kept the maintenance people on their toes.

It also kept the hotel in shape and gave him the chance to be alone with Yoel and Martine. It kept them close to him, and that was important. He knew they enjoyed it, too. It gave them a chance to bring him up to date on their departments.

They finished back down in the main entrance lobby, and Jordan summed up:

"Try and get as much as possible done by the next tour, Yoel. Also, please ring the gardener and ask him to come see me. The lobby plants need attention. It's not the first time I've had to remind him. Martine, one more thing, please call pest control. I got a letter about mice in the pool area, so get him to put down some traps. Thanks, both of you. Good job. I'll see you later." He turned toward the office.

The same feeling washed over him again as he walked by the front desk, and he knew that he had to find out what it was that was bothering him. It was strange, like a ghost from the past that had come back to haunt him. He still could not put a finger on it.

He had told Irit about Josh's accident, but not what he had whispered to him as he lay dying. He did not want her to worry unnecessarily, especially after all he had told her about his past. He hoped he could sort it out without telling her. She thought it was an accident. Jordan knew that Arabs had run him off the road. Deep down he suspected that Josh had been caught up in something ominous, something very dangerous. He could not remember even one instance when an Israeli had been killed by Arabs in the Arava. What did it mean? Was it random, or were Josh and the agency involved?

Perhaps it was in some way connected to the upcoming Taba convention. The Arava was close to Eilat after all. Every time that there had been a summit meeting between the U.S., the Palestinians, and the Israelis, radical Arabs had tried to derail it by an upsurge in violence, suicide bombers, or rocket attacks.

The last thing he wanted was for Irit to be involved or even know about it. She would try and stop him, but he knew that he had to find out what Josh had been trying to tell him. A thought suddenly occurred to him: maybe Josh had died because of what he knew. Maybe it was a targeted hit. He shivered and pushed the thought aside.

Fridays at twelve the hotel entertainment team always gave out punch in the pool to the adults and ice-lollies to the kids. He went down to watch the carnival atmosphere on the deck where clowns played among the children while distributing the lollies. A band played sixties music on the sundeck. Some of the guests were dancing on the deck by the snack bar in their swimming gear.

Jordan loved to see the hotel full and feel the guests having a good time. He could sense that this weekend would be another success, both financially and in terms of guest satisfaction. He walked through the poolside grill and listened to the pre-service briefing being given to the waiters by the headwaiter.

Jordan missed being in the food and beverage department. He felt that it was the engine room of every hotel; after all, didn't people always talk about the food at hotels after their stay? They certainly didn't talk about the furniture or the comfortable beds. They talked about the food and entertainment. Every day brought different problems, different guests, and different challenges. That was what he liked about the department. That plus the fact that in food and beverage management you cruised the hotel and were not stuck behind some front desk answering stupid questions from guests all day.

He took the stairs up to the ground floor two by two and went up to the front desk. Once again that feeling of unease came over him. He looked around the lobby again and saw some guests taking a light lunch at some tables. At other tables some played cards, and a couple was booking a Red Sea day cruise at the sports and local tours desk. A guy wearing jeans and a red T-shirt was standing in line to make a booking.

Jordan shook his head as if to clear it and returned to his office. He settled down into his chair and checked a backlog of guest questionnaires. Since Fridays were short work days, he welcomed the chance of using it to go over the comment sheets. This was his way of keeping his thumb on the hotel pulse—a way to see where the service needed improvement.

The questionnaires were a valuable source of information to Jordan. As he read, he learned of staff that had been especially helpful and others that had not. In the top corner he jotted down his comments. He knew that Linda would photocopy the relevant sheets and distribute them to the different department heads. After he read them, the comments were fed into a computer that gave monthly satisfaction statistics in each department category for the whole hotel.

This batch, as usual, was complimentary to the hotel, which was gaining a reputation for pleasant service and good food. The main complaint as usual was that the guests had to pay an entrance fee to use the health club and that there was not yet any room service. Fully stocked mini bars were in every room, but Jordan could understand the guests wanting room service. It was being taken care of. A suitable location had been found, and the kitchen designers were working on a plan based on the brief that Jordan had written. Hopefully it should be operational soon.

He finished going over the papers and placed them in the out tray. He tidied up his office for the weekend and went over some memos that he had not read. He made some notes and put them, too, in the out tray for processing the following Sunday. He glanced at his watch and saw that it was nearly one o'clock. He decided to check on lunch preparations in the pool grill before heading home. He left the office, locking the door behind him.

The aroma of charcoal-grilled meat hit him as he entered the restaurant, and he could see the chef arranging the colorful salad bar. Many guests, having enjoyed a late breakfast, liked a light lunch from the salad bar, especially in the summer heat. The chef, therefore, put a lot of emphasis on the salads and the colorful variety of both fresh vegetables and salads was a feast for the eyes.

The guest in the red T-shirt was talking to the cashier at the health club entrance, and Jordan thought how out of place he looked among all the guests in swimming gear.

He left the restaurant and took the stairs up to the entrance level and the hotel shop and approached the counter.

"One *Jerusalem Post* and one *Yedioth Ahronoth* please, Shirley." Jordan liked to read the English paper as well as the Hebrew weekend press, while Irit read only the *Yedioth Ahronoth*.

"One sec and I'll be with you, Jord," Shirley smiled.

She handed another customer a bag and some change. She put the two newspapers into a plastic bag and handed it to Jordan.

Looking through the shop window, Jordan again saw the guest with the red T-shirt by the front desk chatting to the clerk.

Suddenly he knew why the guy looked out of place among the guests. They must be fucking amateurs to think that he would not spot the tail, even if he had been gone a long time. Anger built up inside him. Stupid, he thought, putting an inexperienced agent on him. Who in the hell did they think they were? Did they think they could get away with this? Why in hell were they tailing him at all? He would show them how things work in the dirty business. He started angrily out of the shop toward the man.

Quick reasoning and common sense caught up with him as he approached the tail. He brushed past the man and went into his office once more to think things out. If he caught the guy and questioned him, then they would know that he realized that he was being followed and that he maybe had something to hide. On the other hand, he could let the guy follow him around a couple of days and chances were the tail would be pulled. Only then could he take further action. It must be big, thought Jordan, something really big. Was this tail connected to Josh's death? Somebody had seen him at the crash scene and also on the TV news that same night, he reasoned. Someone who knew him from the past.

Jordan wondered how far this thing went, how many were involved, and who they were. Who had ordered the tail? He felt his cold, operational mind taking control, and a thrill went through his body. He realized that his old training was taking over, Agent Jordan Kline taking over from hotel General Manager. He did not like the feeling; it was something he thought he had put to bed many years ago. Still, he realized that this was inevitable if he was to find out the truth behind it all.

Jordan knew that he could do nothing for the weekend. He had to act normally in every respect and not let them realize that he knew he was being tailed. He would know when they pulled it, and then he would get moving. Even then he would have to act swiftly and not arouse suspicions. They could put the tail back on him at any time.

He sat back into the soft armchair in the corner opposite his desk to think things over. First the facts: Josh had been killed by Arabs. He was being tailed. There was a peace convention coming up in Taba and many factions were sure to try and derail it. Damn few facts. Now the questions: What did Josh try to say before he died? What did Apple mean? Think Jordan, think. Many dead…what did that mean?

He expanded his thoughts and tried to remember the people in the agency. Then it hit him. Applebach. Josh must have meant Applebach, the agency controller. Perhaps he would know more about what was going on. Jordan decided that he would visit Applebach at the control apartment on Hayarkon Street at the earliest opportunity next week. He knew him well from his days at the agency, so he was sure that he could get some more information from him.

There wasn't much else he could do at this stage. Jordan hoped that they would pull the tail by Sunday afternoon, by which time he would be finished with his boss Rami Benatan. Perhaps he could catch a late flight to Tel Aviv. From then on he would have to play it by ear and see where it would lead. In the meantime he could look forward to a weekend with Irit.

CHAPTER FOUR

EAST JERUSALEM.
FRIDAY, AUGUST 17TH.

Hassan Fawzi sat at the head of the oval table. He was pleased, very pleased with progress on Operation Break Peace and was now taking care of other business. Just because the PLO was trying to derail the peace conference did not mean that terrorism had to stop in the meantime. On the contrary. The more dead Israelis there were the better, the more satisfying. He pulled a cigarette from the box lying on his desk and lit it up. He took a deep drag and thought about events as he contemplated the smoke curling upwards towards the ceiling.

Of course the Chairman had to renounce terrorism on the international stage, but that did not mean that he wanted the terror attacks to stop. On the contrary, the enemy had to be kept busy, wondering from where the next blow would come. The mainstream PLO would not accept responsibility. It would pass the blame on some splinter group, maybe even the Hamas.

The Intifada had died down, and the movement was getting a lot of adverse publicity from the lynch killings of informers that was going on in Gaza City and Ramallah. The people were nervous, scared of the gangs that killed even those suspected of collaboration. More than one mistaken killing had been made. It did not look good, but the Israelis were damn good at infiltrating the ranks, and informers had to be taken care of. The lucky ones managed to get away before they were caught and lived under new identities in Israel where they were shielded from revenge.

It was time to trigger some of the planned raids, something that would raise the dampened spirits and morale in the refugee camps and the Arab villages. There had been nothing to rejoice about since they had cheered on the incoming scuds from Iraq to Israel during the brief Gulf war, and that was too long ago.

Apart from belonging to the mainstream PLO, Fawzi was also the coordinator and contact for terrorist missions originating from Lebanon, Jordan, and from Arab villages inside Israel. During the past weeks he had been busy working on organizing the Break Peace project and had transferred considerable sums of money in Switzerland to the organization's secret account. It was time to put the funds to good use.

Fawzi looked down the list of possible operations, including potential launch sites and preparation time for each one. Why not launch a few at the same time, perhaps the repercussions could delay even the Taba Convention? Maybe force it to be held at another more convenient location not on Arab territory. If he, Fawzi, could accomplish this he would be looked upon very favorably by the central command. He would become a hero to the most rabid, anti-peace splinter groups within the organization. He cracked a smile at the thought.

He knew that many of the other groups such as the Hezbollah in Lebanon would be coordinating with Islamic parties within the Arab and Muslim world to stir up violence in the streets. They were still trying to pressure Arab governments into rejecting the Taba Convention.

He ticked off three choices from the list on the paper in front of him and picked up the telephone. He dialed a number in the Arab village of Umm El Fahm in the north of Israel.

"Control Palestine Central," he whispered into the mouthpiece and the voice on the other end requested the code.

"Code Stormy Night. Please inform Hezbollah southern Lebanon, action number attack seven, letter L. May Allah be with you." He disconnected the phone and dialed again, this time a number in a small village near the Gaza Strip.

"Control Palestine Central, Code Stormy Night, Letter E. Please cross into Egypt via the Taba crossing and report to Control Sinai. Please repeat to him: Action number attack twelve, letter E. Do it today. May Allah be with you." He disconnected the line and dialed again, this time a local number.

"Control Palestine Central, Code Stormy Night. Cross into Jordan via Allenby Bridge and report to Control West Bank. Please repeat to him: Action number attack ten, letter E. Go now. May Allah be with you" He put the phone down. He smiled.

Within twenty-four hours three terrorist attacks would be carried out, hopefully causing more chaos, confusion, and Zionist deaths. Fawzi chuckled through his yellow-stained teeth and shouted at Samira to bring him his Arak. He settled back contentedly in his armchair. He took a last drag and threw his cigarette into a dirty glass with coffee dregs in it.

Hopefully the central command would soon confirm authorization of firearm use for the Intifada, thus escalating the battle on all fronts within Israel. Up until now their only weapons had been stones. For a long time now the activists had been requesting permission to use guns. "Neshek Ham," hot arms as the Israelis called them. The Palestinians felt helpless in the face of the Israeli army who used rubber bullets, teargas, and guns when they felt it necessary. If the use of guns was not authorized soon, Fawzi felt that some fanatics would run out of control, bringing bloodshed to the camps rather than to the enemy. No, the guns must be used cunningly, in ambushes against the army, and not near populated areas. It would be a dangerous escalation, but so much better and effective than stone-throwing.

Fawzi was hopeful that the situation could be controlled, avoiding unnecessary escalation while raising the enemy casualties. Yes, guns would certainly help, but in the meantime he would wait with pleasure to hear the results of his latest commands. He fished another cigarette out of his pocket and lit it between his yellow tobacco-stained fingers.

EILAT.
SUNDAY, AUGUST 19TH.

The hot summer sun beat down mercilessly through a cloudless blue sky. The temperatures often reached forty-three in the shade during August, and today was no exception. Dry heat and hot winds from the north drove down through the Arava desert all the way to the Red Sea.

Many unsuspecting tourists visiting town who did not drink enough liquids ran the risk of dehydration. The local hospital, Yoseftal, treated many visitors during the hot months.

Shalom Biran, Chief of Security at the White Sands Hotel, watched as the ambulance drove away down the driveway with the old lady from room 232. Usually, he thought, it was the younger ones that were more prone to dehydration. The sweet old lady would be all right after a day on a drip at the hospital.

Shalom turned and walked into the hotel. He fought his way through the Sunday crowds at the front desk and entered the offices.

"Linda, I just packed the dear old lady from 232 off to Yoseftal with dehydration. Please inform Public Relations and the front desk. She said it's okay to pack her things for her so we can get the room ready. I'll send a guard up with someone from housekeeping to pack the case. Remind me in an hour and we'll go see her with some fruit. We can take the hotel van up. I'll go and fill in the incident report and fax it to the insurance."

It was common procedure to fill in incident reports and inform insurance as guests sometimes tried to sue for compensation for just about any complaint. It was also common hotel courtesy to visit guests that had been hospitalized. Usually a head of department would go along with the public relations officer. Linda made a note on her desk to remind herself to organize the visit in about an hour.

She remembered that Rami Benatan was coming down to Eilat today and realized why Jordan was a little edgy. She didn't know if he was staying overnight but took no chances that Jordan may have forgotten. She picked up the phone and dialed housekeeping.

"Martine, Rami is coming to town today. I know how bad it gets on a Sunday, but its red alert I'm afraid. Please get three rooms ready and inform the desk which ones they are. No VIP preparations in the rooms—they must look normal. Give me a buzz when you've done it. Sorry, dear," Linda apologized as she put the phone down.

She wondered how nice it would be if Rami were different. Each time he came down to Eilat it seemed that the whole hotel was on edge. A long letter with the hotel shortcomings, especially those faults that he found in his room, followed each time he stayed. Each visit she could sense the dislike between Jordan and Rami, even though it never surfaced.

On one occasion Rami had written that there was dirt behind the lavatory bowl in his room. Jordan had tried to find the dirt but couldn't. He had asked Rami to point it out to him. Rami had taken him up to the room and, lying in the bathtub, pointed out a small speck of dirt on a tile that could be seen only from a certain angle while lying in the tub. A flaming row followed, and Jordan had been in an angry mood for the whole of the following week.

Two completely different people, she thought. Many times Rami had demanded the firing of an employee for minor infractions, and she knew the employees disliked him. Rami was prone to pre-judge people and believed too much in hearsay upon which he made decisions. He had a built-in lack of trust, and although the hotel ran smoothly, she felt that he disliked Jordan for his independent management style. Why, she thought to herself, did Rami care? The hotel was running very smoothly and the figures were great. She knew that from the profit and loss meetings that she attended.

It was already two o'clock, and Linda was wondering when Jordan would get back from the airport with Rami when they both entered the office. She heard Rami complaining about the congestion in the lobby as they walked right past her into Jordan's office and closed the door.

Jordan knew that he was still being followed, although it was a different man today. He hoped that he could get through the work he had to do with Rami in time to catch the last flight to Tel Aviv. He had told Irit that he had to try to get up to town today if possible. He had packed a few clothes in an overnight bag and put them in the trunk of the Audi. Still, if they didn't pull the tail soon it looked like he'd have to catch a morning flight.

Rami pulled out the White Sands "outstanding matters" file from his suitcase and opened it on the desk. He took the capital investments list off the top.

"Where do we stand on the new cool storage container, Jordan?" he inquired.

"The parts came in at the beginning of the week, and the supplier is almost through assembling it. It should be operational by the middle of next week. It'll take a lot of pressure off the chef. He'll be able to store a lot more vegetables down by the delivery ramp in the container rather than overcrowding the kitchen fridges," Jordan explained.

"The rest of the list you've taken care of, except for replacing the lobby ceiling and redoing the woodwork in the main dining room. I know it's being taken care of. I hope the room is in better shape this time; the last one was God-awful. Hope you took care of all the faults in my letter to you. Seems Yoel can't take care of business. I'd look around for another engineer if I were you," Rami stated in his usual staccato style.

Jordan could feel the anger surfacing but did not want a fight with Rami today. He was careful to be courteous. They went over some more papers and Rami got up and stretched. It was almost four o'clock.

"Let's go do a tour of the kitchens," he said to Jordan, who realized that food was the reason. They got up and left the offices, going past the reservations office on the way out.

Jordan saw his tail on the phone in the lobby and hoped that he was getting orders to back off. They had been with him all weekend, and he had felt almost naked under their invasion of his privacy. At the beach, in the hotel, on the road, and below his apartment, they were there all the time. He was getting tired of the game, even though Irit was blissfully unaware of it.

Rami changed his mind and sat down in the lobby. He ordered a smoked salmon and creamed cheese bagel. Approaching fifty, Rami was a thick-set man with a bulging stomach. He still had a lot of thick brown hair curled above a fat, round face. He usually dressed in jeans and a polo shirt. Jordan could not imagine how a company director could allow himself to dress so sloppily on visits to the hotels. On the other hand it was difficult to imagine how he would look in a suit; Jordan smiled to himself at the image.

"I'm going to take a shower," Rami stated bluntly as he got up and went over to the desk.

"Give me a room," he said without a "please."

Jordan had to smile as he refused the first two rooms offered him by the clerk. It did not seem to bother the girl, and he knew that Linda had not forgotten the arrival, even if he had. She was the greatest, he thought, as he watched Rami disappear into the elevator. The prevailing joke in the chain was that there were some rooms that were smaller due to the multiple layers of paint that covered them in preparation for a possible Rami overnight visit.

He looked around and saw that his tail was dutifully waiting for his next move. He went back to his office and closed the door behind him. He settled into his chair and put his feet up on the table. Tel Aviv was out of the question for today.

He must have dozed off, for he woke up with a start. It was five to seven. Dinner was about to start. He yawned and rubbed his eyes. He looked through the window. It was still light outside, and he wondered absent-mindedly whether his follower was still waiting for him.

At the very same moment in the Jordanian Red Sea port town of Aqaba, three frogmen entered the water. They were no more than three kilometers from the beach below the White Sands.

They were armed with submachine guns and grenades. Each was equipped with a submersible motor that would pull them silently underwater. They were on the way to a deadly mission in Eilat. They would hug the seabed and give wide berth to the Israel Navy Hornet patrol vessel anchored just inside territorial waters. Their guns and ammunition were stored in waterproof bags strapped to their bodies. Once ashore, it would be essential to get the guns ready very quickly as the Israelis did not take a lot of time to respond.

The terrorists knew that this was a suicide mission, but they did not care. They were there to kill as many Jews and tourists that they could. They were martyrs. After death they would ascend to the virgins waiting for them in Heaven, as did all "Shaheedim," Holy Warriors. It was great to die for Allah and get paid with virgins for their trouble. They were happy. They knew that their families would be greatly respected by their actions and would be well taken care of after they were killed in action against the Zionist enemy.

They were pulled silently by the motors, three black deadly fish on their way to kill. They would sow terror into the Israeli hearts to deepen the suspicions of the peace process. It would help to ruin the tourism industry and economy.

Up above them, in the bay of Eilat on board the navy Hornet, Samuel Cohen read the newspaper while keeping one eye on the sonar and radar panels. It was hot and humid on board the navy vessel, and he was sweating profusely. The white cotton navy shirt stuck to his back. The strong smell of diesel fuel and oil mixed with the hot air and was suffocating. Through the windows he could clearly see the lights of Eilat. He killed a few more minutes of the boredom by trying to figure out if he could make out the lights of his apartment in the sea of twinkling lights.

Most of his newspaper was taken up with the upcoming peace conference, and he could imagine the building preparations going on in and around the Taba Hilton. Samuel was getting really bored. He was used to the yearly army reserve service, but each year it seemed to get even more boring. Time just did not go by, especially sitting in the bay of Eilat waiting for something to happen. It never did. He got up and stretched. Then he headed for the galley to boil some water for yet another strong black mug of "botz", or "mud" coffee as it was fondly called.

The border with Jordan was the quietest of all. Apart from one or two infiltration attempts over the years, nothing had really happened to disturb the quiet enjoyed by both countries. That is why Samuel and all the sailors on duty did not bother to call for a replacement while making coffee, going to the toilet, or going for a breather up top. He would therefore never have noticed the suspicious dots tracked briefly by sonar on the outer edge of the screen. By the time he was back with the coffee the dots had disappeared from the screen. He sat back down at his desk. A casual glance at the screen assured him that all was normal.

The three terrorists knew that their only chance lay in going far out into the bay in order to go around the patrol boat. They came ashore at the underwater observatory, just a few kilometers out of town. They quickly slipped out of their wetsuits and donned the tracksuits that they carried with them. They unpacked their guns, loaded them, and silently climbed up onto the bridge connecting the main area with the observatory that was about forty yards out at sea. They could make out a security guard with a flashlight patrolling the attractions and silently made their way towards him. He would have to be silenced. The guard walked through the building housing the giant aquariums and circled past the shark tanks. He climbed up the stairs and came up on the bridge above the tanks. It was a favorite spot with visitors.

The guard watched the sharks circling endlessly and looked in on the giant turtles in the next tank. He always enjoyed looking at the fish on his rounds. It was as if the whole area was open only for his viewing pleasure. Anyway, time passed a whole lot faster this way; it was better than sitting in the office.

The terrorists watched the guard looking down into the tanks. One of them approached him silently from below, entering the lower level of the shark tanks. He passed by the thick glass windows. The sharks circled slowly around the thick glass outside wall of the tank. He slowly approached the stairs leading to where the guard was standing.

The guard saw what he thought was a shadow move across one of the viewing windows on the lower level. Speaking into his communication mike as he went, he moved towards the stairs.

"Michael, hi. This is Eran. I am here at the observatory above the sharks," he informed his partner in the offices. "I think I see some movement on the lower level. Probably only some animal or maybe even a kid shut inside after closing. It's been known to happen. I'll go check. Please stay on line."

The guard reached the top of the stairs and started going down. The Arab waited behind the aluminum stairs in the darkness where he could not be seen.

Almost all the way down, a sixth sense told the guard that he was not alone. He turned around. The bullet caught him in the side of the chest.

He was dead before he hit the ground. Blood seeped out of the hole in his chest and stained his jacket.

The Arab dragged the body behind the stairs and propped it up against the wall. He took off the guard's jacket. He pulled off his track suit top and put on the jacket. The bloody hole would be hard to see in the dark. He picked up the Jew and threw him over his shoulder. He climbed up the aluminum stairs with the body until he was above the shark tanks. He backed up against the tank and pushed the limp body backwards over his shoulder into the tank. It fell in with a loud splash. The sharks immediately zeroed in on the blood spreading in the water.

"Dinner time," he whispered gleefully as he heard the thrashing sharks attacking and ripping the body apart. He thought it would have made a great scene in one of the Jaws movies.

"Eran, Eran? Can you hear me? Can you hear me?" Michael shouted into the microphone in the offices in Eilat. He had heard something like a shot followed by what seemed like a fall. He couldn't be certain that Eran had not inadvertently hit or dropped the Motorola. Michael was still trying to listen to the Motorola that had been attached to Eran.

The Arab had not noticed that the Motorola had fallen off Eran when he was shot and could not have known as he signaled the others to join him that it was company policy to leave the walkies on at all times during the patrols.

Panic welled up in Michael. It couldn't be happening. He could not understand what they were saying, but he knew that it was Arabic. He sensed that it was terrorists and he knew instinctively why Eran was not answering. He must not panic, he thought, as he put a call through to the police in Eilat.

The Arabs reached the main road and saw the headlights of an approaching car stabbing the darkness as it wound its way along the coastal road from Taba. The car was briefly hidden by the mountainside as it came around the corner and approached them.

The driver slowed down as he saw the man dressed as a security guard flagging him down. The old Volvo stopped on the shoulder.

The Arab came around to the window. As the driver wound down the window, the terrorist shot him through the neck and caught him through the window as he fell aside. He opened the door and dragged the body out of the car. He reached in and took the keys out of the ignition and ran around to the back to open the trunk. The other Arabs picked up the body and dumped it into the open trunk, slamming it shut as they ran to get into the car.

They slammed the car into gear and skidded on the asphalt surface as they raced out onto the road to Eilat, opening all the windows as they went. No one had ever come back from such a mission in Israel. They knew and believed that their place in Heaven was assured. They were on a spiritual high, knowing that Allah had sanctioned this Holy War against the occupying Zionist infidel. Their names would be written down in the book of martyrs, their families proud of them. They were not talking to each other now. They were praying aloud in Arabic and reciting verses of the Koran to themselves as they hurtled past the coral beach and approached the Club Med hotel.

There was a group of tourists making their noisy way down to the road from the hotel. They had almost reached the road when the Volvo came alongside them. The terrorists laughed with delight as they cut them down with automatic fire. They saw briefly the surprise on the tourists' faces as they were punched back by the force of the bullets. The Volvo accelerated past the hotel and towards the port. They sped around the bend leading to the navy shipyards and suddenly the driver slammed on the brakes with all his force, burning rubber on the humid asphalt and coming to a halt in a cloud of dust and smoke, all of the men inside the car cursing and shouting.

A hundred yards in front of them the outline of three police cruisers blocked the main road with blue lights flashing brightly. The outline of a couple of docked Navy Hornets lit up intermittently in blue as the police lights flashed. The Arabs had not been expecting this; they were taken by surprise. They sat for a moment in shocked silence. The driver's mind was racing now. The other Arabs looked at him. What could they do? He slammed the Volvo into reverse and threw the wheel around, turning the car around in a violent spin. Thick white smoke billowed from the wheel wells as they finally caught traction on the road.

The car accelerated back in the direction from which it had come. The three police cars gave chase and followed the Volvo at high speed past the Club Med, lights flashing, sirens blaring. The Volvo swerved into the dolphin reef, one of the seaside attractions, and screeched to a halt spraying a wave of gravel to the side. The terrorists jumped out, leaving the doors open, and ran down the uneven stairs through the entrance. They ran towards the stairs going down to the beach and dolphin pools. They could hear the police approaching clearly now.

The police had turned the sirens louder in order to attract the attention of the people on the beach.

It was a futile effort to try and warn anyone at the reef of the approaching danger. The Arabs ran along the beach, running with difficulty through the soft sand towards the pub at one end.

Only the dolphin trainer and the staff of the pub were on the beach at the time. They were unarmed and could only watch in fear as the terrorists approached. They raised their hands in the air. They quickly surrendered to the Arabs; they had no other choice. By the time the police arrived the Arabs held the hostages as human shields and threatened with bullets to the heads if approached.

The police captain did not have experience in hostage situations and called immediately for backup from the anti-terror squad based in Eilat. He then ordered his men to back off and stand down at a safe distance from the pub. He did not want to escalate the situation. He did not want anyone to get hurt. The ATS would soon arrive and they could decide on a plan. So long as the terrorists did not move, they would wait for the anti-terror squad to arrive.

The telephone rang on Jordan's desk. It took him a while to answer as he finished signing a few cheques on his desk. He picked up the receiver and listened intently to the voice on the line.

"Okay, I'll be there as soon as I can," Jordan said. Since leaving the secret service he had volunteered to be part of the anti-terror squad in Eilat but had never expected any attack. What the hell was happening? First Josh gets taken out in the Arava and now a terrorist attack in Eilat? Was it an escalation in violence connected to the upcoming Taba convention? Could be, but he didn't have time to consider it right now. Perfect, he thought. First I am being tailed, and now I am being pulled against my will back into violence, and all this just after I've opened up to Irit. He pushed the thought out of his mind and concentrated instead on the task at hand. There would be time enough to do damage control with Irit later. The other thought he pushed aside was that this attack would not do much good for the tourist industry. No matter what this had to be dealt with as quietly and as quickly as possible. He picked up the phone again and punched zero.

"Operator. How can I help you?"

"Rosy, please get the chief of security to ring me ASAP, and I mean as quick as possible!"

Jordan liked Shalom, his head of security. The guy had been with the paratroopers. He had been with Yitzhak Rabin when he had captured the Temple Mount and the Old City during the six-day war. He was with Jordan in the anti-terror squad. He was definitely a useful guy to have around when in trouble. Solid and dependable. Shalom must be over fifty by now, calculated Jordan, but he still looked very fit for his age. He was a heavy-set guy, but you could tell that he was still muscular and strong. Ever since his service with the paratroops he had sported a crew cut, and he still had it. He had a large angular head perched on a thick neck that connected to broad shoulders. For a guy that looked rough he was kind and gentle with everyone and had endless patience with guests. He had been offered the top security job in the hotel chain. He had preferred to stay with Jordan at the Sands.

The phone rang again and Jordan pressed the voice answer button.

"Jord, You looking for me?" Shalom's familiar deep voice came on the line.

"Get out the night glasses and the rifles with the infra sights and meet me at the ramp now!" Two minutes later he was in the Audi waiting by the ramp for Shalom. He could already see him with a large canvas bag rushing quickly down the long service corridor to the ramp.

"Must be bad," he stated, getting into the car.

"Very," replied Jordan. He guided the car out of the service area and onto the road to town. "Three came by sea, through the observatory. I don't know how the Hornet didn't catch them on the sonar. They're holed up on the dolphin beach with three hostages.

"As far as we know they killed a guard at the observatory and then hijacked a car on the road into town, an old Volvo. We don't know whose yet, but the owner is almost certainly dead. On their bloody way into town they killed at least three tourists and injured four. The cops found out through the security firm whose guard was killed. The other guard listened in on the open Motorola that the dead guard had on him. He heard the terrorists speaking Arabic and was clever enough to call the cops. They put up a roadblock pronto by the navy yard. The bastards saw it too early and turned around, ending up at the dolphin beach. Shalom, we've got to free those hostages. We've got to take the terrorists out cleanly. They are relying on us. We don't want prisoners...it's not good for tourism. Let's give them their virgins," he said. He looked over at Shalom who smiled.

The traffic lights at the new tourist center turned green and Jordan turned left towards Taba. He used the shoulder and overtook the cars lining up at the roadblock. He flashed his ID and was waved quickly through by a cop who knew him. In a short while they were on the hill overlooking the pub where the terrorists were holed up with the hostages. Jordan could see that Alex, another member of the anti-terror squad, had already gotten there and was assessing the situation down below.

Jordan went over to him. "What's our play, Alex?" he asked and looked at Alex. A small, wiry string of a boy with intelligent light brown piercing eyes, he could not have been out of the army for more than maybe a year, thought Jordan. He knew that Alex had come to Eilat after service with an elite unit, and he liked the kid a lot. He was always volunteering to help in the anti-terror squad in any way he could. He was a decent guy doing his bit for the community when he could just as easily have sat back and enjoyed a normal life. Jordan appreciated his army experience, and that was the reason he sought out Alex to see if he had thought out an initial plan.

"Dicey business down there. I can't see how we're going to get three clear shots at the same time, Jordan. They are pretty professional, each bastard taking a different side of the pub but keeping within talking distance of each other. One of us will have to go out to sea and come in with a shot from the dolphin pontoon area. Another will go over on the south side and one will stay here. We'll coordinate by walkie-talkie, headsets. When all of us have our man clearly in the sights we'll fire together. It's the only way and it's bloody risky," answered Alex in a tone like battlefield talk, short and to the point with no time wasted.

The boy was right, thought Jordan, appreciating him even more. He considered what the boy had said for a brief minute. A feeling of dread and panic welled up in him. Could he kill again? How would he react? How would Irit react? If he killed he would have to tell her. He couldn't keep it a secret. And only yesterday he had told her all the truth about his past. For a moment he thought about pulling out of the team, allowing them to carry out the proposed rescue with a cop instead of him. But he couldn't do it—he could not let the squad do it without him. It just wasn't right.

He turned to Alex. "Agreed, Alex. It's risky but the only option as I see it, too."

Jordan turned to talk to the Chief of Police. "Please get me three head mikes, one waterproofed and the others regular. Just make sure that they are good for five hundred meters at least."

Jordan went with the dolphin reef manager into the diving hut and came out wearing a wetsuit. "Since I'm best trained at this sort of stuff, I'll go by sea," he said to Alex. "You stay here, and, Shalom, you go south until you've got your man in the sights. Take a head mike, and both of you wait until you hear me communicate from the dolphin pontoons. Oh, and make sure you shoot straight."

A policeman approached and gave each one a set of head mikes. Jordan disappeared into the darkness to skirt around the northern edge of the beach where he would not be seen entering the water. The warm water gave him a feeling of safety. He put on his mask and adjusted his mouthpiece. Like being back in the womb he thought to himself, a womb at war. It seemed to him for an instant that the water was a deep blood-red color, beckoning him back into the bloodbaths of so long ago. He shuddered at the thought as he slowly immersed himself into the water.

Jordan did not go deep but kept to a depth of about three meters so that he would not miss the pontoons that would be outlined against the clear moonlight filtering through the water. He hoped that the dolphins would not get excited and start to jump up out of the water. That might alert the terrorists. There was no doubt that they would not hesitate to kill if they felt in any danger. Jordan smiled at the thought that it took this kind of an emergency to get him into the waters of the Red Sea.

Here it was, one of the world's best diving areas, and he could not remember the last time he had enjoyed a dive among the fabulous tropical fish that swam these waters. He made a mental note to correct this shortcoming as he came up under the pontoons. He slowly brought his head up above the water. He disturbed one of the sea lions on the pontoon who growled in surprise at the intruder and dove into the water.

The disturbance caught the attention of one of the terrorists nearest the beach. Already on edge, the Arab leveled his automatic at the pontoon and started firing in panic. Another sea lion screamed in agony as it was hit and floundered around until it fell into the sea. Bullets hit the woodwork and the sea indiscriminately. A dark red stain was spreading in the water where the sea lion had fallen in. Jordan had ducked down into the water as the shooting started. He knew that there was no real danger as long as he was protected by the pontoons. The water would also slow the bullets down considerably as they impacted deeper into the depths. He saw the bullets as they traced their way through the water below the pontoon. The shooting subsided and he resurfaced quietly, shielded by the wood. He waited for a long minute before deciding that it was safe to move.

He quietly placed his waterproof package on the wooden surface and unpacked the rifle and the head mike. The rifle he unpacked was the Galil Sniping rifle, an Israeli rifle with a folding wooden stock and adjustable cheek piece. It also had an adjustable integral bipod for greater stability. He had used the Galil throughout his army and Mossad days and felt very comfortable and confident with the rifle. It was, in his opinion, the best sniper rifle around.

He focused the night glasses on the pub and scanned the beach for the Arabs. He could see the outline of two people standing on his side and could see that the Arab had a handgun as well as the automatic. He zeroed in with the rifle sights. It would have to be a bloody clean shot or else there would be more bodies to add to the tourists and the Volvo driver, wherever he was. Probably in the trunk of the car, he guessed. He was grateful now that he had kept going to target practice with the ATS, but could he still hit the target from this distance, and at night? He canceled the thought and put it out of his head.

He would never have had self-doubt in the agency—another sign he was getting soft. He put the head mike on and adjusted the mike placing it very near his lips.

"Hi guys, a great night for diving, although the smaller sharks will be here soon. I'm swimming in sea lion blood. You probably heard the wails of the poor creature," he whispered. There were sharks in the Red Sea, but they were usually small and stayed well out to sea. In the past ten years there had been only one shark attack near Eilat when an unfortunate tourist had lost a hand while swimming far out.

"I'm in perfect shape, no hits. So let's get on with the job. I've got a fucking hotel to run, you know," he whispered into the mike. He could almost sense the others smile; he had said it to get them more relaxed, and perhaps even more to do so for himself. The lives of the hostages depended on each shooter making one clear shot, and only one shot—no second chances. Jordan knew they were all doing the same thing, adjusting their sights on the pub and looking for their assigned target.

"A is ready" Alex reported, and he continued to repeat the letter slowly every two seconds to inform the others that the target was in his sights clearly all the time. If he stopped saying it then this would mean that he was off target and would only repeat the letter when he was back on target with a clear shot. Jordan would wait until Shalom reported his target in sight. Satisfied that both Alex and Shalom were ready, he would then zero in on his target. Only with his target in his sights and the others still reporting their letters would he give the signal.

Jordan kept his rifle trained on his terrorist and felt a surge of adrenaline as he heard Shalom join Alex in reporting: "a...b...a...b...a...b..."

Jordan still had the man right in his sights. In the split second that he shouted the command to shoot into the mike, the hostage raised his hand in an upward motion. The three shots rang out almost as one, followed only by screams from the pub. Jordan swam towards the beach as quickly as he could, weighed down by his equipment. He could see Shalom and Alex running low towards the pub. The two hostages were in shock, and another was sitting holding his mangled, bloody hand. Blood dripped from the wound onto the sand. The dazed man looked at his hand as if it did not belong to him. He was in shock.

"Sorry. I did that, but unfortunately you raised your hand at the wrong time. Anyway, better this than the alternative. Call an ambulance please," Jordan calmly instructed a cop. He went around to the back of the pub. The last hostage, a waitress, had fainted as the terrorist's head had exploded like a ripe watermelon beside her. It had splattered her with blood and brains. The dead terrorist had fallen back into her.

The three Israelis inspected their work. All the terrorists were dead, neatly taken out by their bullets. Their bodies had been laid out in a row on the sand, stained dark with their blood. Sure it was messy, but apart from the hand, the work was totally professional. Jordan was hardly to blame for the hand. Soon the place would be crawling with people. The sooner the bodies were taken away the better. Jordan huddled with the Chief of Police and then went into the diving room to change. He came out and motioned with his hand for the others to join him. "Well done, boys. I'm proud of you. Alex, you did great—good plan in such a short time. Till next time then. We'll do the press stuff tomorrow. Let's go, Shalom." Jordan turned and went off towards the Audi. The cops could take care of the cleanup. Jordan did not want to be around when the reporters turned up

It was around ten o'clock when Shalom and Jordan came through the entrance to the hotel. The lobby was full of the usual summertime Israeli families, and the pianist was busy playing the same old tunes. An older couple danced in the small area in front of the piano. As he went down the walkway towards the main bar, Jordan greeted the bartender who was shaking a cocktail. Then he went into the a la carte restaurant where Rami would surely be.

"Where the fuck have you been all evening?" Rami asked in his usual way.

"Oh, had some urgent work to attend to," Jordan said in a matter-of-fact way. "By the way, there was a terrorist attack tonight on Eilat. Three frogmen came in from Aqaba and managed to get onto land by the undersea observatory. They killed an undersea observatory guard, hijacked and killed a poor bastard in his Volvo, and killed at least three tourists by the Club Med. The anti-terror squad took care of the motherfuckers. It remains to be seen just how quiet we can keep this. And how was your meal?" he asked nonchalantly. Rami was more into the meal than the attack.

"Great meal. It's the best restaurant in the chain. Good thing you brought the a la carte chef from Germany." Rami was referring to the foreign cooks that Jordan contracted through a headhunter in Zurich. It was common policy for the luxury hotels to bring over European cooks, especially Swiss, French, and German. They came on yearly contracts to practice their trade in the specialty restaurants. The main kitchens were manned by Israelis who were well experienced in the art of Middle Eastern cuisine. They prepared the meals for the main dining rooms where most of the guests usually dined from the evening buffets. Of course, the executive chef of the hotel was still in overall charge of the restaurants. This was largely because the whole hotel was kosher and the foreign cooks needed guidance in this. Since many Israelis were observant, it was common practice that all hotels carry the kosher certificate. If your hotel did not have the kosher certificate, it meant that there would be no Israeli groups.

Rami carried on, changing the subject. "I'll call for a meeting of the Hotel Association in the morning to see what we can do to limit the damage to our winter business from the fallout of this attack. Don't forget, the first charter flights start towards the end of September. All the operators from abroad—Thomson in England, T.U.I. in Germany, Holland International—to name but a few have all reported record reservations for this year due to the new atmosphere of security. The Taba Convention was supposed to crown the achievements so far, to announce to the whole world the dawn of the new Middle East. Now this! This could spoil all our progress. You'd think that they would have had enough, that they would want to get on with a new life with peace and security. Bloody Arabs. I guess that the Hamas and the Izzadin al Kassim are making a last-ditch effort to sabotage the convention."

Rami threw his napkin on the table and got up. "I'll see you in the morning. Until then see what ideas you can come up with regarding damage control. Goodnight." Rami was already in the doorway and on his way out.

Jordan cut through the lobby to his office. He picked up the phone and asked once more for Shalom. He checked with him to be sure Shalom had locked the rifles back in the safe.

It was not necessary for everyone to know about their partici-pation in the operation to liquidate the terrorists. He tidied the papers on his desk and folded the *Jerusalem Post* and placed it on top. He was stretching for the switch to turn his table lamp off when one of the death notices in the paper caught his eye. He picked up the paper to take a closer look.

A feeling of horror came over him as he took in the notice:

"Dvora, the beloved wife of David Applebach, is sad to announce the passing of her dearest husband, father to Ben and Odelia. The private funeral was held yesterday with only fam-ily in attendance. Please do not send flowers, but donations to charity will be welcomed. The family is sitting Shiva at his home."

Jordan dropped back into his chair still holding the paper, horrified. Applebach must have been taken out as well. It was too much of a coincidence to happen right after Josh. Had others been killed? Josh had rambled about "many dead." Had they found out about an Arab conspiracy to sabotage the con-vention? Had Josh been on his way to Jordan when he was taken out? Hell, he had died before he could reveal any more information. God, this must be big. So big that Josh and Applebach had died because of what they knew. Applebach was a control, and the Arabs had gotten to him as well? How had they infiltrated the agency? He admitted grudgingly that the Arabs were getting better at this game.

The first step he would have to take now would be to go to the Applebach control apartment on Hayarkon Street and see if there were any clues left. There wasn't much else to go on. Could he get there before they cleaned and stripped the house? He doubted it. They would already be taking care of that. He knew that the agency would sell the compromised property on the open market. Maybe he wasn't too late. If he was, he would need to find other clues as to why they had died. Could Applebach have left a clue?

He got up and left the office, switching off the lights on the way. He wanted to get back home in time to catch the late night news. He swore silently under his breath as he went through the revolving door. He had once again caught sight of his tail sitting in the lobby sipping a soft drink.

CHAPTER FIVE

EILAT.
SUNDAY, AUGUST 19TH.

Jordan was walking into the apartment as the late-night bulletin came up on the television. He had seen his shadow following him in the side mirror but was not bothered by it. He guessed that the man would be pulled in the morning. That would allow him the freedom of movement to get to Tel Aviv to try and check the Applebach control apartment.

Irit, dressed sexily in an oversized T-shirt and panties, was watching the news. Her long bronzed legs were curled up under her on the sofa. She acknowledged his entrance with a wave of her hand. Jordan went to the fridge and took out a can of chilled Goldstar, his favorite local brew. He pulled the tab and took a sip. He went over and sat down next to her and kissed the top of her head as he settled in and put his arm around her.

There was ample coverage of the terrorists' suicidal mission in Eilat, but Jordan was pleased to see that the report had been doctored. They made it look as if they had been caught on the Hornet radar prior to landing. They had managed to evade a first trap but were then nearly caught at the roadblock before being taken out by the Eilat anti-terrorist unit at the dolphin reef.

Irit briefly glanced across at him and he nodded. She frowned and glared at him.

The deaths of the two Israelis was reported as were those of the unfortunate tourists caught in the hail of gunfire by the Club Med. The report was angled to look as if the incident had always been under control and that the terrorists never posed a threat to the center of town or to the main hotel areas.

The report was followed by another on an attack against Israeli troops in the security zone in southern Lebanon. A suicide bomber had tried to fly into one of the camps on a hang glider but had blown up too early, killing only himself. Another few seconds of flight and there would have been a massacre. The Israel Defense Forces had slapped a curfew on the local Arab villages. They were doing house-to-house searches. They wanted to know where the terrorist had come from. When they found out which house belonged to the terrorist, it would be destroyed. It would be bulldozed to the ground as per army procedure for the residences of convicted or known terrorists.

The breaking news from Egypt was that fundamentalists had shot at a busload of tourists, killing one and injuring dozens. The authorities had countered by arresting known activists who were members of the Brotherhood of Islam. It was by far the largest and most organized outlawed opposition in Egypt. These violent attacks were happening all too often, wreaking havoc with the tourism industry and confirming Jordan's line of thinking for the future of Egypt. The fundamentalists were gaining ground, and it didn't look good for the regime. The upsurge in violence and terror attacks all pointed to a deliberately planned conspiracy to delay the convention or, perhaps, even get it cancelled. The Egyptians were, after all, hosting the convention.

There followed some uninteresting home news and a brief look at tomorrow's weather—more of the same searing heat. Another day in the oven to look forward to, thought Jordan.

Irit had already risen and was in the kitchen putting together a cheese toast that she knew would be welcome. "And I thought that you were through with that stuff, Jordan!"

It came out more as a soft cry from the heart rather than a question.

"You bastard, only last night you swore that you were through with the killings and today you're back at your bloody hobby again. How could you, Jordan? What is it with you? When is it going to finally end?"

She cried softly under her breath. The tears coursed down her face. She was hurting.

"You know that I am through with this," he answered firmly, "but I couldn't refuse them. I didn't want this, Irit. You know that. I never thought that when I volunteered for the squad we would ever have the slightest trouble here. What could I do? Let them come and massacre more of us? You know damn well I would not do that. It's not in me. I couldn't turn my back on the guys when they called. Oh, I thought about it but couldn't back out."

The question went unanswered. An uneasy silence separated them. He thought about going over to hug her but decided against it; it would only make the situation worse. Tonight he had had about as much punishment as he could take.

The delicious cheese toast came just as he liked it, with thin slices of onion stuffed in with the cheese. He washed it down with another can of iced Goldstar. The two beers brought on the fatigue following the tough day.

He and Irit did not exchange a word throughout the evening. He knew she was mad as hell at him, and he felt helpless against it. Maybe she was right. He finally got up, took a long hot shower, and got into bed. He was so tired he was asleep before his head hit the pillow.

Irit turned off the television and cleared the table. She tidied up the kitchen and put the dirty plates and glasses in the dishwasher. She stood silently for a moment in the kitchen and contemplated what Jordan had said. She reached for a tissue and dried her eyes. In the past twenty-four hours Jordan had swung back to violence, back to a killing machine. She considered his options as part of the ATS Eilat. She'd known he was a member of the squad, so she should have expected that if there were a terror attack he would be called. Could he have refused? Doubtful. There were Jewish lives at stake. She knew in her heart that he was right this time. She had been too harsh to jump in judgment on him earlier and now she regretted her outburst. She would make it up to him.

Even though she had gotten home much earlier than Jordan and had already taken a shower, she still enjoyed another. By the time she got between the sheets Jordan was in a deep satisfying sleep.

She looked at him lovingly for a long time as he slept peacefully. She marveled at what he was still capable of doing. She could not blame him for tonight's violence; he was right. But when would the violence finally stop, when would Israel be allowed to rest? When would Jordan finally put down the guns?

She wondered if this Taba Convention that everybody was talking about would help. She prayed that it would. It seemed as if Israel was destined always to be at war with her enemies. Families would always have to give their sons to the army. Perhaps Taba would put an end to that.

Irit thought again about that night that she had always known would come. The night that Jordan had told her of his past, of his yearning for the future. She had always suspected that there was a lot more to Jordan Kline. Through her love for him she wanted him to come to her, and he had. She had waited patiently for that night. He was sleeping peacefully beside her now. She felt tremendous pride and pity for the man lying beside her. A man filled with both love and war—a man of so many contrasts.

She lay down beside him. The events of the past few days turned over in her mind. After a few minutes she turned to him, put her arm around him, and drifted off to sleep.

EILAT.
MONDAY, AUGUST 20TH.

Jordan was first to wake up from a deeply satisfying sleep. He got up and went to the kitchen to put some water on to boil. Although it was only half past seven, he already felt the threatening heat streaming through the glass as he stood next to the window.

He had to get to Tel Aviv today and take a look during daylight at the Applebach apartment. He remembered it well and had always wondered how such a beautifully placed apartment could be wasted as a control center. Or maybe that was the idea: put a top-secret Mossad operation right in the middle of one of the best real estate areas in town. No one would notice, except maybe some of the neighbors. They would think it was one of the many small businesses run out of countless apartments all over the city.

The three terror attacks yesterday had to be part of a concerted effort to destroy the Taba Convention or, at the very least, delay it. It would not be surprising if there were more suicide attacks in the coming few days. He hoped that the Shin Bet, the Israeli General Security Services, would be able to avert attacks like the bus bomb in the center of Tel Aviv that had claimed thirteen lives not so long ago.

He made two mugs of coffee and took them into the bedroom and put one down on Irit's bedside table. He pealed the sheet back from her. He bent down and kissed her on her warm, flat stomach. It aroused him, and he could feel that she was pressing her stomach up to meet his mouth.

She woke up and playfully pulled at his hair. "Jordan, I'm sorry for last night. I was out of line and I apologize. You had no choice. And anyway, what's the time, St. George, and how many dragons you going to kill today?"

He took her face between his hands and looked into her eyes. "Quit that," he said sharply. He could tell by the changed look of her face that she was surprised by his harsh reaction, but he had to make this clear. "I did not want to do what I did yesterday, but at the same time I could not run from it. You know they will never let us rest. We cannot afford to show the slightest weakness. You know that. That is why I had to do what I did. Now, drink that coffee, get dressed and I'll drop you off on the way to the Sands."

Twenty minutes later they were in the Audi slowly descending the hill towards the new tourist center. There was an uneasy and tense silence between them.

She was hurt by his outburst—he understood that. But even though he was sorry he had raised his voice he was unrepentant about what he'd said and felt.

Jordan guided the car across the lights and after two hundred yards turned right towards the Neptune. Irit pecked him curtly on the cheek as she climbed out in silence. He watched her go through the revolving door and disappear into the reception area. He put the car into gear and headed towards the Sands. He glanced in the wing mirror and realized with a smile that they had pulled his shadow. My God, he must be getting old if he had forgotten to check until now. Still, better late than never. Now all he needed was to get through the meeting with Rami and catch a plane to Tel Aviv.

He parked the car and went into the hotel and straight to the dining room where he knew Rami would be. He filled a pot with chilled chocolate milk and sat down opposite him.

"Good morning, Jordan. Hope you got a good night's sleep," Rami said between scoops of Shakshouka, a Middle Eastern specialty made of cooked spiced onions and tomatoes topped with fried eggs. "I've fixed a meeting at ten o'clock at the hotel association offices regarding last night. Everybody is going to be there, including the mayor, the chief of police, the fire people, the army guys and all the rest who may or may not be involved. It is vitally important that we put up a united front on this and issue only one report for the public. You remember what happened when we had the earthquake a few years back. Every Tom, Dick, and Harry was giving interviews with the press and television, and each story was different. That got all the tourists running away in panic with their tails firmly between their legs. No. This time only one press release. We should send it out to all the wholesalers and travel agents before they come asking. That way they'll know that we aren't running scared." He wiped the plate clean with a piece of bread roll and got up. The plate looked like it had just come out of the dishwasher.

"I'll see you at the meeting then." He strode out and left Jordan sipping his chocolate.

The man could have been a cowboy, thought Jordan, a cowboy in the Wild West. He laughed to himself as he remembered a joke about cowboys. How did it go?

A cowboy was standing in a saloon next to a friend. The saloon was full of other cowboys drinking beer. The pianist was tickling the ivories, the atmosphere was clouded with smoke, and the ladies were looking for a nights' work. The cowboy points to another cowboy on the other side of the saloon and asks his friend, "See that guy in the six-gallon hat over there?"

"They're all wearing six-gallon hats," answers his friend.

"Yeah, but look at the guy wearing the six-gallon hat and the six-shooters," he says to his friend.

"Yup, but they are all wearing six-gallons and six-shooters."

The cowboy gets annoyed and taking out his guns he blazes away and shoots dead all the cowboys in the saloon, leaving only one standing. "Now," he says turning wearily to his friend, "do you see the guy over there in the six-gallon and the shooters?"

"Yup," says his friend.

"Well, I really hate that guy!"

The small meeting hall was already packed with people by the time Jordan got to the association offices at five past ten. The air was thick with the smoke of the ever-present Israeli chain smokers. People looked tense and nervous. There were heated arguments going on in all corners of the room. It took a while for some semblance of order to be restored and for the meeting to finally get under way. As was the practice, everybody got his chance to speak out about how he thought the incident should be handled. Everybody knew that for the good of the town this thing had to be handled differently and better than the earthquake had been.

Around twelve o'clock a rough copy of the agreed-upon press release was drawn up and left to the public relations people to fine-tune before being issued. At one o'clock the document was issued to the waiting press corps and by the evening it was faxed to most of the European wholesale travel agencies.

The association had designed the contents of the release to be up-front and truthful, not to deny the tragic events of the day before but to calm fears of any potential catastrophe. After all, the navy Hornet had caught the terrorists on their sonar equipment, and the police had put up a roadblock. It was a quick reaction that had prevented the terrorists from entering the town. The matter had been dealt with so efficiently, it seemed, that only the minimum loss of life had been incurred. Eilat was looking forward to the Taba Convention across the border and looking forward very much to receiving record numbers of winter tourists. The release ended with a note of thanks to all the authorities who had helped bring the matter to a speedy end and a thank you for the continued support of all "our European friends."

The Taba Convention would be back in the headlines again and only a few cancellations would be received due to the attack. Minimal collateral damage. Tomorrow it would be yesterday's news.

Jordan drove straight back to the hotel after the meeting and booked a flight out of Eilat at three o'clock. He would ring Irit from Tel Aviv and tell her that he had been called on some urgent business and that he would get back as soon as possible.

The Arkia Airways De Havilland rumbled down the runway as it gained speed to take off. Powered by propellers, the Dash carried only fifty-two passengers and was for years the quickest and most reliable way to get to Tel Aviv. Granted, there were sometimes many delays, but since it was the only airline running the route, everyone took the delays good-naturedly.

Jordan glanced at his watch as the plane lifted off. Good. They were only five minutes late in take off and would be at the Dov Airfield at about four o'clock. As the plane climbed slowly to an altitude of thirty-five thousand feet, Jordan looked down at the Arava desert and the magnificent mountain ranges framing the valley. The pilot came on the public address system to inform the passengers that their route would take them due north along the Arava valley. They would fly over the Dead Sea, turn west just south of Jericho, and then north of Jerusalem on their way into Dov airport. They would come in over the Reading Power Station, fly out over the Mediterranean, curve around in a southern loop towards the ancient port of Jaffa, and land on the runway adjacent to the sea.

The route took them over the Ramallah airstrip used by Arkia on the Jerusalem flights. Jordan wondered, as did many Israelis, if the PLO or any of the splinter groups like the Hamas or the Izzadin el Kassam would one day think of trying a rocket propelled grenade against one of the inbound flights. Any of the surrounding rooftops would do; an Israeli plane could be brought down easily by an RPG.

Jordan thought of the winter flights from and to Tel Aviv. Windy, rainy days meant flights that would be really rough. On many flights people would get sick to their stomach due to the unstable weather conditions that threw the small plane around like a toy in the sky. He had seen many an arrival at the Eilat airport with the passengers looking pretty damn rough as they staggered out of the terminal.

The Dash Seven dropped out of a clear blue sky above Tel Aviv and came in for a perfect landing. The passengers were not long in disembarking after the plane had taxied close to the small terminal.

Jordan had sat in row one, the first row in the plane and the one with the most legroom. It was also the one nearest the exit door. He was the first to step off and walk across the tarmac and through the security doors. He crossed the road, got into one of the many cabs waiting at the curb, and requested to be taken to the Ramada hotel on Hayarkon Street. The drive was a short one. The taxi followed Hayarkon Street past the old port of Tel Aviv and along the shore past the Hilton. It drew up outside the Ramada and he got out.

Jordan crossed the road, bought a newspaper in the hotel lobby, and went out onto the sundeck. He ordered a coffee from the waitress at the bar and sat down at a table facing the control apartment waiting for his coffee. He sat with his back to the sea and scanned the building. From here he would be able to see any suspicious activity.

Even though it was already four-thirty the sun was still hot, but a pleasant breeze coming in from the sea brushed the bulk of the heat and humidity aside. He held the newspaper open and sipped the coffee. As expected, he could see major renovation work going on in the apartment. There was already a "For Sale" sign up just by the entrance to the block of flats.

Jordan remembered the death notices in the *Jerusalem Post*, both the one from the government and the one placed by the family. He figured that Josh had tried to tell him that Applebach was dead. He knew that it was much more than an ordinary terrorist attack. The terror organizations preferred very public attacks that would have an effect on the citizens of Israel, instilling fear. Public attacks would strengthen their powerbase in the West Bank and Gaza. It would keep the dollars flowing from the Iranian Mullahs.

So it all pointed to covert Arab action, but what could Applebach have known to have necessitated his elimination? He must have stumbled onto something, perhaps inadvertently, and this had instigated his death. How on earth could the Arabs have infiltrated the most efficient secret service in the world? Was it possible, he wondered, that the Arabs had an insider? If they did, it would be the first traitor in the agency. No, it just didn't figure, not with the Mossad. The Arabs also had intelligence, and they must have found out that the agency was onto something that got Josh and Applebach killed.

He hoped that Applebach had been, as most controllers were, unusually efficient. Perhaps he had hidden some sort of clue as to why his life was taken so brutally. Jordan remembered that he too had always hidden information away in case he were ever captured on a mission. It would enable the ones that followed to get a decent start, or at the very least a clue to go on.

He drained his cup, got up, and put a ten-shekel note under the cup so that the breeze would not blow it away. He folded the newspaper and put it under his arm. He went back through the lobby, out of the hotel, and waited with a small crowd for the pedestrian light to turn green. Once across the other side he turned right and walked along until he was at the entrance to the block of flats.

He pushed the light button and started up the dimly lit stairwell. The smell of new paint drifted down as he approached the apartment. The door to the apartment was open. There were three painters at work as well as a plumber in the kitchen. The floor was covered in old sheets to catch paint drips. There was no furniture at all.

"Come to look around." He nodded at one of the painters in white overalls. "Anglo-Saxon Real Estate sent me along. I always had a mind to buy me an apartment facing the sea. So rare for one to come on the market." He went into the bedroom. He had been here a few times during his service and remembered that there was a balcony running around three sides of the apartment.

He walked through the bedroom and out onto the narrow balcony from which there was an outstanding view of the seashore. Even though it was getting towards late afternoon, there were many people on the beach and still quite a few in the water. There was a white flag flying above the lifeguard hut indicating calm conditions for swimming. A multitude of different colored umbrellas gave welcome shade to the tourists lying below them. A little further down a game of handball was in progress.

He walked back in and went down the hallway to the kitchen, which he also noticed had been stripped of all appliances and cupboards. The renovators had done a clean and thorough job, leaving nothing that Jordan could even check for clues. If he didn't find something to go on he would be at a loss. He needed some small sign that would point him in a direction that could lead to something.

He went through the kitchen and onto the back balcony overlooking the sandy yard. He leaned on the wall and looked down. There were a few stray cats congregating around the garbage bins sifting through the garbage that had spilled out from a bin that had been pushed over. Occasionally a fight would start, with the victor walking away to sit in a corner and chew at his find. On the balcony opposite a middle-aged woman hung washing on the lines below her. She used the old-fashioned clothes pegs.

While shifting his legs, Jordan's shoe came into contact with one of the small marble panel tiles running along the bottom length of the wall. He could feel that it was loose and bent down to press it back into place. As he did so it fell over on its side. A small key that looked like a safe key lay in the crack behind the loose panel. He bent down as if to do up his shoelaces. Taking a pen out of his shirt pocket he scooped out the key and put it and the pen quickly back into his pocket. He pressed the panel back into place and straightened up just as the plumber appeared. Jordan smiled at him and quietly stepped back into the apartment. He walked around once more as if looking around in a final inspection. He thanked the painters and went down the stairs and back out onto Hayarkon Street.

At least he had something, although he would have to visit the widow to find out where Applebach kept his bank account. He hoped that the key would be for a safety deposit box in that particular bank.

Jordan remembered that Applebach used to live at the very end of Ben Yehuda Street, towards the old port of Tel Aviv. The newspaper had said that they were sitting Shiva at home. It was most probable that they had not moved, since most of the older generation had bought apartments and had lived, worked, and retired in them. That was the way of the old folk that had built the country. They were modest and frugal.

Jordan decided to walk down Ben Yehuda since he had time on his hands. The late afternoon sun caressed him as he walked past all the shops and crossed the Boulevards on his way. In the old days Ben Yehuda used to be one of the better streets of Tel Aviv, but time had gone by and nowadays the shops looked worn and old. Many of them had not changed their display windows. They were from a bygone age.

Traffic had increased tenfold since the early days of the state, and many Egged Cooperative buses ploughed down Ben Yehuda spewing out enormous clouds of thick black smoke in their wake.

As he approached the end of the street, Jordan started looking for Applebach's name on the apartment mailboxes at the entrances. God, all these buildings looked the same. Third time lucky he thought to himself, as he found the address at number 274.

He knew that all the family would be there, and it was natural that Jordan would come to pay respects to the widow.

Mrs. Applebach was clearly pleased to see Jordan, remembering better times. She invited him to sit with the small crowd in the sitting room. The conversation was centered on Applebach's death. Dvorah Applebach recounted how he couldn't have been happier towards his retirement and days to be spent sailing on the Med with the sailboat. Did Jordan know that he had bought a sailing boat with a partner? No, he probably did not since he had left the service a long time ago.

"David had never felt better," she said, "and that is why I cannot comprehend the fact that he died so suddenly of a heart attack."

So that was the official line they had sold her. The agency had covered this up as a natural death because they did not want adverse publicity.

"Well you know, there are so many people that are healthy throughout their lives, and then suddenly they get a heart attack out of the blue. I guess it is something that creeps up on you with time," ventured Jordan.

"Yes, but even as little as six months ago the doctors gave him a clean bill of health after his yearly physical. How can things go so wrong in that time?" she asked no one in particular.

If only Dvorah knew the truth behind the "heart attack." Jordan sipped on a grapefruit juice and after ten minutes of small talk he asked for the directions to the washroom. Going down the narrow corridor towards the washroom, he walked past the bedroom and then the study. The old wooden parquet floor creaked under his footsteps. Family pictures now yellowing with age hung on the walls on either side of the hallway. Suddenly he had a thought. Maybe Applebach had a safe in his study or bedroom. Perhaps he had kept the confidential material at home rather than in the bank safe which would be more difficult to access.

Jordan walked softly back to the corridor entrance and closed the door silently so that he would hear if someone were to disturb him.

He went into the bedroom and checked the cupboard but found no safe. He then went into the study. He quickly located the small safe in the right hand cupboard of the desk. He pulled out the key and prayed that it would fit. It was a perfect fit, and he opened the small old-fashioned safe. Not a very strong safe, nor a clever place to put it, he thought. On the other hand, Applebach had probably not expected anything to go wrong, shielded as he was, being a control. He'd had no idea what he had stumbled across, and right now neither did Jordan, but it was something that had cost Applebach his life.

The safe was small and there were a lot of papers stacked in it. Jordan saw a cassette tape squeezed in between the papers on right side of the safe. He was reaching for it when he heard the corridor door opening. He quickly grabbed the cassette and in one movement he put it in his pocket and straightened up. He had no time to lock the safe but only to push it and the cupboard door closed.

Above the desk there was a picture of Applebach among a bunch of people that included Ben Gurion, Israel's first Prime

Minister. Jordan pretended to be looking at it with interest as Dvorah Applebach entered.

"He always spoke highly of you, said that you were one of the best the agency ever had. He even lamented a few days ago the fact that the new generation is so different and—" Dvorah left the sentence unfinished, her face pained.

"I liked him and respected him, too, very much, Dvora. Times are different, and I can imagine how much he was looking forward to his sailing...it's a tragedy he didn't realize his dream." Jordan hugged the widow. "I better be going. I'll give you a call in a few days and see how you are doing. I'll try and visit you when I am in town."

"That would be very nice of you, Jordan. I'd like that. I will look forward to the visit," she answered in her kindly, matronly voice.

Jordan was keen to get out of the flat since it might be under observation. He was not in the mood for the small talk and memories that were part of the mourning period. God how he wished he had had time to lock the small safe and take the key! The agency would know that someone had gotten there first. It was surprising that they had not already found the opportunity to go over the Applebach's apartment. It would come, no doubt about that. They would be there soon, no loose ends. He was eager to hear what was on the cassette. It would have to wait until he got back to Eilat.

He walked out onto Ben Yehuda Street, hailed a cab, or rather a dirty beaten-up Mercedes that passed for a cab. He directed the driver to take him back to Dov Airport where he hoped he would not have to wait long to catch the next flight back south. The interior of the cab was hot and stank of the sour sweat coming from the driver. It was overpowering—didn't the guy get his shirts washed? He buried his nose in the crook of his arm to shield the smell. Jordan was really pleased when they pulled up at Dov Airport.

He quickly passed the security checks, flashing his Arkia airline club card, and was in time for the seven p.m. flight on which there was a free seat. In the few minutes before the flight was called he had enough time to grab a Kif Kef, the Israeli equivalent of the Kit Kat, and a bottle of mineral water to sip on during the flight down.

Jordan's plane touched down just short of eight p.m. and taxied to the gate. After a short cab ride to the hotel, he walked into his office and sank down into one of the armchairs in the corner. He turned on the mini stereo on the shelf behind his desk, took out the cassette, snapped it into the holder and punched the play key.

The voice on the tape was that of a frightened but determined old man. Applebach recounted in his hardly intelligible cockney that agent Eisenstadt had not reported in from Switzerland on his mission to follow Mohammed Iyad, a Palestinian activist that Jordan had heard of. This meant that he was very probably dead. He reported on the mission that he had assigned to Gilad Dolev to follow David Hofstein to Italy. He listed the facts that Gilad had reported in his call to control. He was calling from outside a "Castelfranco" marble company in Italy and gave the number plates of a Ford Sierra that he was following from Bologna. Following the call he had not heard any more from Gilad. He was probably dead too, said the voice on the tape. Jordan listened as Applebach told of Hofstein's name being found on a document seized in a raid on a PLO cell in Ramallah.

Jordan felt a surge of fear welling up inside him, and realized in an instant that all three agents, Josh, Eisenstadt, and Gilad were all under Applebach's control.

God, thought Jordan, I am the only one who knows about this, and I don't have any pieces of the puzzle. Why have they all been killed, and how is David Hofstein connected? How and why did his name come to be in a PLO file? Had he found out about the Arabs' plan to derail the conference? Were Applebach and his team trying to get more information about the Arabs? Was Hofstein a target now? The questions filling his head unnerved him.

Jordan stopped the tape. He sat back in his chair and held his face in his hands. He had to think clearly. He knew that he had to hide the tape in a very safe place, somewhere even the Mossad would not think of when they came looking. He opened the deck, took out the cassette, put it in his pocket, and walked out of the office.

He strolled across the lobby and entered the entertainment lounge. The entertainment team was preparing for the evening show and was discussing the timing and choreography in their dressing room behind the small stage. Jordan climbed a couple of stairs and went into the DJ booth from where he could view the whole bar and entertainment area. The guests were beginning to congregate in the lobby, some ordering drinks from the waitresses, others making sure that they had good seats for the show. Jordan took out the cassette and slipped it into the end of one of the many rows of cassettes lined up like books on the shelves in the DJ booth. They were rarely used now since most of the music was on discs. Applebach was still using cassettes. He made a mental note of where he had placed it and quickly exited the booth to go say hi

110

to the entertainment team. He hoped to God that the DJ wouldn't choose that tape to play, but since it was unmarked that was highly unlikely.

"Full house again tonight," he said to Uri, his chief entertainer and organizer of all the entertainment at the Sands. "Make sure you don't fuck up the show. I know it's a new production, but I do not want complaints in the morning."

Uri, just putting on his costume, laughed with Jordan. "Why don't you stick around to see us making asses of ourselves?" Uri was very talented. Many of the stars on Israeli TV came from the entertainment teams at the Eilat hotels.

"No, too tired today. Maybe I'll take in the next show. Don't want to be around when they start throwing the eggs," Jordan said over his shoulder as he left the room laughing and walked back over to his office.

He picked up the telephone and dialed the Neptune Hotel. "Hi, chicken. Still at work?" he asked Irit.

"Another long day, another dollar short," she said. "Please pick me up on your way and quickly, Jord. I am dead tired and I've missed you!"

She sounded like she needed a relaxing evening and a good night's sleep.

"I'm on my way," he said dutifully as he put down the phone, picked up his briefcase and keys and exited his office.

He was outside the entrance to the Neptune before Irit came out, waiting in the car for her to join him. He watched as she approached, loving every second of it and looking forward to being alone with her in a few minutes at home. She opened the door and slid into the passenger seat. Her skirt rode high on her thighs. She gave him a playful slap on his cheek, knowing that he had watched her approaching.

Five minutes later they drew into the car park under their apartment and took the elevator to their floor. Irit unlocked the door to the apartment and pushed it open. A look of horror came over her as she walked into the living room.

"We've been broken into!" she said in a faint voice, stunned, as she surveyed the shambles. The place was a mess; everything was upside down. Cushions, papers, and books were strewn all over the place. They had emptied the kitchen cupboards and thrown china and glassware onto the floor. Thousands of bits of broken glass and china littered the floor. The walk-in closet had been searched, their clothes thrown onto the bedroom floor. The sheets had been torn off the bed. They had even ripped the mattress in several places. They had given the flat a thorough going-over, but as far as Jordan could see, they had not stolen anything. Then again, they were not looking to steal anything. He knew that. They were after the cassette, or something of similar size. Something that could have fit into Applebach's safe at home.

My God, thought Jordan, they were even quicker than he would have guessed. He realized that this time he was under suspicion, and that they would not let go. He must act very normal if he was to gain time. He had to think. They had prob-ably discovered the open safe with the key still in the lock at the Applebach's and had put two and two together. After all, he had just left the apartment. He knew that they would check the place, including who had paid condolence visits. He picked up the phone and rang the police to report the break-in. He answered their questions and asked them to come over the next morning to dust for prints.

"There has been a rash of break-ins during the past month in this area, Honey," he lied to Irit. "We'll take a room at the hotel tonight. I'll have housekeeping clear up the mess after the police have been tomorrow. It'll look good as new tomorrow noon, you'll see. I promise. Everything will be fine. I'll take care of it. No need to worry, my love."

Irit cried as he hugged her close to him.

"Why us?" she asked. "Why'd they do this to us?"

Jordan picked up some clothes for both of them from the pile on the bedroom floor and tossed them into a backpack. He guided her down to the car and out towards the White Sands.

CHAPTER SIX

EILAT.
TUESDAY, AUGUST 21ST.

Jordan passed a sleepless night at the hotel, his head filled with thoughts of the past week. They had asked the chef to send them some sandwiches and drinks and had eaten in their suite. Irit was sullen and withdrawn. They had showered and gone to bed early.

He could not get comfortable. He could not sleep. He turned over listlessly in bed, careful not to disturb Irit sleeping beside him.

He didn't know where or how to begin putting the pieces of the puzzle together. He didn't have many pieces of it in any case. He needed time to think, to try and reason this thing out. He was embroiled in something very sinister, of that he was in no doubt. It had cost the lives of four people already, and one of them a control. He thought briefly of poor old Applebach, so near his dream of sailing.

He realized the he was under suspicion now, and probably in danger. If they thought that he might compromise an operation, they would be ruthless. They had already proven that. It would take all of his rusty operational experience to ride this one out. He thought of going to the agency and reporting what he knew but decided against it. Whom could he trust there now? They had placed a Goddamn tail on him. Why hadn't they come to him with explanations? They knew him from his past. The Arabs must be up to something serious this time, he figured, for the agency to be acting like this. They must be near to cracking open a case, maybe a conspiracy connected to the Taba convention.

One thing he knew for certain. He could not and would not tell Irit. That would put her in danger too. She must know nothing of this; she had to carry on with her life normally. She had to be oblivious to what was going on. He had to do this alone.

Somehow he managed to grab a couple of hours sleep.

Irit was showered and dressed and ready to go by the time he put the finishing touches on his tie. He grabbed his jacket and they rode the elevator down to the car park. He drove her over to her hotel.

"See you tonight, Jord, and don't forget to have them clean up the flat, please," Irit said. She was not in a good mood today, not the usual Irit. It was understandable.

Jordan could sense how upset she was about the break-in as he accelerated down the ramp and back to his hotel. He blew a kiss at Linda as he entered his office, closed the door behind him, and sat down at his desk.

He analyzed the situation again in his mind, careful not to put anything down in writing. He knew that there had been four murders and made a mental note of the names involved: Yuval Eisenstadt, Gilad Dolev, his friend Josh, and Applebach. He also added to his list two names Applebach had mentioned on the tape: David Hofstein, the contractor, and Mohammed Iyad, the activist. The first four were dead, leaving the other two somehow connected.

Apart from being a very well known Palestinian, Jordan recollected that Iyad was also a known furniture dealer. Perhaps this was the connection to Hofstein. It wasn't that out of the ordinary for a large contractor to travel to Italy to arrange a contract for marble. Although surely a man of his standing would send one of his purchasing agents to do the deal? It was also commonplace to purchase furniture from Palestinian businessmen, though he could not understand why. The two sides were virtually at war with one another. Some people seemed to be going to great lengths to try and sabotage the Taba Convention. The short-lived terror attack must have been designed at the very least to delay the convention. It had proved a mere distraction, thanks to the anti-terror squad and their quick reaction.

Jordan knew he was clutching at straws, but that was all he had. The only thing that he knew for certain was that the Taba Convention was to be held at the Hilton on the eighth. He figured that there was a conspiracy to undermine and destroy the convention. All this violence and killing must be connected in some way to the convention.

The only thing he could think of as his next step was to visit the Hilton Taba and see if he could pick up some sort of lead from there.

He picked up the phone and dialed John Macdonald on his direct line. John was the Scottish manager of the Hilton and well known among the Eilat hoteliers. He was a really colorful character. On certain occasions he had been known to turn up in his kilt with the inevitable jokes and bets as to whether he wore anything underneath. He had invited Jordan and Irit to many functions, and they had gotten to know one another quite well. They had spent many a Saturday lazing on the beautiful beach below the Hilton and had enjoyed meals together in the Marhaba restaurant situated just above the beach area. Jordan smiled at the thought that "Marhaba" meant "welcome" in Arabic. He probably wouldn't be very welcome there soon if he was right.

"Hi, John," he said as the Hilton manager answered. "I was wondering if you could show me the expansion going on at your hotel. Perhaps you could show me the plans for the convention. It sounds really interesting especially on the professional level."

"Be only too glad, bonnie lad. Come on over for a beer, and I'll take you around," John said in his thick Scottish accent.

"I'll be there around noon, and you can stretch that to buying me a humus, tehina, and a kebab at the Marhaba," Jordan added.

"Sure, we'll do lunch too. I was looking for a partner. You can fill me in on the terror attack in Eilat, you big hero of a lad. See you in a wee bit."

Jordan spent the next hour going over the guest satisfaction forms and signing the never-ending cheques for suppliers. The volume of the summer business was reflected in the large pile of cheques that the chief accountant had dumped on his desk. The hotel was running at over ninety-seven percent occupancy during the month. Jordan hoped that Rami would be complimentary about the record profits forecasted for the month. Perhaps it would buy him some quiet so he could concentrate on his investigation, though he was doubtful about that.

He glanced at his watch and saw that it was time to move.

It was a clear day, and he could see right across the narrow gulf to Aqaba. Looking further south he could make out the Saudi Arabian shoreline. It was regretful that there was no peace in the area. He knew that the beaches on the Jordanian and Saudi side were really wide with fine yellow sand. The water was deep blue and inviting. The towns would really complement each other in peacetime.

The road hugged the shoreline taking Jordan past the Israeli Navy docks and past the "bonded customs" car park. Hundreds of imported Japanese cars were lined up in a large fenced-off area. They were waiting to be freed from customs and delivered to their new owners. He passed the port and rounded the corner. The Princess Hotel came into view. It was one of the newest, largest, and nicest of the hotels that had been built during the tourist boom. He had enjoyed many a cold beer sitting in the panoramic lobby. The lobby was situated almost on the shoreline, as if above an infinity pool. The lobby blended straight into the sea.

He arrived at the border post and quickly passed through to the Egyptian side, processed by border guards on both sides that knew him. He swung a left around the Hilton tennis courts and guided the car around the beautifully manicured lawns in front of the main entrance to the hotel.

John was taking care of a guest at the front desk but soon broke away and came over to greet him. Together they went down to the Marhaba restaurant and sat down at a table on the deck overlooking the Red Sea. In an attempt to humidify the dry desert air a system was installed that sprayed a fine mist of water into the air above them. This went a little way in alleviating the intense August heat. Together with the immense sunshade it was reasonably comfortable. They ordered their grilled kebabs from the waiter who came over to their table quickly.

"So how are preparations going for the convention next month?" Jordan asked his host.

"Not bad at all," replied John in his heavily-accented English. "As a matter of fact the building has almost been finished. They are laying the marble floors now and putting the finishing touches to the place. The furniture is already in Israel and should be here within the next couple of days. Great stuff. I can show you some samples so you can get an idea of what it is going to look like. We're definitely going to be ready, and the convention will bring great exposure for us. It should help us reach record occupancies this winter. Who wouldn't want to stay in the hotel where the historic peace agreement was signed? The Europeans will be scrambling for more rooms come October."

"I'd love you to show me around," Jordan said, "and if you know the timetable of the events and where they are going to be held it would be interesting if you could walk me through it."

"You are invited in any case, you know. I sent you the invitation a while ago. You must have received it by now." John said laughing, "'Not planning on any disturbances are you?"

"No, I am all for this peace stuff, but the Mossad must have planned plenty of security around for the convention. There are many that would rather it not take place." He was fishing now. Just over a couple of weeks to go to convention time and not much time for him to get to the truth. He had a long ways to go in a short amount of time.

They washed down their grilled kebabs with a fruity glass of Gamla Merlot from the Golan Heights winery. They ordered strong Turkish coffees to help offset the lunchtime sleepiness coming over them.

Jordan fished his cell phone out of his pocket to make a quick call to Irit, but John waved it down. "Can't make a call from the Marhaba Jordan, my lad. We put in wireless cell phone blocks in the restaurant. There were too many complaints. People want to enjoy their meal without the constant ringing of the damn phones. It is supposed to be a top restaurant, right? The blocks work a treat, too, up to fifty feet. One blocker covers the whole restaurant and deck. Nearly all types of cell phones are blocked. They keep updating the things to block more phones as the companies design more models. Pretty good, eh? Also, they are really small nowadays. Take a look over there. Small, but efficient, and all they need is an double-A battery." He pointed to a corner of the restaurant through the glass windows. A small white box no more than six by five centimeters was attached to the wall right in the corner behind the last booth. It was placed just before the corridor to the toilets. It was barely visible and looked like so many of the new smoke alarms that were made these days. He made a mental note to source them out for the Sands restaurants after this mess was over. They could come in handy, though Jordan doubted that they were legal. They could draw some lawsuits over in Eilat from irate cell junkies. But this was Egypt, and people here were much more laid back about these things, almost welcoming the opportunity of silent phones during meals. They were perfect for the Hilton and the Marhaba. He returned his cell phone to his pocket.

John signed the check and they walked towards the new convention center. As they approached Jordan saw workers completing the sidewalks and approach roads. Gardeners were busy planting trees and flowers in what looked to be a magnificent garden that covered the complex. Just below the steps leading to the new conference hall there were very large piles of Italian marble stacked high in wooden crates. John pointed out that they were waiting to be laid on the floor of the hall. What caught Jordan's eye made him stop dead in his tracks. His heart missed a beat—the labels on the crates. In bold black lettering imprinted on each crate was the name *Castelfranco Marble Co. Italy*. The bold lettering stared back at him as if daring him to put this piece of the puzzle in place. My God, he thought, Castelfranco was the company that Hofstein visited while being tailed by Gilad Dolev in Italy. It was in the verbal report that Gilad had managed to send in before being eliminated. Hofstein was involved in some way, and the marble was also a part of the puzzle.

The "piazza" in front of the convention hall was impressive. A large expanse covered on three sides by the new complex, the piazza was paved with cobblestones in the old European tradition. There was a magnificent fountain in the middle decorated with sculptures of lions in a circle, as if they were defending the hall. Jets of water spurted from each lion's mouth and from a central pump water gushed to a height of four meters above.

Jordan could already imagine the motorcades entering the piazza and dropping off the VIP's after driving around the fountain. John explained that after entering the hall for dinner, the Prime Minister of Israel, the President of Egypt, the President of the United States, the King of Jordan, and the Palestinian leader would appear before the gathering. They would make speeches from the top of the steps at the entrance where they were now standing. They would then sign the agreement at a desk that would be placed to the right of the entrance.

If there was going to be an attempt to sabotage or blow up the event, Jordan thought, it had to be here during the signing ceremony or inside the hall. For maximum effect and exposure, the best place was on the steps in front of the whole world. Multiple chief executive assassinations on center stage. The CNN, BBC, SKY TV, all the international channels would all be there. It was hard to imagine a more spectacular setting for potential terrorists.

Workers had not yet finished laying the marble at the entrance to the hall, and Jordan had to step over pipes. He followed John into the grand hall.

Jordan was impressed by what he saw. The hall was large, about nine thousand square feet in all, he guessed. The flooring was completely covered in shiny beige marble tinged with a delicate pink. There was a black marble border around the hall that framed the flooring. The lion motif was carried into the hall. There was a huge golden lion in a coat of arms inlaid in the floor at the entrance. Massive wooden panels covered the walls and four large crystal chandeliers hung from the ceiling. Jordan could see that the hall could be divided into three sections so as to achieve maximum practicality in banquet and convention sales. Large windows invited guests to enjoy the panoramic view of the Red Sea from one side and the desert from the other. It stretched out almost as far as the eye could see.

Jordan thought of the convention business that the Hilton would lure away from Eilat in the future. In one corner of the hall there was a seating arrangement. Made of wood and stained a dark brown, it looked very comfortable. It was covered in soft velvet cushions in a dark burgundy.

He followed John through the almost complete casino where the slot machines were being put in place in long rows. They passed the roulette and crap tables, and into the new wing of the hotel. He was shown a new room in the wing, and taken through the royal and presidential suites that would soon be occupied for the convention.

As they came out once more onto the piazza, Jordan could see the large billboard that that stood in front of every new building site. It offered passersby information regarding the companies involved in the project. It was a usual feature on building sites. He read down the list of architects, engineers, and suppliers. Again it hit him between the eyes like a well-delivered jab. In bold lettering the name of the developer screamed back at him. *Building Contractor: D. Hofstein.* How in hell's name was Hofstein involved? Had he found out something about Iyad and the Arabs?

Jordan had a sudden thought and turned to John. "I am thinking of replacing some of the furniture in the lobby. I was wondering if you could give me the supplier information for your project. It looks good and maybe they have a couple of lines that would suit the White Sands."

"Sure I can," John answered. "I'll give you a copy of the project file with all the information and plans, including the furniture. The complex is almost finished, and I have a spare copy anyway. I don't have a problem with that. Pretty soon the files will be gathering dust for years in some filing cabinet after we open. Keep it to yourself, though."

A few minutes later Jordan thanked John for the lunch and his hospitality and accepted the project file with thanks.

Back in his car he took the project file out of the brown envelope and opened the section that dealt with suppliers. He found the furniture section and it almost jumped out at him. Another piece of the puzzle. The East Jerusalem Furniture Company, the company owned and managed by a certain Mohammed Iyad,

124

had supplied all the furniture. It really was coming together now, Jordan thought. Now he had a definite connection between Hofstein and Iyad. They were both working on the new Hilton Taba complex. My God, he thought, if the Arabs were to blow up the convention it would really send any chance of peace back into the middle ages.

Jordan sat in his car and wondered what his next move should be. Once back across the border in Israel, they would be following him again. This time there would be no losing them short of disappearing altogether. That would really put the cat among the pigeons and would lead to an all-points alert for him.

He must not put Irit in any danger. He had to find a solution to keep her out of harm's way. How could he accomplish that? He knew the way the Mossad operated. They would quickly take her in and play her as a pawn against him. Jordan needed time to think this out, to make some sort of a plan that would give him at least a chance to get more information. While he did that he had to hide Irit in a safe place. They would take her to flush him out. They would not waste any more time before taking him in. But why? He had done no more than happen upon Josh's death, go to the funeral, and visit the Applebach family in mourning. He knew that they had found out about the safe in Applebach's study, and he knew that they suspected him. They were quick, the bastards. They had placed a tail on him after the funeral, and they had his apartment broken into and searched even before he got back from Tel Aviv with the cassette. The tail was definitely a Mossad agent, and he was equally convinced that the agency had ordered the break-in. It was strange behavior from the Mossad, but he had to know more. The Arabs must be planning an attack on the convention, the Mossad was onto the conspiracy, and he was caught in the middle. The Arabs knew the Mossad was right behind them and they had killed Applebach and the others. They knew about the Mossad, but not about Jordan Kline. He could help best by staying independent and working from outside, he thought.

Although difficult, he had to act as naturally as he could, summoning all his experience in the field. He needed to burn at least a week before starting what would surely be a suicide mission.

Jordan turned on the ignition, backed out of the space and drove out of the Hilton towards the border crossing. He waved at the guards on the Egyptian side as he passed by. He conversed briefly about the recent terror attack with the Israeli border policemen and was soon at the entrance to Eilat. He turned right at the tourist center and guided the car towards the hotel.

"Hi Linda. Anything new?" he asked as he entered the executive offices.

"No, except that Irit called this morning to see if the apartment has been cleaned up and put in order. I told her that the crew was already back at the hotel. We also replaced the wooden door with a steel safety door. She says for you to be home by seven tonight. She's cooking you a special dinner. Five years is a hell of a long time to put up with someone like you she says. She still wants to celebrate, though I cannot imagine why." Linda laughed cheerfully as she always did, though Jordan didn't find it so humorous.

My God, our fifth anniversary together, and Linda reminding me like a fool!

"Linda, please order a gigantic bunch of white carnations for me; Irit's favorites. Should keep me in the good books for a while. And thanks for the reminder, you've saved my life," he beamed.

It was a quiet afternoon, and Jordan spent it going over his paperwork. He finished up at about six-thirty, in time to go over and check the dinner buffet that was already spread out in the dining room. It was ready for the massive onslaught it was about to experience from the crowd of ravenous guests. Funny how they were always so hungry on holiday he thought to himself.

He exchanged a few words with the duty manager, picked up his car keys and the flowers, and went out to the car park. He could sense that he was again being followed, but paid no attention to it. He had already decided that there was no point in acting now. In any case he didn't have a plan yet.

Coming out of the elevator on his floor, he opened the door softly. The smell of home cooking filled the apartment. Irit was working in the kitchen.

He came up quietly behind her. He reached around and cupped her breasts softly in his hands. He whispered softly in her ear, "Guess who's home for dinner?"

Irit smiled without turning around, and leaned back into Jordan.

He knew that it always stirred her desire for him.

She stroked him through his trousers. "Maybe we can wait until after dinner, Honey?" she murmured weakly, still with her back to him.

"I can't wait, Irit. I want you now," he answered quickly, breathlessly.

Jordan was in a hurry now, pulling up her cotton skirt and stroking her smooth silky stomach as she undid his belt and unzipped his trousers. He pulled down her panties as she was bending over and entered her from behind. They made love in the kitchen. They made love among all the pots and pans, among the aroma of their anniversary dinner. They were oblivious to the world for a few wonderful shared minutes. Afterwards they kissed passionately. Jordan hugged her close to him, not wanting to let her go.

Drying off after a shower, Jordan put on a pair of shorts and a t-shirt and went into the kitchen.

"You sure cooked up a great appetizer. It was real tasty," he whispered into Irit's ear.

"Stop that at once, Kline, or it will be the main course and dessert, too," she answered. "And then there will be nothing after coffee." She turned and winked at him. She was back to her old self.

She turned serious and looked into his eyes. "I have to tell you this again. I don't know why but I feel I have to. Jordan, I love you more now that I really know the real story. I know the pain that you must have gone through before telling me, but I admire you more for it. That took a lot of courage, Jordan. Someone has to do the dirty work for our country. You are a decent man and you followed your convictions. In the end they led you back, back to me and the love we have."

He looked at her and knew that she was the woman he would love all his life. "Happy anniversary, my love," he said as he brought the bunch of white carnations around from behind him.

She squealed with delight. "You didn't forget—you didn't!" She took one of the carnations, cut it short with a kitchen knife, and put it in her hair. The rest she arranged in a tall vase and placed it on the dinner table.

She dimmed the lights in the dining corner and lit the candle on the table. She poured them each a glass of Gamla Cabernet Sauvignon and they toasted the occasion. Then she served Jordan all the food he loved: first the shrimp tempura followed by veal cordon bleu accompanied by garlic potato puree and "gurken salat," cucumber salad cut very thinly in lemon and olive oil dressing. For dessert she prepared a favorite that reminded him of the Cafe de Venise in Paris: profiteroles filled with vanilla ice cream and smothered with a deliciously thick hot chocolate sauce.

They were quiet during the dinner, content to be with each other, knowing that the first five years were only the beginning.

Jordan scooped the last spoon of chocolate sauce and smiled contentedly. He got up, went over to the cutlery drawer, and took out a long meat knife. He went over to Irit and placed it on her shoulder declaring, "I, Jordan Kline, General Manager of the White Sands Hotel, do hereby confer on you the title of Lady Executive Chef of the Hotel and private chef to the Right Honorable J. Kline. Seriously, Irit, that was a masterpiece of taste. All the food I love rolled into one dinner. Thank you, my love. What an anniversary dinner." He kissed her on the mouth and went over to prepare two cappuccino coffees on the Pavoni espresso machine.

He opened a bottle of Veuve Clicquot, poured some into champagne flutes, and they toasted their anniversary again. They spent the rest of the evening in the comfort of the living room reminiscing about the past and planning the future, totally engrossed in each other. It was late when they climbed into bed and made love again. This time they enjoyed each other longer, satisfying each other by kissing, touching, and exploring before finally coming together.

As she was falling asleep, Jordan whispered softly, "I am going to marry you, Irit." She pulled him closer to her and they fell into a deep sleep in one another's arms.

CHAPTER SEVEN

EILAT.
WEDNESDAY, AUGUST 29TH.

Jordan sat as his desk at the White Sands going over some memos and guest questionnaires, but his mind was not really concentrating on the forms. He had lain low for over a week now. He had not really come up with the slightest viable plan that could work against the organization he was up against. He had thought of everything, even of going to the Prime Minister himself. He would only sound crazy. He couldn't prove a thing. Going to the Mossad was out of the question, and they worked too closely with the General Security Services. Besides, he didn't know how far this thing went. He knew only that he was alone.

He knew that he had to put together a small, trusted team in order to have any chance of success. He had to get Irit to a safe place for the next week and hope that he would make it back alive to see her again after it was all over. How would he begin to tell her that he needed her to disappear for a week? She would immediately suspect something, perhaps that he was back in the service. He thought of the possibility of losing her forever. He had only just recounted his past to her, promised her that this was over. After that he had taken out the terrorists at the Dolphin Reef. And now this. How much more could Irit take?

Well, he would have to think of something good, he thought, wiping a hand nervously over his face.

He had thought about letting it all go, letting them blow up the convention if that was what they wanted. What did he care? He had his own life now. But he knew that he just couldn't do that; it wasn't in him to let them slaughter all those people. He couldn't just give up and let them ruin this chance for peace. It just wasn't Jordan Kline.

Suddenly it came to him. After all, what was the Eilat Anti-Terror Squad all about? To fight terror, to keep the peace. There were ten members in the ATS, but Jordan did not want all of them involved, just the two he really trusted.

Jordan picked up the phone and called his security officer. "Shalom, please call a meeting of the ATS as soon as you can. I want to go over the action at Dolphin Beach, see if we can learn something from it," he lied.

"Let's say at ten-thirty, in about an hour?" Shalom answered.

"Good enough. We'll hold it in your office as usual, if you don't have anything scheduled that is."

He felt a sense of relief that he had now taken the first step in setting up his team. He had just stepped over the starting line. He would not be alone for much longer.

It was a little after a quarter till eleven by the time the members of the ATS had gathered in Shalom's office. They sat around the table sipping cans of soft drinks. After initial greetings, they went over the detailed report on the incident and found that they had acted both quickly and efficiently. The only thing that they found, as usual, was a lack of equipment. They made a note to request further communication gear in their next budget meeting with City Hall. The group agreed on a date for target practice, and Jordan thanked them for coming.

As they were filing out of the office, Jordan added, "Shalom, Alex, please stay behind for a moment, I have something to discuss with you both." They both turned and sat back down at the table.

"Shalom, please lock the door after making sure that no one is in the corridor outside."

"Sure thing, but why the secrecy, Jord?"

"When I tell you, it will blow your mind, Shalom. I promise."

Shalom locked the door and sat back down at the table. He and Alex looked at Jordan with puzzled expressions that indicated they had no idea what to expect or why they had been asked to stay behind.

Jordan looked at them and said, "Before I start, I want you both to know that when I am finished, we three will be the only ones that know about it, apart from the bad guys. This is a matter of international consequence. I am not joking. Also, you two are the only ones that I can trust with this, the ones that I have chosen to help me. The odds are stacked against us. This is a matter of life and death and could put each and all of us in harm's way. Should either of you not want to risk this, please say so now. You can leave before I tell you what it's all about. Please note, I repeat that it may turn very dangerous, even deadly. I ask you to decide and I will not blame either of you should you decide to get up and leave the room."

Shalom spoke for the both of them, Alex nodding his young head in agreement, "Come on Jord, what the fuck is this about? You know that we're behind you whatever happens. You can count us in, but it better be fucking exciting. We need a bit of that around this sleepy one-horse fucking town." His deep laugh echoed around the room.

"As if the Dolphin Beach wasn't enough for a while," Jordan replied then added seriously, "Let's get down to business. Both of you know about the Taba Convention planned for the eighth, right?"

"You must be joking, right, Jord?" replied Alex. "The ATS has also been involved in the security on site, or had you forgotten?"

"Right, I had forgotten, but that's not the point. I have, through no intention of my own, come across what I think is a conspiracy to disrupt and possibly blow up the convention. It is possible that they want to assassinate all the leaders gathered there for the signing." He carried on despite the incredulous expressions on their faces. "Now both of you may know that I was once an operative control in the Mossad. I gave it up after becoming disillusioned with the life. Not that I didn't do my share of the killings mind you. I plead as guilty as the next man. However, I left that and came down to a different life in the hotel with you guys and, of course, Irit."

"Just over two weeks ago, on my way back to Eilat in the Audi, I came across a fatal car crash. The guy killed was an old friend from the firm, Josh. Before he died, he managed to whisper some stuff to me. He also managed to tell me that 'Apple' was dead before he too died. He meant Applebach. Applebach was a control in the Mossad whom I knew very well. He sent me on some of my missions in the old days. I did not want to become involved, but you two know me, especially you Shalom. So I followed up during a quick trip to Tel Aviv.

"I found a key that Applebach had hidden in the control apartment before being taken out. Lucky he hid it well, because the safe apartment had already been cleaned, ready for sale. I visited his wife during 'Shiva,' where I found this in his safe in his study which the key opened. Take a listen, and I will fill you in with what I found out after."

Jordan had collected the tape on his way down from the DJ's box and put it in the recorder on the desk.

Shalom interjected, "Before you play it Jordan, I must tell you something which now makes sense to me. A General Security Services agent came to visit me this morning and asked if he could look in my security department safe. He asked me if you had given me anything for safekeeping lately."

"Very interesting. Well, thank God I didn't give it to you, though I thought of it," Jordan admitted.

He pushed the play button and let them listen to the tape Applebach had put together and had hidden behind the panel.

"My God, if this is true, then it really could be dangerous," Alex said, and then added, "As you may know, I was in the 'Sayeret Matkal,' the Chief of Army Staff's unit, the elite commando unit of the Israel Army. It takes a lot to scare me, and this is really frightening."

Shalom spoke first. "Jordan, you know that before we move we will have to get Irit to a safe place. That in itself will be hard. Hard on her, even harder on you. Also, since you told us that you were being watched, we have to be very careful where and when we meet. Since they do not suspect us yet, Alex and I are in the clear to carry out a plan if we have one. Until we are compromised ourselves. Then the game changes and gets rough."

"What do you want us to do Jordan?" Alex asked.

"Well, firstly we must not let them suspect that you both are even remotely involved. However, I would like you, Alex, to take a few days off from work, tell your employers you need to go up to Tel Aviv to visit someone. Tail Iyad and see if he leads us to someone connected to this affair. Shalom, I want you to take a good look at the project file, and then I will send you to Tel Aviv on some errand. You can follow Hofstein for a while. See if he does something suspicious. For God's sake, don't let them make you. Follow from a distance and observe. Be very careful. You both now know what happened to the last poor sods that tailed them. I wouldn't want either of you on my conscience. I will ring you from a payphone tomorrow evening, but in case you need to phone me in an emergency, Shalom will give me one of the spare cellular phones that we keep. I will keep it on at all times. When we decide to move, I will take care of Irit. We can't breathe a word of this to anyone if we are to stand a chance at foiling this in time. Once we move we will have to stay one step ahead of them all the time. They will use all their force, deadly force, against us if we get in their way. We all know what that means. We shall talk tomorrow."

Alex said good-bye and walked out of the security office. Shalom opened the safe and gave Jordan the spare phone. He took the project file from Jordan. He was already ringing Arkia inland airlines to make a flight reservation for the next afternoon as Jordan walked out of the office.

Jordan spent the rest of the day going over some papers, dictating letters, and doing the rounds of the hotel as he usually did. He talked to the staff and exchanged small chat with some of the guests. He was well aware of the agent watching him, but carried himself as if everything were normal as always.

CHAPTER EIGHT

TEL AVIV.
THURSDAY,AUGUST 30TH.

Shalom noticed that Alex was on the same flight to Tel Aviv as he was and greeted him warmly as a fellow ATS member. He was, however, careful not to sit next to him. He chose a window seat a couple of rows back. He didn't know if someone was watching the passengers and didn't want to draw suspicion to either of them. He was wondering if Jordan had been right to involve such a young guy in their plans. He was already past fifty, but Alex could not be more than twenty-three. His whole life lay ahead of him. Had he not paid his dues in the elite unit? Then again, Alex had eagerly agreed to join their cause. That's just the way the lad was, Shalom decided.

He listened to the constant whirr of the propellers and the rattles and vibrations in the cabin of this old DeHavilland aircraft. The valley unravelled below him, mile after mile of dusty yellow desert. The Dead Sea was drying up at an alarming rate. Many of the hotels were located further back now that the shoreline was receding. They really had to get the canal project going to get water from the Galilee into the Dead Sea; otherwise, the sea would dry up completely. That would be disastrous for tourism. Many tourists from abroad, mostly Germans, came every year to take advantage of the magical cures of the Dead Sea waters. Tourists flocked there to experience for themselves the fact that you actually floated on top of the water.

They flew on just to the north of Jerusalem and south of the Palestinian city of Jericho, the world's oldest known city. On the left of the plane the golden dome of the Mosque of Omar in the Old City shone in the sunlight. Then they circled over Tel Aviv and landed at Dov airport.

Since he didn't have a bag, Shalom headed straight for a cab and asked the driver to take him to the Azrieli Center. It was a huge complex comprised of two towers, one round and the other triangular. They stretched up into the sky above a large shopping mall in central Tel Aviv. The offices of the Hofstein Building Co. were located there. Shalom knew that the company was building apartments in Eilat. He decided to check out the prices and floor plans in their offices. Maybe he could even see and follow Hofstein if he was at his office. Maybe pick up a clue.

The cab driver joined the Ayalon Expressway, the main artery that ran through Tel Aviv. He took the "Shalom" or Peace exit that ran right in front of the center. Same name as me, Shalom thought as he did every time he came this way. He paid the driver and walked over to the entrance to the round tower.

He rode the high-speed elevator and soon arrived at the thirtieth floor where he casually entered the Hofstein corporation offices.

"Welcome to the world of Hofstein Development, sir. How can I help you?" the pretty girl in uniform sitting at one of the reception desks asked, almost automatically. She sounded as if she were a taped answer message on a phone.

"I saw that you are building apartments in Eilat and would like some information—size, layout, prices, that sort of thing if I may? Maybe you have a project file with the info?"

"Certainly, sir. Please take a seat and I will give you a file with our Eilat projects. Would you like a bottle of mineral water?"

He accepted gratefully. He had already seen a Hofstein construction project file, he thought to himself. A different file, but nonetheless a Hofstein file. He had not found anything suspicious in it. He wondered where they would plant the bomb. It was there—right on the plans—but he didn't know where to look. On which plan was it? God he wished he knew where to look.

The girl came back with the Eilat apartments project file and explained the locations and plans of the various apartments and buildings. Shalom pretended to study the file while sipping from the bottle of mineral water. Suddenly Mohammed Iyad walked into the offices. He strode passed the reception desks and marched straight into Hofstein's office.

Shalom was taken aback by his entrance. This was not a meeting between two managing directors, the one selling the other furniture. An Arab businessman would wait to be announced. He would be escorted into the office of one of the largest developers in Israel. Yet here Iyad had marched in unannounced, like he was a close friend, like it was his right to go in whenever he chose. Perhaps the hostesses were used to this, but it sure looked suspicious to him. There was more than just a business connection between these two.

Shalom closed the file and got up. He thanked the young girl for her help, promised to think about a purchase, and caught the elevator back down to the entrance floor. He almost ran into

Alex leaning against one of the massive pillars holding up the tower. Although their eyes met, he walked right past him and went out into the sunshine. He lit a cigarette and waited for developments.

Alex and Shalom did not have to wait too long. About a quarter of an hour later Iyad came out of the elevator and walked out of the building. He went across the pedestrian bridge leading to the railway station.

Shalom quickly figured that he could be of more help to Alex and followed him across the bridge to the station. He saw Iyad purchase a ticket and climb onto the Jerusalem-bound train. He saw Alex get on the train on a different carriage. Shalom waited a couple of minutes and jumped onto the train just as it was about to depart.

The line to Jerusalem had only opened a couple of months earlier and already complaints were piling up. The journey was slow, about an hour and forty-five minutes. It was way longer than it would take by car or bus. Also more often than not there were delays that added to the overall time. You couldn't make any plans for meetings in Jerusalem by following the official timetable.

Apart from the time it took, Shalom couldn't understand what all the fuss was about. New carriages, beautifully appointed and air-conditioned had been introduced on the route. There was even a mobile snack trolley operator that came past offering sandwiches and drinks, even hot coffee. Shalom bought a cheese baguette and a can of Coke and settled down to enjoy the view. The tracks took the train past Ben Gurion International Airport and on past lush fields of corn and bright yellow sunflowers. Half an hour later they were starting the steep ascent towards Jerusalem through magnificent forests that shielded the carriages from the sun. As it climbed ever higher Shalom caught glimpses of the rolling hills of Judea, golden yellow in the late afternoon sunshine.

He acted as if he didn't notice Alex sliding into the seat alongside him.

"Listen Shalom, you shouldn't have come with me," Alex said. "Since you are here, follow us at a safe distance and give me back-up if necessary, though I doubt that will be necessary. Maybe we'll get lucky today."

Then he was gone, having left as silently as he came.

The train pulled into the station located behind the Teddy football stadium, named after Jerusalem's famed Mayor Teddy Kollek and home to the Betar Jerusalem football team of the Israeli premier league.

Iyad climbed into one of the cabs in the long line of taxis waiting as the train disembarked. Alex got into the following one and Shalom slid quickly into the one behind it.

"Follow the cab in front," Shalom ordered his cab driver. He smiled at the thought that this was exactly what Alex was requesting of his driver in front. He wondered if anyone else was following them. Funny if there were ten taxis all following one another, he thought, laughing out loud in the cab. It could easily have been off the set of a comedy film.

The cab ride wound through the heavy traffic out of the Talpiot area of Jerusalem, past the Liberty Bell Garden, and up the incline past the famous King David Hotel that stood majestically overlooking the Old City walls and the historic Jaffa Gate.

The King David had been taken over by the British army during the war of independence, and the Jewish underground had blown up one wing with devastating loss of life for the British. It was probably the most famous hotel in the Middle East and almost always full. It had welcomed many heads of state through the years.

The driver turned right onto Agron Street and approached the traffic lights near the walls of the Old City below David's Citadel. Shalom could just about recognize the outline of Alex's head through the dirty back window in the cab two cars ahead of his. About eight hundred meters above sea level, the evening air in Jerusalem was cool, and almost all the cars had their windows open. A mix of Israeli and Arab songs issued from the cars in traffic, and Shalom thought how sensible it would be to make peace. After all, he thought, we live one among the other. He smelled the distinct scent of the Old City, the spices and herbs and the smoke of the countless grills in front of the typical Arab restaurants serving their "shish kebabs." A strong aroma of Turkish coffee wafted through the traffic from the ancient walls.

As he sat waiting patiently for the green light, he saw the cab carrying Iyad start to pull forward even though the lights were still red. What in hell was happening? Had he noticed Alex's cab following? Then a Vespa motorized scooter passed his window, weaving quickly in and out of the traffic to get to the front of the queue at the lights as they always did.

The lights changed to green and Iyad's cab hung a right, tires squealing as it took the corner fast. The scooter drew alongside the cab carrying Alex. Shalom saw it screech to a halt. Calmly, the man riding it took a revolver from the inside pocket of his short leather coat, aimed carefully, and calmly shot Alex in the head through the open window at close range. The windows of the cab turned red as the bullets tore into their target. Almost in slow motion the scooter driver replaced his gun in his coat pocket, revved up the motor, and took off towards the lights which were still green. The scooter glided across the crossroads and disappeared into the Old City through the Jaffa gate. It was out of sight in a second and would be hidden very quickly in one of the old Arab houses that lined the myriad alleys of the old city.

Shalom thought quickly, pushing all thoughts of Alex aside for the moment, and snapped at the driver, "I'm in a hurry. Please get past this accident and follow the dirty white Skoda taxi over there that just turned." He was trying to think fast, his mind reeling. My God, I just called Alex's murder an accident. It wasn't an accident; it was a cold-blooded public execution. Jordan was dead right; they had stumbled onto something really big if they killed you just for tailing them. Someone, maybe a bodyguard, following Iyad must have made Alex. God, they hadn't thought of that. He had better be very careful. He hoped that no one had seen them together in the train or he would be next on the execution list. He hoped that the cab he had asked to follow was Iyad's cab since this was a calculated guess. There were so many Skoda taxis in Israel and all of them as dirty and beaten up as the next.

The cab quickly skirted the "accident" and turned right at the lights, hugging the Old City walls. Shalom had tried hard not to look at the cab as he passed, but his gaze was drawn to the horrific scene. Almost all of Alex's head had been blown off, and blood and brain matter was slowly dripping down the inside of the back window. He turned away quickly and choked back the feeling of nausea coming from the pit of his stomach.

The cab driver didn't want to get stuck in the mess that was going to happen when the police got there any more than Shalom did. He would lose precious road time, the one thing that he depended on for his livelihood. He followed the Skoda that headed down the road, passed the Sultan's Pool, and continued under the ancient walls of the old city. He drove on, hugging the road as it climbed around a small hill.

After a short ride the Skoda come to a halt near a large car park, and Shalom remembered that this was the nearest car park to the Western Wall, the most revered and holy place for all Jews. It was also situated right below the second most holy place for the Islamic religion. The Temple Mount included the Mosque of Omar from which Mohammed was reputed to have ascended to heaven. It was also home to the El Aksa Mosque. He instructed the driver to carry on a little further and stop. He paid him in a hurry and exited the cab just in time to see Iyad disappear down one of the many narrow alleys.

He followed quickly so as not to lose sight of Iyad, while at the same time trying to blend in with the many tourists crowding around. Iyad went quickly through the Jewish quarter. He was probably uncomfortable among the many haredim Jews, the ultra orthodox that had taken back and built up the area surrounding the Western Wall with synagogues and learning places since its capture during the six-day war.

There were many of them going about their business, all dressed in black suits with long jackets and black fur hats. The strands of their Tzitsiot, the prayer shawls, hung down around their trousers.

It wasn't hard keeping track of Iyad among this crowd, following his Kefiya headdress among the crowd. Shalom kept a very respectful and healthy distance from the Arab.

Iyad went up the steps opposite the Western Wall and disappeared down an alley flanked on both sides by the distinctive shops of the Old City. He was just in time to see him duck through a doorway and enter one of the Arab houses on the street. He followed and continued past the entrance, memorizing the number as he passed: Thirty-three Via Dolorosa.

Shalom retraced his steps back to the car park and waved down another taxi, instructing the cabbie to take him to the King David Hotel. They pulled up at the entrance a short drive later.

He paid, exited the cab, and entered the hotel through the magnificent Jerusalem stone archway.

He chose a secluded corner of the magnificent colonial style lobby and sank down into one of the soft, deep armchairs. He let the air out of his lungs in a long sigh of relief and instinctively brushed the sweat from his forehead with the back of his hand.

Shock finally began to set in. He thought again about poor Alex and how suddenly and brutally he was murdered. He figured that since they knew that Alex was following Iyad, they had probably already made the connection through Eilat to Jordan. Jordan was now in very real danger and had to be warned.

He fished his cell phone out of his pocket and punched in the number of the phone he had given Jordan from the hotel safe. He had to warn Jordan and then get the hell out of here fast. A group of Americans sitting nearby looked over at him. He hoped that he did not look as anxious as he felt.

"Jordan, hi," he whispered as loud as he could. "I don't have too much time, but Alex has been taken out, bullet to the head. Very professional job. I could almost swear the guy who took him out was Israeli. Probably also because it was so professional. Funny why I would think that, right, Jordan? Anyway, I followed Iyad and know his address. Thirty-three Via Dolorosa. I'll SMS you when I get back to Eilat, but you have to move quickly. They must be on to you. Get the hell out of Eilat now!" He snapped the phone shut.

He got up quickly and went out of the hotel and turned right towards the Paz gas station at the corner of King David and Shama'a Streets. He saw a branch of the Eldan car rental firm on the corner. He crossed the busy street, entered the office, and quickly rented a car. He requested a white Skoda. It was an added advantage since there were so many. He hurriedly went to the washroom to relieve himself and wash his face before the long drive ahead of him.

He navigated the car out of Jerusalem and past French Hill onto the road leading to Jericho. He decided to take that route, feeling safer going that way. With luck, he figured that they still had not made him, had not connected him to Alex. With any luck they hadn't thought about the possibility that there were two people following Iyad. He floored the accelerator and made good time, hardly noticing the turn to Jericho as it flashed past. He was soon skirting the Dead Sea.

EILAT.
THURSDAY, AUGUST 30TH.
EVENING.

Jordan was in total shock. He was still holding his open cell phone in his right hand. My God, what butchers. Alex was dead. Jordan blamed himself for drawing him into this mess and for his murder. He should have thought before they left that Iyad would be suspicious, would have his people watching for anyone following. They had caught this so quickly. They were fast and ruthless. He hoped that Shalom was in the clear for the moment. He felt a wave of anxiety wash over him. He realized that he was still holding the open cell in his hand and snapped it shut. They would be coming for him soon. Even worse, they would be coming for Irit. He knew the way they operated.

He had to move quickly, get Irit out of the way, and then disappear. He had to leave the hotel in a different car; his would be on all the lists by now. They would be watching.

"Linda, mind if we swap cars for tonight? I have to pick up an anniversary present for Irit and can't be seen in the Audi. Everyone will know about it."

"No problem. I'd kinda like to drive the Audi around town, make me feel like a rich bitch for a while." She smiled and tossed him the keys to the small green Fiat Punto she drove.

He gave her his keys and ran to the car, jumped in, and drove quickly out of the hotel car park, connecting with Irit on her cell phone as he drove.

"Irit," he said, "No time to talk, but an emergency has come up. Do as I say. No questions. Please go straight home, pack some things for about a week, and I'll pick you up outside the flat in ten minutes sharp. Don't argue, just do it." He closed the phone before she had the time to react. He definitely did not need a debate right now. The debate would certainly come later, but for now he needed silence.

He drove over the intersection after skirting the airport landing strip and turned left past the new tourist center. He guided the small car behind it into a narrow street where all the loading docks were situated behind the shops. He squeezed the Punto into a narrow spot and cut the lights, leaving the engine idling. He had about five minutes to burn until he could drive out to pick Irit up.

He scanned the darkened road for any sign that he was being followed. A drunk came out of a pub and relieved himself behind a garbage bin. Apart from the drunk and the stray cats he saw nothing that caught his attention. He glanced at his watch. After five never-ending minutes, Jordan eased the car out back onto the road leading up to the apartment. He approached the building slowly. He saw a car idling not far from the entrance to his building, the lights cut. He could make out two men sitting in the car. He knew that they would not be expecting the Punto and probably had not yet been informed about Irit. He sure hoped not.

They were waiting for him. He was getting nervous now. He scanned the area. Where the hell was Irit? Why hadn't she come down? Had others gone up to grab Irit? Then he spotted her coming out of the entrance and eased slowly up to the curb as she neared it.

He stretched over and opened the door. "Quick, get in, Irit," he ordered.

She did as he said and he pulled away from the curbside, looking back in the mirror to see if the other car had followed them. They weren't in the wing mirror. They were still waiting for the Audi.

He drove in tense silence down the hill, left at the tourist center and out onto the Arava desert road. Darkness was setting in now, and Jordan welcomed that and the chance to put some distance between them and Eilat. Irit had tried to speak to him a few times since he picked her up, but he had silenced her quickly with his hand. There would be time enough to talk later on when he reached their destination. It was the place where he was as sure as he could be that she would be safe for the few days he needed.

The road wound its way through the desert, the hot wind whipping up sand all around them in small tornado like circles. He sped on down the road into the night. He was trying to think clearly, not prepared for the speed of events that had led to his quick exit from Eilat. Things had happened way too quickly and he needed time to collect his thoughts and build a plan.

He drove hard and fast and finally turned into Kibbutz Yotvata, a cooperative farm famous for its chocolate milk. He had a good friend from his army days who had come to live here. They had been in touch on several occasions. There was no way that they could connect the two of them—at least not for a while—until they did a thorough background check on him. For this reason he figured that Irit would be safe here on the kibbutz. It was a settlement among the many that had sprung up during the first years of the state, where everybody owned a piece of the action. Things here were run on a semi-communist basis. Nowadays most of the kibbutzim were outdated and were turning into cooperatives. Each member was given his own house and shares in the companies that the kibbutz owned and ran. Ilan owned such a house.

Jordan knew where Ilan lived. He had once visited his friend a while back when he had moved to Eilat. Ilan had invited Jordan down for a weekend. He chose a spot shaded from the streetlights and parked the Punto opposite Ilan's house. He cut the lights and engine and turned to Irit.

He could see that she was frightened now, her face creased with fear. She was shaking visibly and right on the verge of breaking down.

"Irit, please, you have to stay strong, you have to keep it together," he spoke authoritatively.

"Jordan, my love, can you please tell me now what the hell is going on here?" she pleaded with him.

"No, Irit, I cannot right now, but you have to trust me. I cannot tell you for fear of endangering you, too, and that would kill me. If you really love me, then please do as I say and, God willing, we shall meet up in a few days after all this is in the past."

"In the meantime, I will ask Ilan my friend to put you up at his place for the next week or so. You must promise to do exactly as I say. First, please do not leave the house during daylight. They will be looking to get back at me through you. They will succeed if they get you. Secondly, do not, and, I repeat, not ring anyone on your cell phone, no friends, no family, nobody. They will start tracking your cell phone very soon if they haven't already. If you do call you will also be putting whomever you call in harm's way. More importantly, it will give your location away."

"I will contact you, but I can't tell when or from where. I will contact you, I promise you that, my love. Third, do not under any circumstances contact anyone you know from any other telephone, either family or friends, since they will be listening on all lines at the other end as well. This could also endanger the people you call. In short, you lie as low as you can for the next week. Don't even try talking to the other members of the kibbutz, since they are a very talkative bunch. Kibbutzim are like soap operas, no secrets."

He took a deep breath and looked at the face he loved so much. "Honey, I am so sorry for all of this, but you have to believe that I was dragged into this unwillingly. You have to believe that if you are seen and taken my life will be in danger. The one thing that I ask you is to believe that I wanted none of this. I know that is a lot to ask, but you have to believe me. I am only doing the honorable thing in following this through. I have no other option. Please believe me."

Tears streamed down her cheeks. He stretched over to wipe them from her cheeks with his thumb. Then he held her close. Sobs racked her body as he held her. He couldn't think of anything to say except that he was sorry over and over again.

In between the sobbing, Irit once again turned to Jordan and looking him in the eyes, said to him, "Jordan, I shall follow your request. I do not know why and I do not ask. I know that it is very dangerous. All I ask is that you be careful, for if there is something I fear more, it is losing you, my love. Quick, you are in a crazy hurry, and I must hide. Oh, and one more thing, please make it the last mission. You promised that you had left this way behind, and you lied," she added sadly, looking away.

They climbed out of the Punto, walked up to Ilan's front door, and knocked. Ilan was a bachelor, and this helped. Ilan opened the door and a look of pleasant surprise came over his face.

"Great to see you, Jordan, my old friend. Come in, come in," the tall, mustachioed man wearing a blue bathrobe insisted.

He showed them the way into the small cozy house. Jordan motioned for Irit to follow him in. Ilan's hair was wet from showering and he was drying it with a small towel.

He threw the towel on a chair, pulled a cigarette from the pack on the small glass lounge table, and lit up. He exhaled and looked at Jordan with a puzzled expression. "Haven't seen you in a ton of time, my man," he said in an unmistakably upper-class British accent. Ilan had been in Israel since childhood and yet still had that annoying bloody accent.

"Listen, Ilan, I do not have much time to stay, and this is an emergency. I need for you to allow Irit to stay here for about a week, no more. Hush hush as possible. No one knows her here, and she will be fine. Please do not tell anyone that she is here. If anyone sees her, tell them it's a cousin come to stay or something, but don't invite anyone over. I am sorry to lay this on you, but I really need your help. I couldn't think of anyone else to turn to. By the way, if I'm on the news at some stage, don't believe a word they say. Trust me on this, please," he said.

"Glad as always to help, my dear fellow," Ilan said as Jordan headed for the door. "You can rely on me, of course. No one will even know she's here. Mum's the word."

Jordan turned to Irit and gave her one long, last hug. He kissed her hard on her lips.

"Irit, once this is over I will tell you all about it. I have to go now. Please follow my orders and I shall be back for you soon, I promise. And it will be the last time, I promise," he said unconvincingly.

Jordan did not go far. He drove across the main Arava road into the gas station and parked around the back. He made sure that he was well out of sight of the main road. He cut the engine and lights and sat in the quiet darkness of the car park. From here he could still keep an eye on all the traffic entering the car park. He desperately needed time to think, and he needed to get in touch with Shalom. He must be well on his way back down to Eilat from Jerusalem by now.

He got out of the car and went over to the snack bar to grab a sandwich and a drink. He noticed a few truck drivers sitting in a corner but apart from them the place was deserted. It was late for tourist traffic. The barman looked like he was getting ready to close for the night.

Jordan took an egg salad sandwich that had seen better days from the display fridge, filled a glass with Fanta orange from the self-serve unit, and paid at the counter. He sat down at a table to eat. On the TV the weatherman was just going over the next days' temperatures when a breaking newsflash was suddenly announced. His attention was drawn to the screen.

The anchor came on and announced that there was what appeared to be a gangland slaying in Eilat. It was followed by some initial amateur footage. Jordan was sickened by what he saw. Fear and nausea filled him. He felt numb. He felt a cold chill go through him. God no, not this. He looked at the screen with horror and shock.

Caught clearly in the middle of the screen was his bullet-riddled Audi. He could make out a body slumped in the driver's seat, the head resting on the steering wheel. My God, Linda, what have I done? Tears welled up in his eyes. Poor Linda, the bastards hadn't even checked to see who was in the car before they had opened fire. She had paid the price because he had swapped cars. She had paid for his anonymity. First Alex, now Linda. He couldn't take much more of this.

Right now I am not the best guy to be around or to know, he thought grimly to himself. This was not the agency he knew. They were not even checking whom they shot, just doing it in cold blood. My God, what was this all about? He felt weak and helpless.

He collected his thoughts. It would not be long before his face would be on an APB. He had to get out of the snack bar fast. He walked slowly out of the snack bar. Nausea caught up with him as he approached the car. He bent over and retched, tears falling on the sand as the shocking reality of Linda's death sunk home. When he finished retching, he wiped his mouth with his sleeve and stood up, breathing heavily from the exertion. His throat was on fire, the taste awful. He opened the door and climbed back into the Punto.

He took out his cell phone and sent a short SMS message to Shalom: "where r u?"

He waited anxiously for the answer.

It was not long in coming. Shalom answered that he was halfway down the Arava on his way back. Jordan sent him a message back telling him to pull in at the Yotvata gas station. He hoped that they were not yet tapping in to this cell phone, or Shalom's for that matter. It would come soon enough. They had until morning to come up with another, better solution for communications between them.

About a quarter of an hour later Shalom pulled off the road and entered the car park cautiously, looking for him, for the Audi. Shalom parked a few rows over from Jordan. Jordan waited for a few minutes before getting out of the Punto. He came out of the shadows and approached Shalom. He had waited to make sure that nobody had followed Shalom.

"Hi, Jordan, you were right. We're in some real big trouble."

"There's more, Shalom," he said. "I swapped cars to get away unnoticed and took Linda's Punto. They didn't even check who was in it before they ambushed her. They thought that they were eliminating me. Linda is dead because of me. As simple as that. Who would have thought that they would just open fire and not try to arrest me? Anything but this. My God, what the fuck have I done?"

"What's done is done, get a grip. Snap out of the self-pity shit, Jordan," Shalom said coldly with an urgency that brought them back to concentrating on their present situation. They had to focus.

Shalom broke the short silence, "Now I am not sure that I have been compromised, but probably not, since I am still alive. On the other hand they will be looking for you all over the country. We have to find a safe place for you to lie low until we figure out what we are going to do. I thought about it on the way down, and I have a plan. I have a very close friend that runs a tourist company called The Dust Riders. He lives in a place called Nof Ha Arava which he founded. He lives there with a few dogs, cats, and, of course, camels that he uses to sell treks to the tourists. Most if not all of his business is with the foreign charter traffic in winter, and now is a very quiet time for him. I already spoke to him and he is expecting us, so let's go. By the way, Ronni served in the "commando Yami," the Sea Commandos. He could be useful, never asks questions."

"Agreed. Let's leave the Punto here, since they will already have realized that I swapped with Linda. They will be searching for it already." Then Jordan said, "On second thought I'll drive it into the desert and cover it with some brush. It will take them a little more time to find. Follow me."

He climbed into the small car, switched on the ignition and drove onto the road. He spotted what looked like a suitable place where the shoulder was shallow. He left the road and drove into the desert. He heard and felt the thud of rocks as he drove over them, but did not drive with any care now. The car was a danger to him. Its usefulness was over. The longer he could put them off his trail the better. He drove round a small mound, made sure that the car was out of sight, and cut the lights and engine. He found some brush and threw it over the car, covering it as best he could. He ran back to the road, scrambled up the shallow embankment and joined Shalom in the Skoda.

"Shalom," he said, "I need to go back to Eilat before we go to Nof Ha Arava."

"You must be fucking crazy, Jordan. Are you out of your mind? We cannot go back now, at least not you," he retorted.

"They will have figured that I am long gone by now and will be looking for the Punto. The last place they will be looking for me is Eilat. Please, I need to get back just for a few minutes." He looked over at Shalom.

"Okay, call me an idiot. Here we go," he answered, shaking his head.

Twenty minutes later Jordan guided Shalom through the industrial park and into Eilat the back way. Jordan told him where to park and Jordan got out of the car, instructing Shalom to wait in the darkness, ready to move.

This was something that Jordan needed to do before they drove to Nof Ha Arava, someone he needed to see. He had thought a lot about the events as they had unfolded so quickly. They had affected him deeply. Beyond the fact that he had become embroiled once more in violence, it was the first time that a Jew had raised a hand against a fellow Jew in this way—if Shalom was right about Alex's murder. It looked very much like a professional job, one that could easily be the work of the Mossad. It shook his faith for the first time. He needed reassurance. He could not grasp the reality that the four had died and that Israelis might be behind the events, or at least connected. He was a secular Jew. He respected and loved the traditions of his faith and observed the holidays. He did not attend synagogue except when he accompanied Irit on Yom Kippur, the holiest day on the Jewish calendar. He believed rather that it was important to be a good human being, to respect his fellow humans. He respected all faiths and the right to believe in them. It was fundamentalism that perverted the people, the radicals that preached hatred and death. There were extremists of all religions and nationalities, no faith had a monopoly on that. It had been that way down through the centuries and would probably be for many more.

He believed fervently in the rule of law. The government was elected democratically to act on behalf of all the citizens. You may not agree with some of their decisions, but they were the government. They decided and you followed. The armed forces acted on their decisions, as did all the branches of intelligence. Could it be that someone in the Mossad had taken the law into their own hands and had decided to act against his own government? It certainly seemed that way, and yet Jordan found it hard to believe and grasp the full meaning of his suspicions. That was why he was here to see the Chief Rabbi of Eilat, Yitzhak Carlebach.

He was standing in front of the Chief Rabbinate building on The Six Day Street named for the war. The Rabbinate was an ugly two-story grey concrete building. The same design flaw could be seen in many other buildings in the town. The windows faced the town rather than the inviting panorama of the bay of Aqaba spread out below. He wondered who had designed all these drab buildings and not taken advantage of showcasing the view. He focused on his visit and thought about the questions that he needed to ask the rabbi. He got out of the car. A stray cat was licking milk from a dirty bowl on the top step. He circumvented it and entered the Rabbinate.

Rabbi Carlebach saw him as he entered and came over to him. "Jordan, how very nice to see you on a social visit. It makes a pleasant change from your weekly visits to discuss infringements by your chefs cooking on the Sabbath!"

On many Saturdays the cooks had of necessity broken the Kashruth laws and cooked food on the Sabbath. They had done so because they had run out of the food prepared prior to the Sabbath and because they enjoyed playing a game of cat and mouse with the Rabbinate supervisors. On most occasions they had been caught, resulting in Jordan being called to the Rabbinate on Sunday to apologize and beg that the Kashruth certificate not be revoked. It was a ritual that many managers went through on a weekly basis. Rabbi Carlebach took these infringements good-heartedly.

Jordan laughed with the Rabbi. "Yes it does make a pleasant change, although you receive us with grace and patience every week. Probably much more patience than I would have in your place."

The Rabbi smiled. "We are here to correct wayward ways, Jordan, to teach the correct way and to have patience. It is our way." The Rabbi was a small man, no more than five-two Jordan guessed. He was approaching retirement but looked older. His skullcap sat on his head of white hair that seemed to blend in with his long unruly beard. It too was white and stretched down to the fourth button of his waistcoat. The waistcoat was part of the black suit with the long jacket commonly worn by the religious Jews. His intelligent brown eyes looked out from behind thick glasses perched upon a large straight nose. His skin was wrinkled beyond his years, his complexion pale and white. He was a wise man. Many of the townsfolk turned to him for advice, religious and secular alike.

"Please come to my office and enjoy a cup of coffee and cookies with me, Jordan. Then you can tell me what is on your mind. I will do my best as always to help you in any way, my son." He took Jordan by his arm and guided him down the corridor past classrooms full of young men studying the Torah.

Rabbi Carlebach poured Jordan a cup of coffee, took a sip from his cup, and settled back into his armchair.

He looked across at Jordan. "Now, what is on your mind Jordan? What is so important that you seek out my advice?"

"Well," Jordan started unsteadily, "first I would respectfully request that our conversation be in confidence."

"Of that you have my word," answered the old man.

Jordan collected his thoughts before he spoke. "Rabbi Carlebach, I served in the Golani brigade and many years in the service of the Mossad. During those years I saw unspeakable horrors. Worse, I committed many acts of violence myself, acts that I am not proud of."

The Rabbi cut in. "Jordan, please do not speak to me of these acts. I cannot forgive. I am not even a Catholic priest who can order you to repent with Hail Mary's." He smiled and continued, "What I do know is that Israel has to survive. It is our country, the only safe home for us Jews. In order to survive we sometimes have to act in ways that are not in our character. But you did not come to tell me of your past I am sure."

"No, Rabbi, it is for something much more important and deeply troubling to me. I have learned of a plan to destroy the Taba Convention. I have learned of the deaths of four Jews that were in the Mossad." Jordan looked up at the Rabbi who was listening intently. "I have learned that other Jews may be behind their deaths, even if they did not murder them with their own hands. I have been taught that life is sacrosanct. I was brought up believing that never must one Jew take up arms against another. This is the cornerstone of our state, of our religion. Rabbi, I do not know how to understand and grasp this reality. I am lost. I am not sure how to react to this. It is the reason I came to you for guidance." Jordan finished and sat back in his chair, a troubled look on his face.

Rabbi Carlebach sat silently in his chair, his arms folded across his chest, his gaze on Jordan. Minutes went by, and then finally the Rabbi spoke.

"Jordan, I do not have all the answers, they are the property of "Ha Shem," the name. I am but his servant. I can however tell you this. This world is made up of many different people. Most live normal happy lives and contribute to society in many ways, some small, some large. Some are led astray by their beliefs and some act on those beliefs. The Nazis believed that we were not worthy to live on this earth and wiped out six million of us. The Arabs believe that we are living on their land and have done their best to throw us off this holy ground. In both cases our faith has carried us through the dark times. Now we have achieved independence in our own land, a Jewish state for all Jews who care to come and join us. We have reclaimed the land that is rightfully ours. The Jewish nation has risen from the ashes of the Second World War and must not be allowed to fail. It must not be allowed to fail at any cost, any cost however hard and brutal that may be. The army, the Mossad, the General Security Service—all act under the government, all act as one to defend the state." He paused and continued, "But all this you know. I only tell you to underline that whatever you did in the service you did for the state, and you did faithfully. You are not to blame for this service but to be proud of it. Our land is sacred."

The Rabbi looked at Jordan and sighed, "I too am deeply affected by what you have told me of this plan to destroy the peace convention. I am not in favor of giving land for peace, especially the settlements that have taken so long to develop and grow. Good people live there Jordan, true Israelis, true believers. The government has taken the decision to give back land and we must live with that decision. We can argue, we can demonstrate, that is our democratic right. What we must not do, cannot do, is to take up arms against each other. We cannot do this however negatively we feel."

"As it is we are a diverse people. Sephardic Jews feel downtrodden and they were right for a long time. No longer is that true. Some Ashkenazi Jews still feel superior even today, but this is fading now. We are a complicated nation, Jordan. We live among each other, the Orthodox, the religious, and the secular. Many are right-wing, many are liberal, but we are finally coming together as one people. What you speak of will lead to civil war, to the destruction of Israel as we know it. I do not want to know more of what you know but I can tell you this. A Jew who saves a life is as if he has saved the whole world. Sometimes we have to take lives to save the state and our world. Yes, it is against our religion and our inner beliefs, but we do it only in self-defense. It is saddening and regrettable, but it has been that way since our forefathers

161

walked this land. We only do what we have to do. We may not be able to win on the world stage of public opinion, but we must save our homeland at all costs. While it saddens me deeply, it is still necessary to defend our way of life. It is against those that would take it away from us. It is just."

He paused, thought for a minute, and then looked over his glasses at Jordan. "I know that I may not have answered your questions directly with my words, my son. However, please reflect upon them and let them guide you in the future. I am glad that you have come to me, and I hope that I have been of help to you."

"Rabbi Carlebach, I thank you for your time. I believe that you have answered my concerns. You are a wise man, your words comforting and clear. Thank you again for your time." Jordan got up and shook the Rabbi's hand. "I will see myself out. May you live a long and healthy life, Rabbi Carlebach. Hopefully we shall not meet this Sunday."

He could still hear the Rabbi laughing as he went out into the heat of the night. He glanced at his watch. The visit had taken longer than he expected. He got into the car and told Shalom to start driving. The Rabbi had answered him. Jordan knew what he had to do and was at peace with his decision. The burden had been taken from his shoulders. Thank God he had thought to go to the Rabbi for guidance.

They headed north into the Arava until they came to the sign to Uvda, the largest Air Force base in the south of the country. The base was only used for visiting squadrons now. It was also used for the European charter flights that would soon be landing there in winter.

The Uvda base sat up on top of the western ridge of the Syrian African Rift, and a little westward on a flat plain. Nof Ha Arava and the Dust Riders were lodged right on the ridge above the Arava. It was a place where you could view the whole valley during daylight hours. It was also a hell of a good place to hole up for a while, a great vantage point from which you could see anyone coming up from the airbase.

The road wound up to the plateau and was beautifully lit up by the full moon. Not a single car passed them on the way, a good sign, thought Jordan. They left the main road before coming to the base and started up a dirt track that led to Nof Ha Arava. The car kicked up a hell of a lot of dust and sand behind them, but under cover of darkness no one would notice. No wonder the company was called the Dust Riders, Jordan thought.

Coming around a bend in the dirt track they drove in among a group of Bedouin tents. They could see a group of camels a short distance away. There was one small brick house and Jordan guessed that this was what Ronni of the Dust Riders called home. Some mongrels got up from the dust and barked their welcome. A dusty, beaten-up Nissan pickup was parked by one of the tents. A faded Israeli flag flapped in the wind atop a makeshift pole. Jordan could see why the tourists would like this place. It had a unique and authentic atmosphere. A camp that Lawrence of Arabia could have used.

A tall thin man came out of the house wearing the sort of turban that the Bedouin used on his head. As he approached, Jordan could see a pleasant weather-beaten face with large smiling eyes above a two-day stubble. The transformation to Bedouin tribesman was rounded off by his Arab dress which he wore with a leather belt at the waist. The man was totally at ease here in the wilderness. He looked much more at ease than in town, Jordan reckoned. The guy was probably right. It was so serene and peaceful up here, no traffic, no buses belching smoke. Only you and the stillness.

"You must be Jordan, a real pleasure to meet you. Any friend of Shalom's is a friend of mine," Ronni said warmly, greeting him with a firm handshake. Jordan was already beginning to like the man.

Ronni continued, "Probably nicer to meet you under other circumstances, but we'll make do. I understand that you need to lie low for a few days, no better place than among the camels up here. Nobody visits during the summer, too damn hot and dusty. Smells of camel shit most of the time. Give me a day or two and you'll look and smell like a Bedouin too," he laughed.

Not a bad idea at all, thought Jordan. It could work and help him evade his would-be captors. He got out of the car and tucked the project file under his arm. He had no change of clothes, but that looked less than necessary out here. Ronni showed him to a small room in the house, and they sat down to a steaming and very welcome cup of brewed Bedouin tea. It was very sweet and made with herbs and plants that grew in the desert around the encampment. A whole pot of it simmered constantly over glowing coals on the small balcony.

After a short time Shalom got up to leave. He had to get back to Eilat under cover of darkness and return the Skoda first thing in the morning. He shook hands with Ronni and Jordan and left the house. They heard him drive away, the noise from the engine carried by the desert wind until it faded away slowly and left them in silence. They talked for a while, but Jordan was reluctant to tell Ronni anything that might put him in danger. After a while Jordan excused himself and turned in. He fell into an exhausted but fitful sleep on the multicolored pile of Bedouin cushions that made up his bed.

CHAPTER NINE

EILAT.
FRIDAY, AUGUST 31ST.

Shalom knew that they would come asking questions. He had arrived back in Eilat early in the morning and had drunk a welcome mug of hot coffee in his kitchen before snatching a few hours' sleep.

The General Security Agent was waiting for him when he arrived at the hotel. He knew that the questions would be probing and that he had to be good, bloody good.

"Agent Cohen. Pleased to meet you, Mr. Biran," the agent said and sat down in Shalom's seat behind the desk.

Yeah, right. Mr. Cohen for sure. Shalom wondered what the man's real name was. Cohen in Israel ranked with the Smiths and Jones in England.

Shalom cut in quickly. "Please take a seat," he said sarcastically. "What can I help you with, Mr. Cohen?"

"Agent Cohen. Please call me 'Agent Cohen.' I would like to ask you, since we know you took the train to Jerusalem yesterday, what you were doing up north?" the agent asked curtly, as if he had every right to question Shalom and demand answers.

Shalom felt a wave of relief flow over him. They hadn't seen him around the Azrieli towers or in Hofstein's office. "Who's asking, and what business is it of yours?" Shalom spat back, trying his best to look annoyed. "Official hotel business is of no concern to you. I would like to remind you that you are not my employer."

"The General Security Service is asking, and I repeat my question to you, so do us both a favor and answer. *We* don't want to do it the hard way, do *we*?" said the agent softly.

Shalom bet that there were many other Agent Cohens out there, all lookalikes, all clones. All of them would now be looking for Jordan.

"If you really have to know, I was at the King David Hotel checking their new sprinkler systems which have to be installed into all our hotels during the next two years. This is to comply with the new fire laws. Every time the bloody Yanks upgrade their systems, the Ministry follows suit and we have to spend a fortune on upgrades. May as well add another star to the stars and stripes and call us Yankee State of Israel," he said cheerfully. He knew that they must have seen him at the King David, so he had been ready for this question. Pretty good answer, since it was true. They could check the story. He had been there recently to check on the sprinkler system.

"Then why did we rent a car to return, surely a flight is quicker, no, Mr. Biran?" Agent Cohen probed, looking for telltale body language. Again the *we*.

"Simple, Mr. Cohen," replied Shalom. "Firstly it was getting late, and with the heavy traffic that's always coming out of Jerusalem on a Thursday evening, I was not sure to catch the flight. I was on the waiting list anyway, didn't have a firm reservation. Secondly, I hate flying, even though I was with the paratroops in the war. By the way, I also love driving, so there's your answer."

It apparently satisfied Agent Cohen, for he got up and said over his shoulder as he left the office, "It is Agent Cohen, Mr. Biran, don't want to keep reminding you. Nasty stuff happening around here, Mr. Biran. Wouldn't want you to get involved would we? Anyway, might be back later for some more questions, so don't wander."

Shalom got up and went around his desk and sank down into his own chair. He had passed that test. Now the tough part: what to do next.

TEL AVIV.
SUNDAY, SEPTEMBER 2ND.

Einhorn was nervous now, very nervous, and extremely angry. He had been quick to act, but Mr. Kline had been even quicker, and much cleverer. The son of a bitch.

The stupid GSS agents in Eilat had bungled the job. How in hell could they mistake a woman for the real target? What the fuck did they think they were doing? He did not order the hit on this Linda woman. Since when did the agents just open fire? It was not like this with the older, more experienced agents; they did the job cleanly and efficiently, not in public as these fools had done. They would pay for this. They'd had to scramble fast to clear this up, right up to the gangland slaying cover-up. It was the best that he could come up with at such short notice. Not good but the best available story.

He knew that he must not underestimate Mr. Kline anymore; he seemed to be very elusive. He had gone underground. No point in looking for a needle in a haystack. No, he would have to wait for Kline to make his move. Then he would catch and kill the bastard.

The APB had been issued, and there were thousands of agents on the lookout for Mr. Kline, following orders, ready to report any sightings. One sighting was all he needed. He would wait patiently. Yes, that is exactly what he would do, wait for Mr. Kline to break cover and then kill him before he had any further chance to meddle. He must calm down, he thought. Keep control of yourself, Einhorn. He realized that he had broken out in a sweat, a cold sweat. He took a tissue from the box on his desk and wiped his face. He patted his face with his palm to make sure it was dry, and threw the tissue in the bin under his desk.

The telephone on his desk rang and brought him back to reality. He picked up the receiver and put it to his ear.

"Can you explain what the fuck has gone down in Eilat, Einhorn? The explanation better be good. Who the fuck is Jordan Kline anyway?" Dan Heller barked down the line. He had seen the APB and was obviously enraged. He was furious. Dan Heller, tall, good-looking, and the Chairman of the House Security Committee was on the line. He was often considered future prime minister material. He had straight black hair neatly parted above an aristocratic face well known to the public who adored this new, young, western type of politician. Dark brown, almost black eyes, set wide apart looked wisely down a strong, straight masculine nose. He was good-looking and knew it. He used it well to his political advantage.

Israelis were growing tired of the old leaders. They quickly started favoring Heller when he entered politics after a brilliant military career during which he was twice decorated for bravery. Israelis loved a war hero, especially a good-looking one that could replace the old, boring generation of politicians. It was very common for military officers to enter politics after army service. Many went on to top cabinet positions, some even to become Prime Minister. Yes, Dan Heller had every reason to believe that he could rise to the highest office in the land. A youngish forty-five, Heller had plenty of charm and charisma to go with his successful military background. He had a radiant smile that oozed confidence and a knack of getting people to like him. He invariably used the sense of touch to get near people: a small hand on the shoulder, a firm handshake with two hands, a delicate arm around the back. That was his way. People liked being around him, liked being part of his success.

"Everything is well under control. You may rest assured. Calm down. Unfortunately the poor fucking bitch was driving Mr. Kline's car, and the idiots didn't bother to check. Trigger-happy fucking bastards. I have had my suspicions about Kline for a while now, but nothing concrete that I could move on. Kline has disappeared, but when he moves, I will eliminate him." He was reining in his temper now, watching his language. He couldn't afford to row with Heller. Not now.

"Einhorn, you better not slip any more. I am not liking this, not liking this one little bit. There better not be any more of this shit flying." Heller slammed the phone down.

Now Einhorn was really annoyed; who the fuck was that fucking junior Minister to be telling him, no, worse, threatening him, the Deputy Chief of the Mossad? He was sitting up in his fucking ivory tower while he, Einhorn, was doing the dirty work. He would settle accounts with the bastard after they had taken care of the convention.

He calmed himself down and looked pensively out at the view of Tel Aviv laid out below him. Where, he wondered, was their Mr. Kline? Had he gone to ground in Tel Aviv? No, he would not do that; he would be too far from Taba in Tel Aviv. He must be holed up somewhere close to Eilat, so that when he decided to break cover and get to Taba, he would be close. Oh, and where was that beautiful girlfriend of his? They must take her in and dangle her as bait for him. That would get the rabbit out of his hole, for sure. He picked up the phone and dialed a number.

NOF HA ARAVA.
SUNDAY, SEPTEMBER 2ND.

Jordan lay on his stomach in the dirt high up on the edge of the plateau and looked down at the valley below. An amazingly beautiful view lay spread out before him: the deep valley way down below him and the pastel-colored Jordanian mountains climbing high on the other side. He could see the cars approaching Eilat on the Arava road and made out the Aqaba-bound traffic on the Jordanian side.

Now and then an Arkia shuttle from Tel Aviv would fly by him, descending or climbing as it flew past Nof Ha Arava almost level with him. He thought about Irit. He could even see Yotvata Kibbutz in the far distance below. He wondered how she was coping, hoping that she was being well taken care of by Ilan.

He had spent the Saturday resting, glad for the company of Ronni. Ronni in turn seemed glad that he had someone to talk to over the weekend. They hit it off immediately, and the more Jordan got to know Ronni, the more he liked him. He was the type of guy that gave you the feeling that you'd known him already for a long time, even though you had just met him. Great sense of humor, too. He could be a real good friend in the future—if Jordan managed to have a future.

Jordan got up and walked back to the house. He looked in the mirror in the entrance hall and liked what he saw. He already had considerable stubble and had picked up a slight tan that contrasted sharply with Jordan Kline, the hotelier. Another day or two and he could really look like a genuine Bedouin, he thought, with some help from Ronni.

He had the basics of a plan in his head, and when he had finished thinking them through he would ask Ronni for help implementing them. His help would be vital, in fact.

Jordan turned from the mirror and went back out into the sun to work on a better tan.

CHAPTER TEN

YOTVATA.
MONDAY SEPTEMBER 3RD.

Irit sat quietly in the salon in the little house at Yotvata and wondered what on earth was going on. She had been here for almost two days now, and no word from Jordan. She was nervous and not a little shaky. She had seen the news and read the papers and knew about Linda and Alex. It was called a gangland killing in Linda's' case and a drive-by shooting by a nationalist Arab in Alex's' case. It was easy to camouflage Alex's killing under the guise of terrorism, but she knew better.

This was certainly part of what Jordan had become involved with, she was sure of that. She now knew why Jordan had to disappear. She was really frightened for his safety. Still, she had confidence in his abilities to get through this one just as he had all his life. If anyone could survive it was Jordan, she thought to herself in an effort to calm her nerves. She thought back to the carefree days in Eilat before all of this—the nights of lovemaking, their anniversary evening. She smiled as she figured that there wasn't a room in their apartment that they hadn't made love in. The places they called their "locations."

She knew that if they got a hold of her, they could flush him out. If there was one thing she was sure of, it was that Jordan would come for her if she were taken. It must be something of huge importance, but what? God, she wished she knew a bit more, sitting in this hot little oven of a house in the middle of nowhere getting very bored.

The telephone rang, breaking the silence, and she rushed over to pick it up.

The voice she loved came loud and clear.

"Irit, my love, how are you keeping? Low I hope. Can't talk for long, but soon all this will be over and we can finally carry on where we left off, from my last whisper to you as you fell asleep. Did you by any chance hear me?" Jordan spoke softly and she could sense his great longing for her.

"Do I ever remember, Jord? And I am going to hold you to it. My answer to your whisper is yes. And yes, I am fine and being a good girl, though I don't know how much longer I can stand this place. How on earth do these people live in this Godforsaken place anyway, Jord? Please come quickly. I can't take much more," she pleaded.

"I will. I promise you. And I meant every word of my whisper, you know that. Got to go now, my love," he said and cut the line.

She replaced the receiver and heard someone approaching the door. She was looking forward to Ilan's company, anything to break the monotony of the silence and loneliness she endured in here.

The door opened, and Ilan walked into the house.

He was in the company of two gentlemen wearing dark grey suits. This was not good. Thank God, she thought, that she had finished talking with Jordan.

Ilan spoke first. "Irit, my dear, these are GSS agents who are looking for Jordan. They have explained to me that he is mixed up in a murder. However friendly I am with him, the dear fellow, nothing justifies my aiding and abetting him in his crime. They would like you to accompany them to Eilat to answer a few questions, my dear. They have assured me that you are safe with them, so be a darling and gather up your stuff and go with them, please," he said curtly, as if he were tainted by the act of shielding her. His posh accent really annoyed her now, the stuck-up British bastard.

"You stupid back-stabbing bastard," she cried out. "Don't you know Jordan? He would never murder someone. He must have stumbled onto something and they are out to silence him. You have helped them by leading them to me. My God, how stupid and naive can you be, you dumb stuck-up English kibutznick bastard!"

She quickly considered her options. She couldn't run, there was only the one doorway out and the grey suits were standing in the way. She turned and went into the bedroom to get her stuff. She didn't have anything to tell them anyway, but she had to show defiance, to try and help Jordan in some small way. She had to gain some more time for him and whatever it was he had to do.

She came out with her backpack and they escorted her to a grey Mazda the same color as their suits. She got in the back with one of the suits while the other suit went around and got behind the wheel. They looked alike, twins.

Once in the car, all semblance of civility left them. The suit with her in the back took out a pair of handcuffs and locked her in them roughly. She cried out as they cut into her wrists. They drove out of the kibbutz entrance, and then the suit in the back spoke to Irit.

"You, my dear, are now suspected of aiding and abetting a murderer and traitor. We believe that he was the perpetrator of a drive-by slaying in Jerusalem. You will tell us all you know, and he will come to us. He will do it for you. He loves you."

She could see that the filthy bastard was scanning her body now, thinly veiled by the summer dress she had on. It was riding high on her thighs. She could see the lust in his eyes. She had heard of the GSS interrogation methods. They stopped at nothing, not even rape or sexual abuse to get what they wanted. They enjoyed their work. They were a law unto themselves.

She had to do something, anything, to try and get away from them. She had her hands cuffed behind her back.

She thought of a plan.

Turning around to the agent in the back and facing him as if to speak to him, she fumbled behind her back with the door handle. She could feel the outline of the handle and gripped it.

"You idiots think that I know something? You think that he was stupid enough to tell me anything? Dumb fucks!" She was playing for time now, trying to get a stronger hold on the handle, and continued, "You don't know Jordan Kline. He forgot all that you think you know a long time ago. If you hurt so much as a hair on my head, he will kill you. I promise you that!"

The suit beside her laughed out loud with the driver. He was certainly not ready when Irit made her move.

The car was just accelerating when Irit in one swift movement opened the door, brought up her long legs, and pushed herself out of the moving car, using grey suit in the back to gain momentum. She felt a sharp pain as her head hit the edge of the door, and then she hit the road hard, rolling over and over. She tried to curl up in an effort to protect her head. She skidded over the edge of the hard shoulder, hitting rocks and brush on the way and kicking up a cloud of dust. Her dress shredded as she skidded over the rough terrain. The asphalt burned and razed her skin. She cried out in pain. She knew instinctively that she had broken her arm, had deep cuts, and was bleeding badly. God, it hurt. She didn't care. She had won, she thought for a fleeting moment. Then she slammed into a tree. Darkness descended on her.

CHAPTER ELEVEN

JERUSALEM, TUESDAY, SEPTEMBER 4TH.

Dan Heller, Junior Minister had every reason to be content. He had just chaired another committee meeting regarding security arrangements for the upcoming convention in Taba. It was just days away now.

He had listened in turn to all the fools and their plans—first the Israel Police, then the Army, and finally the GSS. They all went over their carefully laid plans for security.

It was foolproof. No one uninvited in his correct mind would even try to enter the Taba Hilton complex, let alone try any sabotage. They had it sewn up.

Einhorn had been in touch with him and assured him that although Kline had not yet been eliminated, they had his girl. She was in the hospital with a concussion, a broken arm, and some cuts. They would get any information that she knew about Kline when she woke up.

Heller didn't know whether to laugh or cry at Einhorn. He reminded him of the bloody Marx brothers. He was a totally incompetent clown. Kline was in a different league and he just hoped that Kline would know better than to interfere; they had his girl. Gutsy bitch. She was lucky that she had not killed herself throwing herself like that from a moving car. He had to admit that it had taken courage. Maybe Jordan Kline would attempt to get her back when he found out that she was in Yoseftal hospital. Then they would be sure to capture him, neutralizing any threat still possible.

Heller knew that the Hilton Taba complex was finished and ready to host the convention. He could picture the marble floors, the high ceilings, Iyad's furniture all arranged for the talks and the ceremonies. He could not remember being happier. His career was at a turning point, a point that could take him to the top of the party. All he had left to do was to wait for the eighth, that was all. It would soon be here.

NOF HA ARAVA.
TUESDAY, SEPTEMBER 4TH.

Jordan looked at himself in the mirror and was even more satisfied at the face looking back than he had been before. Two days in the sun had given him a deep tan all over his body, and he now had the beginnings of a beard. Ronni had brought him hair dye from Eilat, and he had dyed it jet black. The face looking back at him was almost that of a real Bedouin. The clothes Ronni had given him rounded off the appearance.

My God, thought Jordan, a long way from the tailored designer suits of the White Sands, and all in just a few days. He looked good, but he would have traded all this in the blink of an eye to be back in his cozy living room lounging on the sofa with Irit and nursing an ice cold Goldstar.

Jordan was used to disguises from the Mossad days, but he had to admit that this was good. He hoped that it would attract no more than a cursory glance when he made his move.

He had spent the past couple of days working on his tan as well as a plan; although, he would have to make a lot of it up as he went along. After careful thought, and since he had little choice, he had decided to try and enlist Ronni. He could be a very valuable member of the team with his army background. He had intimate knowledge of the terrain in and around Eilat and Taba. They could definitely do with Ronni on their side.

"Good morning, Ronni," he said as he almost bumped into him coming out of the bathroom. "Ronni, have you got a minute or two, there's something that I have to ask you?"

"I was wondering when you were going to come around to that. Let's go into the tent and have tea and a chat." Ronni seemed eager to listen. His curiosity over Jordan's circumstances must have been driving him slightly mad.

Ronni finished drying his hair with the towel and poured two teas into glasses from a teapot that rested on embers in the corner of the room. He settled into a pile of cushions opposite Jordan as he handed him a glass of the steaming herbal tea.

"Now, what's this all about? Must be something really serious. You and Shalom in trouble with the law? That why you're here?"

Jordan laughed at the absurdity and answered, "I wish it were, but actually it's more the other way round. This time the law is in trouble with us. By pure coincidence I stumbled over something of national, no, of international importance on my way down to Eilat about three weeks ago. One of my buddies from the Mossad days was taken out, run off the road. He managed to whisper a few words to me before he died."

Choosing his words very carefully, Jordan told Ronni of the events that had unfolded over the past days since he had chanced upon Josh in his final moments.

He left nothing out, since Ronni had to know all the facts if he was to agree to join. It was a while before he finished.

"So you see, as I told you, part of the law is in trouble with me and Shalom." Jordan smiled and added, "Ronni, what do you think of it all, and will you help?"

Ronni seemed amazed by what he had just heard, and it took some moments for it all to sink in.

He leaned back into the cushions and was silent for a few minutes, apparently sorting it all out in his mind. Finally he answered Jordan. "Of my help there is no doubt, Jordan, but we have to be really careful if we are to get out of this thing alive. We are only three men and that's hardly enough. However, we do have some things going for us. Firstly, I operate the Bedouin tent on the beach below the Taba Hilton and the new complex, so I can move about freely. Everybody knows me there."

"My people are also preparing some of the food for the banquet before the signing ceremony. On top of that, I will have some of my people there, and we can use them up to a point. Secondly, I have some arms stashed away here, though not much—some revolvers, grenades, that sort of thing. Never know when they might be useful, living here isolated and near the Egyptian border. Thirdly, although a little rusty, I am a Sea Commando, and have been through a few incidents, believe me. You have the Golani background and the Mossad training, and Shalom has a great action background and experience, too. We are all men of great resources. That has to count for something."

"We still need to know a lot more, though where it will come from I don't know. So long as we have a chance in hell of fucking up their plans, we have to try. Yes, I am in. Might turn out to be the best fun I've had in years," he said. He slapped his knees with the palms of his hands in his excitement.

Jordan had not seen anyone so excited at the thought of violence, perhaps over-excited. He put it down to the boredom of life up here in the compound during the winter.

They sat together for a long time, figuring out their next move and going over and over again what little knowledge they had. Jordan brought out the project file and they went over the plans: architectural, construction, electrical, air-conditioning, and plumbing. The air-conditioning plans held some hope since one of the major ducts led to the area exactly above the entrance to the great hall. Ronni brought up the possibility of positioning an assassin there during the event, but then dismissed the thought.

They laid out the plumbing plans and went over every detail. Everything seemed in order, and they were just about to turn the page when something caught Jordan's eye.

"Don't turn the page just yet, Ronni, there's something strange here." He looked at the plans with renewed interest. He pointed to the plans of the entrance to the hall. "Look, Ronni. All the pipes lead to somewhere and look fine, but what about this one? Where does this pipe lead and what purpose does it hold? It has been staring me in the face all along, I'll be damned. I must be blind."

Running from one side of the steps at the entrance to the hall to the other side there was a pipeline with no apparent connection on either side.

"You're right, Jordan. Even if it was a water pipe for gardening, it's way too big. They wouldn't plan it here anyway, much too ugly. It's not sewage either. My God, you may be onto something. They knew that this was the best way to get the pipe put in since any changes afterwards would definitely have raised questions—especially because of the location. How simple, and yet how extremely clever. No one would know to question the pipe. No one would really look at the plans. They would accept the expert planning. You've got to hand it to the bastards."

The pipeline ran right under the central staircase at the entrance to the hall. How easy to place explosives at one end and push them into place in the middle of the pipe. Close the ends and even the sniffer dogs wouldn't have a clue. Stand at a respectful distance and blow it by remote wireless. God, how easy! How many times had the Mossad terminated terrorists by planting an explosive device in the cell phones and then ringing wirelessly to activate the explosives? Only these were not terrorists, these were the President of the United States, the Prime Minister of Israel, the President of Egypt, and the Palestinian President.

Ronni looked at Jordan and said, "If this is the plan, we have to move quickly, and we have to know who else is involved. Now, Alex lost his life for following Iyad in Jerusalem. That means that he was dangerously close to seeing something. Either that or they are just not taking any chances and terminating everyone that they suspect could get in their way. I think that they did not want Iyad followed. Since Shalom gave us the address, I believe that we need to know more about this Iyad and his connection. I am curious. I want to know more. Don't forget that the guy is a Palestinian militant, and aside from selling Hofstein furniture, he is involved in this up to his fat greasy neck. Apart from that, I don't like the look of where this is headed.

"I believe that this is a plot by Arabs who do not want any peace treaty to be signed. There are those that would go to these extremes. I shall go up to Jerusalem tomorrow and watch the house on Via Dolorosa for a while. We have no other leads. We can't very well go and tell our story to anyone—they wouldn't believe us. In any case we would be taken out by them before we could act. Don't forget, if they can terminate people just like that," he said, snapping his fingers, "they must be bloody powerful. We could never work with the Palestinians to get a successful chance at peace, but boy can we work together with them, at least some of us, to destroy any chance of peace. I wonder who the traitors are among us. We shall see soon, Jordan. We shall soon see their true faces."

"I agree entirely, Ronni," Jordan replied. "To give us the best chance, we must act at the last possible minute. Give them the least opportunity of catching us. In the meantime, you are right, but I shall go with you. We'll go see what we can find out about this house in East Jerusalem and who is involved. Take a pair of the night glasses that you use on the treks. If there is any action, you can bet it will be under cover of darkness. We must be back here by the seventh evening, because we should start moving towards Taba during the night under cover of darkness. We need to be in place well before the start of the convention. Don't forget that the GSS will close off the area early on the eighth, if not before. After that it will be damn near impossible to get into the Taba area, let alone the Hilton complex."

"Yes," Ronni said. "I shall go on a sales trip to Jerusalem tomorrow and see what I can find out. You will be in the trunk. In the meantime I will instruct some of my people to get camels ready for the seventh. When we get back you can prepare the arms we need. By the way, don't forget to charge the Motorola walkie-talkies so that we have communication between us in Taba. Leave them in the chargers until we go on the seventh. We'll leave tomorrow afternoon so as to be in Jerusalem in good time. In the meantime let's go over the plans again and make sure we didn't miss something."

The cell phone on the small table rang just as Ronni finished talking. He picked it up and flipped it open. He mouthed the name Shalom to Jordan and listened intently before answering, "Listen, don't do anything and don't call us. We shall be in touch with you at the appropriate time when we come. Keep low, and the time will come to act. Bye."

Ronni turned to Jordan and spoke softly, "Listen Jordan, Irit is in Yoseftal. Shalom does not know how she got there. He is going to visit her and try to find out what condition she is in and how she got there."

Rage built up in Jordan. God no, not Irit. Had Ilan turned her in? Why? How badly was she injured that she was in Yoseftal Hospital? If they had hurt her, the bastards, he would make them pay.

Ronni looked at him. "Jordan, no, not now. Chill out, you got to chill out. Anger makes you think crooked, and we need you thinking straight. It will have to wait until the seventh when we make our move. Calm down. We will have to get her before we go to Taba. We cannot leave her there to be used against you. The minute she is out of Yoseftal they will use her to flush you out, you know that. In the meantime lay low and get some rest. God knows we'll need to be as sharp as possible when we move. Don't worry, we'll get her out."

Jordan needed to be alone. He had known that Irit was at risk, but he'd thought that they would not find her tucked away on the kibbutz. If it was Ilan he would make the bastard pay. It must have been Ilan. Jesus, they were quick. He needed fresh air. Jordan left the tent, went over to the edge of the plateau and sat down cross-legged to think. He needed to be alone. He needed to get a grip.

EILAT.
TUESDAY, SEPTEMBER 4TH.

Shalom finished up his call to Ronni and walked out of his office towards his car. The general manager at the Neptune had called the hotel looking for Jordan, and they had put him through to Shalom in Jordan's absence. The manager had told him that the staff at Yoseftal had rung him about Irit and that he was looking for Jordan to tell him the news.

Shalom knew that they had found her at Yotvata. Irit had probably tried to get away, injuring herself. It would be so like her to try and help by gaining some time, by not allowing them to use her as a pawn against Jordan. What a courageous woman, he thought, pulling a trick like that. But what had she done to wind up in Yoseftal? He had to go find out. He had to get to the hospital and see Irit and talk to the director of the hospital. She must not be taken anywhere until they decided what to do.

After a short drive through town and up the hill Shalom parked his car in the hospital car park. He walked into the bright, sterile, neon-lit reception.

"Shalom, what a pleasant surprise to see you," exclaimed Dr. Grundman, the hospital director, in his German accent. "And what brings a nice guy like you to a place like this?"

"Can we talk a little, Dr. Grundman?" asked Shalom. He lead the doctor by his arm to his office just off the reception. Shalom closed the door softly behind him.

"Listen, Irit is here after injuring herself. Now, it's very much involved and complicated, and I don't have the time to tell you more. You must promise me that you will keep her hospitalized until I tell you any different. All I can say is that it may mean the difference between life and death for her and also Jordan, so please do me the favor. You owe me one anyway, since I fixed your family that free stay at the Sands, right?"

"No problem, Shalom," the doctor answered shakily. "In any case she should be here at least another day for observation. She looks a lot worse that she really is, I believe. I'll keep her here, no problem. Really bad luck she had falling down those stairs, huh?" The s's came out like z's when he spoke. It was clear to Shalom that he did not know how Irit had hurt herself. The GSS goons who had brought her to the hospital had probably sold him the story about the fall.

Shalom thanked and left the good doctor. He walked down the corridor to the ward in search of Irit's room. He had no problem finding it; a GSS agent sat stationed right outside her door. The agent lounged on a cheap wooden chair with his feet stretched out across the corridor. He read a newspaper, a half-empty glass of coffee on the floor by the chair.

"No one goes in," the agent stated bluntly as Shalom approached him.

"Listen here and listen good, asshole. I am the Assistant Director of the Anti-Terrorism Squad in Eilat. It is my duty to visit all injured Eilati civilians, so do me and you a favor and get out of my fucking way." Shalom spoke with such authority that the agent moved his legs to the side hurriedly. Shalom turned the doorknob and entered the room.

He was shocked by what he saw. Irit lay on her back, her left arm in plaster. Her face was covered with bruises. He dared not think what the rest of her looked like under the hospital sheets. She seemed to be in a deep sleep. They were surely tranquilizing her to keep her calm.

He sat down in the chair beside the bed and took her hand.

Irit opened her eyes and saw Shalom. She whispered, a tear falling down her cheek and onto the sheet, "They came to get me from Ilan's, Shalom, but I jumped from the car."

"Irit, you did great, stupid but great. You could have gotten yourself killed doing that. You have to listen to me now. However bad you feel, make it look worse. You must stay here until we come for you. They must not be allowed to take you out of the hospital. I spoke to Dr. Grundman who promised to keep you hospitalized for now. I can move around because they don't suspect me yet, so trust me, we'll be back for you on the seventh. Have to go now, but make out like you're in a coma or something. Hang in there, Irit. Bye." He turned to leave, but she pulled him back by the hand.

"Please tell Jordan I'm sorry and that I love him. And tell him to be careful, too. Stay safe, Shalom" she said weakly and let him go. Her hand dropped back onto the bed.

Shalom exited the room and spoke to the agent. "Poor girl seems to be in a coma. She really fucked up falling down those stairs," he said.

NOF HA ARAVA.
WEDNESDAY, SEPTEMBER 5TH.

It was early afternoon. Jordan was outside petting one of the dogs. Ronni came out of the house a completely different person. Jordan was amazed at the transformation. He was dressed in a dark grey suit, white button-down shirt, and dark blue tie. The Bedouin was gone, and in his place there was a respectable businessman. The ever-present stubble and the deep tan from a life out in the open were still there, but Ronni looked good. Guess he still couldn't bring himself to shave Jordan thought.

"How did you do that? How in hell's name did you do that?" Jordan asked in amazement.

"Simple. You forget that I come from your side of the street. I do have suits, you know. I run a business. And you don't look so bad yourself, Jordan. Come on, let's go." Ronni carried his attaché case to the beaten-up Nissan. They got in, and Ronni gunned the engine. They drove down the rough track leading to the main road, raising the inevitable clouds of dust and gravel behind them.

CHAPTER TWELVE

JERUSALEM.
WEDNESDAY, SEPTEMBER 5TH.

It had been a relatively easy trip up to Jerusalem and had taken no more than three hours. Ronni had noticed more police traffic than usual on the Arava road and was even asked at the roadblock if he knew or had seen someone resembling a certain Jordan Kline. The photograph he was shown was rather outdated. He was tempted to tell them that he looked a whole lot different now than in the photo. He guessed that the picture was pulled from an old agency file. He thought of Jordan in the trunk and smiled.

He swung a right after the roadblock and skirted the Dead Sea, going past Ein Bokek, the area where all the Dead Sea Resort Hotels were located. He drove on past Jericho and climbed up to the entrance to Jerusalem. They were a little early so he parked the pickup at the King David Hotel and they went in to have a coffee and a bite.

Ronni ordered a toasted cheese sandwich with tomato slices and an iced tea to wash it down. Jordan requested a cup of tea with mint and settled down in the armchair with the day's copy of the *Ha'aretz* newspaper, the English version of the Hebrew daily that came as an insert with the *International Herald Tribune*.

Jordan showed the picture of the woman who'd been murdered in Jordan's car to Ronni under a headline of innocent citizens caught in the crossfire of crime. They should not have killed the woman. That was a mistake, the type of mistake that he would not have made in their place, thought Ronni. They were amateurs.

He had to admit this was getting more and more interesting. He just had to understand more than he knew at the moment. Well, let's wait until dark and see who else is involved in this, he thought to himself.

Ronni washed down the last bite of toast with the iced tea and fell asleep in the armchair opposite Jordan. The long drive had exhausted him.

He awoke with a start. The waitress was shaking him lightly to request payment as her shift was ending. He rubbed his eyes with his knuckles, glanced at his watch, and saw that it was already six-thirty. He saw Jordan still asleep on the sofa. They must have been asleep for over an hour, he thought. He was thankful that the waitress had woken him. He paid the bill and shook Jordan awake. They got up and walked out of the hotel. The short sleep had done them a world of good; they felt refreshed after the long drive.

Ronni took a right onto King David Street and another right at the crossroads. It took them down towards the Old City walls and the traffic lights under David's Citadel where Alex had met his death. He skirted the Old City walls and parked near the Jewish quarter. They exited the car. Under the cover of dusk and the open trunk, he quickly became Ronni the Bedouin once again. He put the suit down carefully on the backseat, picked up the night glasses, locked the car, and the two disappeared quietly into the alleys of East Jerusalem.

Knowing their way around the Old City well, they arrived quickly at the Via Dolorosa. Looking around to find a suitable location from which to view the entrance to thirty-three, Jordan saw one of the typical, very narrow side alleys that separated the houses. With the help of a drainpipe and by using his feet on both sides of the houses lining the alley, Jordan was quickly in position on the roof of the house opposite number thirty-three. Ronni followed him up the same way. They camouflaged themselves as best they could, and Jordan trained the glasses on the entrance to the house that Shalom had seen Iyad enter.

They had both almost dozed off again when they heard muffled footsteps coming from the dark alley. Jordan glanced at his watch and saw that it was almost nine o'clock. He silently trained the glasses at the entrance to the house. It was not long before he could make out three figures waiting at the doorway. They were dressed in suits and were glancing around nervously in all directions. It was clear that they did not want to be seen.

He got a clear unobstructed look at all of their faces in the moonlight as they scanned the alleys, and what he saw hit him like a freight train. It took a while for it to sink in, for he suddenly realized that he was staring down at three of the most powerful men in Israel. Not that he was surprised that Hofstein was there, but Ariel Einhorn of the Mossad, and Dan Heller, the junior Cabinet Minister and Chair of the House Security Committee? No wonder they could have people killed quietly and without question. What in hell were they doing at this time in the evening in East Jerusalem, waiting to enter the house of a known Palestinian publisher and arch-anti-Semite?

He and Ronni watched as the group was ushered in by Hassan Fawzi. So the Arab publisher was also in on this. They waited to see if the men were being watched and guarded by a security detail. Jordan did not see or hear any suspicious activity. He doubted very much that there would be a security detail with the three men for this meeting—it would have been too risky for even the most trusted bodyguard to be aware of the meeting. Jordan whispered to Ronni the names of the three who had entered.

Silence fell again in the alley. They waited for a few minutes before lowering themselves quietly back down the way they had come. They retraced their steps back to the pickup, running softly away from what they had just seen. Ronni threw his Jellabiya into the trunk. He got back into his suit. He opened the door and let out his breath as he sank down into the driver's seat and looked across at Jordan.

"God Jordan," Ronni managed to say between heavy breaths. "How easy it could be for them to sabotage the convention. Between the four of them they have the builder, the furniture supplier, the man in charge of security and planning for the convention. The Mossad deputy could also place anyone he chose at the location to make sure that their plans went smoothly. If a junior cabinet minister and the Mossad deputy are involved, then how far up the ladder does this thing go? And if it does, then who is involved and calling the shots? It surely couldn't be from the cabinet—they were all invited to the ceremony. Suicide is not something a Jew contemplates. Maybe it is limited to these three and their secret army."

"Yeah, right, and maybe pigs will fly, I think they say in the States,"answered Jordan sarcastically. "But think of this Ronni—Jews taking up arms against Jews. Not only that, but Jews plotting with Arabs. It has been staring me in the face all the time, but I just did not want to accept it. I kept pushing the thought out of my mind. Look how easy it is for them to wipe people out. Money is no problem. I'm sure there is plenty of Arab money, more than enough to bankroll this operation. Arab killers are no problem at all. Planning and security are no problem. I can understand the right wing being against the peace treaty, but to go in with the Arabs? Jew and Arab together against peace? How do you relate to that? I mean, I believed that the Arabs are capable of anything, but those bastards we saw? Come on, let's get the hell out of here."

Luck would have to be on their side if they were to have any chance whatsoever to thwart the potential bloodbath in Taba. They headed for Eilat via the Dead Sea, the shortest route from Jerusalem. They had to get back as soon as possible to try and come up with a plan. The nighttime traffic was thin. They soon hit the road to Jericho, accelerating into the night through the Judean hills.

CHAPTER THIRTEEN

JERUSALEM.
WEDNESDAY, SEPTEMBER 5TH.

The Turkish coffee sat steaming in front of them, the aroma filling the small room as they sat around the table in the house on Via Dolorosa.

Hofstein was the first to speak. "Well, we seem very close to our goal now and nothing can stop us. Perhaps we should have put some whisky in the coffee to celebrate. Hassan, your reports please. Keep it brief with no anti-Semitism this time, you fucking Arab. The rest of you can follow up."

Fawzi ignored the remark. "Well, with Allah's help we took care to eliminate the Eilati fellow that was following Iyad here in Jerusalem. I cannot say that Mr. Einhorn is having the same success with his end, huh?" Hassan hissed, turning his beady eyes accusingly in Einhorn's direction.

"I do not see any problem with my end, and keep to your fucking business. I will take care of mine," he answered curtly, but Hofstein interrupted.

"No problem? No problem? You stupid idiot. First you kill an innocent secretary by riddling the car, and her, in public.

Then you bungle the arrest of Mr. Jordan Kline's girlfriend in Yotvata, and you have no problems? That's a fucking laugh. And you don't even have a clue where the guy is. Let me remind you that Jordan Kline was one of the best operatives we ever had in the Agency and could still be a problem, a huge problem. What the fuck are you doing to find him, Einhorn? You are a fucking joke, Einhorn, a bad fucking joke." He had called him twice by his surname taking Einhorn by surprise. Hofstein was attacking him in front of the Arab.

"It's like this," stammered Einhorn, visibly shaken by this onslaught. "The girl is in Yoseftal Hospital and well guarded by my people. The way I figure it is that Jordan Kline will turn up soon at the hospital and try and take her back from us. We do not know where he is. He could be anywhere. We think that he is acting alone. He can hardly succeed on his own. We have no suspicions about anyone else at present. We cannot hide the girl yet. She is in a semi-coma from when she threw herself out of the car and cannot be moved. Doctor's orders. Yes, he will come, and then 'Bam!' we take him out and the way to the finishing line is open. I do not see a problem on my end, no."

"No problem on my end, no," Hofstein mimicked Einhorn. "I, at least, am worried by this man. What I have found out about him over the past week is that although our public does not know him, he is a fucking legend in the agency, and he is only in his mid-thirties. That itself means that the guy is a problem, a real problem. At least he is not a hero to the public. No one will mourn him nationally when you take him out— correction—if you take him out. No problem on my end," he mimicked Einhorn again before continuing. "Please report as soon as this matter is taken care of. It is giving me a headache, no, a migraine."

"Now to business at hand. The bomb is already in place. Einhorn and I have the wireless trigger numbers on our cell phones. You will all, of course, allow me the pure joy of blowing them all to hell. You must make sure that when they all come out onto the stairs that you are all at certain distance to the side and well protected. If not, you will join them all in Paradise. I doubt that virgins, however, will be waiting for you, Hassan, when you arrive. Anyway, look at the size of you. You couldn't fuck them even if they did come to you. You couldn't get your small dick near enough." He chuckled.

Hassan looked pained and frowned.

"We can do no more from our end," Hassan said. "We cannot help at the convention. We are very pleased that our investment in this venture has been very worthwhile. Our leadership is looking forward to many more years of exile and enjoyment in Tunis. Since this is the last meeting I would like to convey their thanks to our Zionist friends and hope that we do not have to collaborate in the future on such ventures. After all, we are enemies and should act like enemies. Personally, to sit with you Jews makes me uncomfortable, and in my own home at that. I would not have done this but for the Leadership. You all understand me, no?"

"We thank our Arab brethren for their backing on this," Einhorn said. "We could not have done this without your help or money. By the way, the attacks you launched after we left the last time were utterly superfluous, you fucking idiot, but what's done is done. We hope that the Leadership spends many years enjoying life in Tunis while we create a whole Israel that will not be disturbed for a long time. Mr. Fawzi, we shall shortly reward you for your efforts. "

"Meanwhile I have issued the tags to my boys that will be in Taba. I have cut them down to ten agents, don't want to arouse suspicion. You will know them apart from the others by the tags that allow them alone to be close to the leaders—orange tabs. Should something go wrong they will be in place to help us. They each are highly armed and can, if necessary, take the leaders out 'manually' on my command. They are completely trustworthy and are with the cause. They think entirely as we do, but obviously know much less. Suffice it to say that they would die for the cause."

Heller broke in: "And I have made the last-minute arrangements for the convention, including the positions of each head of state on the steps for the speeches. Everything is as planned. Tomorrow their security details start arriving for talks in Jerusalem and fine-tuning of the convention timetable. The heads of state will all arrive at the Hilton by separate limos on the seventh evening. They will arrive for the state dinner on the evening before the signing ceremony."

"I will of course be there and will allow for no more changes in the plans as we have made them. The three of us will be there to make sure that all goes as planned. Please make sure that you see me leave the steps before you blow them away. You may be blowing up our next Prime Minister, you know." His mouth creased into a wide grin as he looked around the table.

Hofstein called the meeting to an end and turning towards Hassan said, "What, no arak to celebrate our last and final meeting before victory? Where is your famous Arabic hospitality, my friend? Has it left you already?"

"Of course, Mr. Hofstein," answered Hassan nervously. He shouted in the direction of the kitchen, "Samira, arak and four glasses, please. Now!"

The sound of clinking glasses being prepared came from the kitchen. It was not long before Samira shuffled into the room with a bottle of arak and four glasses on a copper tray. She placed the tray on the table by Hassan and started to open the bottle.

A look of pure terror came over Hassan as Einhorn brought up the pistol fitted with a silencer from under the table. Neither Hassan nor his wife had any time to scream or react as Einhorn put a bullet cleanly in each of their foreheads. Samira slumped to the floor onto her back, dead before she landed. Her lifeless eyes stared up at the ceiling. Her fat legs twitched under her dirty black embroidered dress in her final moments and then were still. Blood started to ooze from her head, staining the dirty carpet in an ever-increasing circle. Hassan slumped forward onto the table, his surprise and terror evident on his face as blood trickled from the small hole in the center of his forehead. His fat chin came to rest on the table—his lifeless eyes stared straight ahead. The blood coursed its way down his forehead around his nose and mouth and onto the table where it pooled.

Einhorn broke the silence. "We hope that you are satisfied with your reward, Mr. Fawzi."

The three men poured the arak into three glasses, clinked them in the air together, and drank the arak down in silence.

"Well, he did say that he found it uncomfortable to sit with us. I would say distasteful would be a better word. Solved that fucking problem for him, haven't we." Einhorn stated rather flatly. They had agreed before the meeting that Einhorn should have the pleasure.

They got up from the table and went out silently one by one into the moonlight. On their way they passed the houses and shuttered shops on both sides of the dark, narrow, cobbled alleys.

NOF HA ARAVA.
THURSDAY, SEPTEMBER 6TH.

It was almost two in the morning when Ronni guided the Nissan off the main road to Uvda and on to the dirt track leading to Nof Ha Arava. There had been virtually no traffic on the way and no problems at the roadblock at the entrance to the Arava.

He was a well-known figure and in any case was not under suspicion. The soldiers had shown him a picture of Jordan again, but apart from saying that he knew him as the manager of the Sands he couldn't help them. They waved him through, Jordan stashed safely in the trunk.

He wondered if they thought it strange that he was driving back at this time of night—whether they would report it to someone. He didn't think so since he had often returned at night after visiting Tel Aviv to escape the daytime traffic.

He drove up the dusty track and parked the pickup in the usual place. His dogs ran to greet him as he got out. He patted each dog in turn.

They entered the house, and Jordan poured them two glasses of tea from the pot on the coals. Ronni settled back into the couch. "Jordan," he said flatly, "we are truly up against it."

"That we certainly are. They saw you at the checkpoint and will come to check out your place just to make sure. We must move out with the pickup, camp in one of the ravines, and camouflage overnight. We will make our move on the seventh evening, go into Eilat for Irit, and then somehow get to Taba. We need to get into the complex and your tent there during the night. I will put some of your arms aside, stuff that may be useful. By the way, you certainly do have some stuff here, stuff that we shall no doubt need." They worked quickly. Ronni put some supplies together and placed them in the pickup. He was sure not to miss anything, water, canned food, a camping gas unit, sleeping bags, and the camouflage netting they would need to hide the pickup. They would need all the equipment if they got delayed at all out in the open.

Jordan, meanwhile, loaded the arms into a kit bag and placed them in the back of the vehicle. There was no point in taking hand grenades; they couldn't use those in Taba for obvious reasons. He loaded four Magnum Desert Eagle pistols with silencers into the bag along with enough ammunition. He added some smoke bombs that might come in handy, some teargas canisters, and stun guns. They had to travel light. They could not use heavy firepower at Taba for fear of collateral damage. He drew the zipper on the kitbag closed. He did not want the blood of Jews on his hands.

They climbed into the Nissan, leaving Nof Ha Arava behind in a cloud of dust as they descended down the rough stony road. Turning left towards Eilat they drove to the border crossing with Egypt before turning off and driving down an incline into a shallow ravine. Here they could hole up and hide from sight for the time they needed. No one would see them here. He backed up the pickup in front of a small cave, and they unloaded what they needed. Then they covered the Nissan with the camouflage netting until they were satisfied that it would not be visible either from the air or the road.

Ronni brewed up some tea on the camping unit, and they sat down on the sleeping bags to enjoy a cup of the strong Bedouin brew.

They worked on a plan, a very simple one that relied more on luck and improvisation than on anything else. Ronni made a few calls from his cell phone before they turned in for what was left of the night. He was used to roughing it from his camel trips with tourists. For Jordan it was like going back in time on his agency missions.

The loud rotor noise of a low-flying helicopter woke them early, and they were just in time to see the Apache flying low over the ravine and towards the Uvda airbase.

Ronni was the first to speak. "Jordan, 'Boker Tov!' 'good morning.' There are no Apache helicopters stationed in Uvda at the moment. They must be going to check on my house. Thank God we got out of there in time, good move. I am sure that they figured that we are connected. They put two and two together when I passed the roadblock. They are checking out all leads just to be on the safe side."

He had hardly finished speaking when they heard the sound of explosions coming from the distance. They looked at each other without talking, understanding what was happening. The sky lit up with a yellowy orange hue. Over the top of the nearby hill clouds of thick black smoke billowed up into the sky. The poor animals, the camels and dogs didn't stand a chance. Ronni would not have anything to go back to if they made it out alive.

What a bunch of bastards, thought Jordan, blowing Ronni's place away just because they had seen him at the check post. The assholes didn't even know if Ronni was involved at all. He could have been there, back at his place. They didn't know, and yet they just razed the place.

Jordan put a hand on Ronni's shoulder. "I am so sorry I got you into this mess. I really didn't think that they would go so far as they did without at least checking on the ground first. They still don't have proof that you are mixed up in this. Even so, I would not go into town and have a meal at a restaurant just yet if I were you. Your face will be all over the news now, wanted for questioning. I know what questioning means in the agency, and it doesn't include coffee, croissants, and sitting around the table. Seriously though, we have to get into your tent at Taba where we will blend in with the other Bedouin. We can wait there until we make our move even though we don't yet have a plan. Anyway, sorry again for this mess, Ronni. I really am."

"No sweat, Jordan. It's not your fault. I'm insured, so when we get out of this I will rebuild and make it better. We have to be really careful, and I mean really careful. They know we are around here. They would not hesitate." He didn't need to add anything; they both knew exactly what he meant.

NOF HA ARAVA.
THURSDAY, SEPTEMBER 6TH.

Wing Commander Dvir Goldfarb, in his cramped cockpit on board the Apache, had received the orders early in the morning at his base near Beer Sheva, about one hundred kilometers south of Tel Aviv.

He had geared up immediately, lifting off a few minutes later and flying low and south towards Eilat. It was early morning and he had the good fortune to see the sunrise over the mountains on the Jordanian side of the Arava. It was a short flight, no more than half an hour and he was flying over the Uvda Air Force Base. He circled just south so as to come around over Nof Ha Arava and the Dust Riders encampment. He knew where it was and smiled at the recollection of the holiday that he had spent in Eilat only a couple of years ago. He had taken a half-day trek with his girlfriend on a camel there. It had been a great experience.

He did not question the orders he had been given, but thought it a shame to destroy the place. Must have been too near the Uvda base, or perhaps the military were preparing something secret. His orders were to destroy it and that was what he was going to do.

Dvir came in low from the south and hovered just above the camp. The rotors kicked up the sand below. He lined up the main house in the sights and pressed the trigger with his thumb. There was a whoosh as the air-to-ground missile streaked off its berth under the short wing. There followed a huge explosion and fireball as it hit the compound. The fires quickly spread to the tents scattered around the house and dense black smoke spread upwards into the sky. Not really much to this camp or mission, he thought to himself. This was an easy one but at least it alleviated the boredom of training flights. He wondered when they would give him a mission over Gaza; that was the real thing. Kill some Arabs, a real mission. That was what would really get the adrenalin going.

Satisfied that his mission was accomplished, Dvir flew over the scene of destruction once and photographed the area. He banked the Apache sharply to the north and his base. He thought about the delicious Israeli breakfast buffet waiting for him. He was ravenous.

CHAPTER FOURTEEN

IN TRANSIT TO EILAT.
FRIDAY, SEPTEMBER 7TH.

It was getting towards dusk now, the sun had settled behind the mountains and darkness would soon come. Ronni and Jordan began to pack up their campsite. They had spent the day resting and in quiet contemplation of the past few days and the impossible mission. The camouflage netting had given them some shade and protection, but the sun had still beaten mercilessly down upon them. The flies had tormented them throughout the long day. They had taken turns scouting the perimeters to make sure that nobody had discovered them and had eaten some of the canned food that Ronni had packed. They had been careful to make as little noise as possible. They had taken turns at trying to sleep. In the dry desert heat it was virtually impossible.

They would need to move fast, get into Yoseftal Hospital with the advantage of surprise on their side, grab Irit, and get out as fast as possible.

They could not stay in the area for long. A massive manhunt would be underway, a manhunt that they could not possibly elude if they lingered. They had to keep one step ahead.

Ronni had given his people in Taba instructions to meet them with four camels at the border crossing to Egypt. It was located a short drive up above Eilat on the Uvda road, across the road from them. They would take it from there. The plan was to cross over into Egypt where they could not be easily found. There they could disappear into the hills under cover of darkness. The Israelis could not follow them into Egypt. It would be much easier to get to Taba from the Egyptian side, but they needed to do this without either the Egyptians or the Israelis knowing, at least allowing them to get to Taba before it was discovered.

They finished loading the pickup and dressed in their Bedouin garb, checking each other to make sure that they looked as authentic as possible. It was not hard. They were dirty as hell, dusty, suntanned and unkempt.

They got into the Nissan, switched on the engine, and drove out of the ravine. Ronni gunned the engine and accelerated to get them up and onto the shoulder of the main road. Safely up he turned left to Eilat. They left behind the mess at the campsite; they would not need it again. It did not need camouflaging any more. Hopefully there would be no roadblock on the way. There was one in place nearer Uvda that they knew of, but that was behind them. There would not have been any publicity about the destruction at Nof Ha Arava. It would have been kept out of the news. With luck they might think that Jordan had died along with Ronni in the bombing of Nof Ha'Arava. Jordan figured that in any case, they would wait for him to make his move if he was still alive. They would be waiting in Eilat. He would be coming for Irit and they would be waiting at the hospital. They did not know about Shalom, so maybe they still stood a small chance. He would not allow her to be used against him.

Well, he thought, we won't disappoint them, will we?

BEN GURION INTERNATIONAL AIRPORT, TEL AVIV. FRIDAY, SEPTEMBER 7TH.

Israel Broadcasting Channel One had been covering the arrival of the dignitaries during the course of the afternoon.

It had been decided that to show solidarity and equality among the leaders, they would all congregate at Ben Gurion International. The President of the United States had generously offered to take them all down to Eilat on Air Force One so that they would arrive together. This would facilitate the security arrangements on arrival at the Uvda base. It was the only airport in the area that could accommodate such a large jet.

The first to arrive had been the Prime Minister of the State of Israel, Avner Dotan. He would receive and welcome the guests before the short flight south. Abu Mahmoud, Chairman of the Palestinian Authority, had arrived in the early afternoon and had entered the VIP lounge without commenting to the waiting press. Much as he disliked the veteran terrorist, the prime minister had afforded him a presidential welcome. He had inspected the guard of honor while looking as statesmanlike as possible in his bulging army uniform and the trademark headdress. At least he was not carrying a gun as he usually did when visiting abroad and as he had when addressing the UN assembly a few years before.

The Egyptian presidential plane had arrived next, followed by the royal Jordanian jet carrying King Ibrahim. He was not only the king but also an experienced pilot who had taken the controls for the short flight from Amman to Tel Aviv. Ibrahim was well loved in Jordan. He had been brought up in England and was an Oxford graduate. Ibrahim was about five-ten in height with brown wavy hair and intelligent green eyes that looked out from under full eyebrows. While still of Middle Eastern appearance, he cut a dashing figure in his dark grey pinstripe suit. He had chosen the suit over the traditional Arab dress to underline his modern monarchy.

Each arrival was greeted with fanfare and carried live by all the major international networks. Children dressed in blue and white greeted each leader as he descended the steps of his plane, and presented the wives with a bouquet of flowers. Each head of state was ushered into the VIP lounge without commenting to the press. It was agreed beforehand that all speeches were to be made in Taba before the signing ceremony. Protocol was strictly adhered to.

Finally towards three o'clock the big presidential 747 that was Air Force One dropped out of the clear blue sky and touched down on the main landing strip, taxiing to its position near the red carpet. Air Force One was impressive and was in the best position for maximum exposure and media coverage. This was a great opportunity for the president to win some foreign policy points back home and get his ratings up. The prime minister and the president of Israel stepped up to greet President Jonathan Cabon as he descended the steps of the giant plane with his wife, Dana.

The president was a tall man, about six-two, and looked like he came from money. Approaching sixty, his hair was a salt and pepper mix of grey and light brown. He had a long face with large intelligent eyes perched above a long aristocratic nose. He looked fit and suntanned. The bright yellow tie was knotted perfectly and contrasted with the dark blue double-breasted suit he had chosen for this moment. Dana, the first lady, was almost a replica of Jacqueline Kennedy, though a poor man's copy, and, of course, older. She was beautiful, the ideal trophy wife. She was wearing a knee-length dark blue cotton dress that complimented the president's suit, as if they had agreed to coordinate their wardrobes for the day. Both the president and the first lady were smiling radiantly for both the cameras and the assembled public.

The *Star Spangled Banner* was played, and then they too disappeared into the VIP lounge after inspecting the guard of honor. The president had been to Israel on at least two occasions before, and was very well liked, almost loved, by the Israeli public. He knew how to work the crowds and was known to be very pro-Israeli. On the tarmac he had gone out of his way to show affection and had shaken the hands of all the parliamentarians and Israeli dignitaries lined up to greet his arrival.

The ground crews immediately got to work on the plane, cleaning and refueling it in preparation for the short flight to Uvda, the Taba Convention and their date with history.

Dan Heller, on hand to guide events, was very satisfied with the progress. It was all going according to his planned timetable. He smiled to himself as he watched the heads of state congregate from the corner of the VIP lounge.

THE HILTON CONVENTION CENTER, TABA, EGYPT. FRIDAY, SEPTEMBER 7TH.

Ariel Einhorn of the Mossad had arrived in the early afternoon on an Arkia flight out of Dov Airport in Tel Aviv to Eilat. He had taken a cab and crossed the border into Taba not long after. He did not delay; he was keen to get to the Hilton.

He held a briefing with his agents in Taba and met with the ten operatives that he had handpicked for backup in case anything went wrong. They did not know anything about the operation planned, but they were ultra-nationalists who would be completely loyal in the event that he needed them. They would follow any command he gave without question.

He had issued them the orange tags that allowed them to be on the steps of the convention hall with all the dignitaries. It also allowed them to roam freely in the "sterile" zone that would be shortly created in the complex. Even now he saw the General Security Services scan the entire area with both agents and sniffer dogs. They had turned the area over to the American Secret Service to make their own check prior to declaring it a sterile zone before the arrival of the president in a few hours. Soon the Egyptian security services would take over responsibility for the whole area.

The bomb that would end this madness had already been in place for two days. It would never be found now, not even with all the dogs and agents. Once the President of the United States and the First Lady of the United States, or POTUS and FLOTUS as they were known by their code names, were in Taba the place would be sewn up tighter than the proverbial duck's ass.

On his rounds he had seen the ends of the pipe running through the center of the steps, camouflaged as fire hydrants at either end of the steps. He pictured the explosives sitting right there under the steps at the entrance to the convention hall and felt the familiar outline of his cell phone in his pocket. It was reassuring; it gave him strength and added resolve. All he had to do was make the call and all hell would break loose. He could imagine the little red lights blinking on the explosives waiting to receive the incoming call to detonate.

Einhorn wondered if Kline would be foolish enough to try and get his girlfriend back at the hospital. His best agents were now with him in Taba, but he had left agents at the hospital in the event that Kline made an appearance. Not too many agents, but enough to take care of Kline should he turn up. He thought it more likely however, that Kline would turn up in Taba. Einhorn would be more than ready to receive him.

He figured that Kline knew by now that his girl was in a coma and could not be moved. Therefore it was logical that Kline would leave her there and go for Taba. A part of him hoped that Kline would not want to be suicidal and would quietly wait this one out and then get on with his life. He doubted this was the case, though, since he guessed that Kline knew he would be a target for execution in any case now. No, Einhorn thought, he will come and I will be ready for him. Maybe he would have the pleasure of executing Kline himself, but only after Kline witnessed and admired the genius of their plan. Yes, he hoped that Kline would come to Taba after all.

Hofstein, too, was in the complex; he had been there since early morning, holding meetings with executives from Hilton International regarding the official handover of the new complex. It was due to take place directly after the convention was over. He had done the final inspection tour of the new buildings with David Champion, the Managing Director of Hilton International, and apart from a very few faults that they had added to the finalization document, they had settled and signed over the buildings. This was the only urgent matter on Hofstein's agenda, since he needed this settled and signed before the convention. He smiled secretly to himself as Champion signed the document. Destruction by explosives was definitely not covered in the building warranty, and the buildings were now in Hilton hands. He smiled with satisfaction at a job well done. He had built the casino and hall perfectly, handed them over officially to Hilton, and was now going to destroy them. What a shame. He who builds will destroy, he thought. He laughed out loud at the thought that they would probably come to him to rebuild the place after he, Hofstein, had destroyed it. Wasn't that poetic justice?

After he had safely stored the document in his in room safe, Hofstein wandered jauntily around the site, well pleased and calmly looking forward to the next day's historic events.

EILAT.
FRIDAY, SEPTEMBER 7TH.

It was mid-afternoon, and Shalom had to get a hold of a getaway car for Ronni and Jordan. They would not be able to leave Eilat in Ronni's pickup. It would be too obvious and easy to follow. Everybody would see it when they made their escape from the hospital. It would be on all news broadcasts. It would also be on a special APB in the area. It was not necessary to remind himself that there was a huge army camp situated just above Eilat on the road to the Uvda base. Soldiers would be unleashed in the hunt for Jordan.

Shalom also realized that he would need his car at the hospital in order to get back to the hotel, so he left the Sands after checking out with the switchboard. He told them that he was going to check up on Irit and a guest who was in the hospital. This was, thank God, a usual habit of his and not unusual. It would not arouse suspicion. He told the switchboard that he would be returning soon.

He took the elevator down to the pool floor and went through the back of the house to the ramp area. He invariably parked his car there during the summer high occupancy months. Here there was always parking as opposed to the guest parking area that was really congested during peak summer months. He just had to be careful to park it so as not to be in the way of the large supply trucks that brought all the necessary supplies to the hotel. The trucks that emptied the garbage containers were driven by a particularly rough bunch. They were the reason for a really deep scratch running down the side of his car. He had not bothered to follow up with the garbage removal company; he knew that there was no point. From that day on he had parked very carefully and well out of the way of the turning trucks. He did not want any further damage. Not that his car was so beautiful, but he had grown attached to the ageing Oldsmobile Omega. It was such a reliable means of transport—and what an engine.

The city industrial area was situated north of the main city. It was home to all the light industrial companies—the garages, the electrical companies, and also the large supermarkets and food and beverage suppliers of Eilat. Huge trucks climbed down the long road from Tel Aviv to Eilat once or twice a week to make their way south like the camel caravans of old. They hauled their supplies to the industrial area where they were stored, sorted, and then distributed to the shops, businesses, hotels and restaurants in the city.

Eilat was a really unique city, Shalom thought as he drove through the industrial area. A city with three very distinctive parts. There was the main city on the west of the Arava desert and stretching up to the mountains overlooking the Red Sea. Then there was the hotel area below the city and located right on the shores of the sea. The airport separated these two areas cleanly down the middle. What a racket the big jets made as they landed and reversed thrust to slow down. The tourists were not warned before they came on their vacations, he was sure. What if some of the English charter crowd lived under the flight path to Luton airport, or maybe Gatwick in London. He laughed at the thought. An Eilat vacation sure would make them feel at home.

To complete this separation of areas there was the industrial area to the north. It was not through any city planning or forethought, thought Shalom, but had rather grown this way over the years as the need for expansion had arisen. In any case, it worked fine for the city—that is, everything except for the sewage treatment plants that had been built just to the north of the resort area. When the wind blew from the north the smell was overpowering around the hotels and the source of major complaints from the tourists. The citizens had it better than the tourists, thought Shalom, as he turned right into Rehov Yafo, Jaffa Street. He eased the Olds into a parking spot behind the Oresh Vegetable Suppliers building.

It was well after business hours. The main supply distribution took place early in the morning hours when the sun was not so fierce. During those early hours the vegetables could sit for a short while on the hotel delivery ramps without fear of getting hot and going bad.

Shalom checked that no one was taking undue interest in him and got into the small beaten up Oresh vegetable truck. Everyone left their cars and trucks open here. There was no theft to speak of, especially when you were in the middle of nowhere: two Arab borders on the one side and a hundred and seventy-five kilometers of desert road on the other side.

He quickly shorted the ignition wires and navigated the truck out of the industrial area and up towards Yoseftal Hospital. He knew that the truck would not be missed until the next morning, so that gave them plenty of time. Shalom passed the hospital and parked the truck in an inconspicuous spot on the road above the hospital, but well to the side so as not to arouse the suspicion of passersby. It was a great spot and very near a small ravine into which Ronni's pickup could be pushed when they swapped cars after they got away from Yoseftal.

He stepped out onto the dusty road and walked about five hundred meters until he was almost back into town and near the hospital. He flagged down a cab, got in, and asked the driver to take him to a supermarket not too far from Oresh Vegetable Supplies.

Arriving there a few minutes later, Shalom paid the cabbie and took a casual stroll back to his Oldsmobile. He climbed in and drove back to Yoseftal Hospital to await Jordan and Ronni as they had planned.

He parked the car in a spot not far from the end of the car park and near the exit. He got out, locked the car, and walked up the road above the entrance to the hospital.

EILAT.
FRIDAY, SEPTEMBER 7TH.

Jordan and Ronni approached the entrance to Eilat from above in the beaten-up pickup on the road that led directly to the Yoseftal Hospital.

They drove slowly down the incline and spotted Shalom waiting for them by the side of the road a short way ahead. They pulled over onto the shoulder and Shalom got into the back seat.

He spoke cheerfully, "Jordan, I hope that you know that you are one of the most famous people in Israel at the moment. Just about everyone is on the lookout for you. Your ugly face is on the TV on every newscast. Anyway, back to business. I took the Oresh vegetable truck after he had closed for the day. You can see it over there." He pointed to the old truck. "I am sure George wouldn't mind, although it may be a problem for him afterwards when they find it. Still, couldn't exactly take the hotel van and throw suspicion on me, could I? You will need to get rid of the pickup after we have taken Irit back. It will be too much of a risk to drive.

"I have checked the hospital, and they have left three agents to watch the place. There are two in the hospital, one by the door to Irit's room and one at the main reception entrance. The third is on the roof. I suggest that I take the one on the roof so as not to give myself away. I can take the guy out and be back in the hotel almost before the actual deal goes down. People will not have noticed that I have been here at all. The switchboard knows that I went earlier to visit Irit and another guest who is in the hospital. In any case this will be overlooked by the chaos you guys will create. Don't forget that I am also invited and will be at Taba tomorrow."

"It will be good for one of us to be able to move freely there. I need to get clean away from this. You take the other two out and get Irit out of there. I will return to the hotel and come to Taba tomorrow as planned. By the way, I brought four sets of the anti-terror squad Motorola's for us to use and some night glasses that will probably come in useful. Here," he said, handing them the gear and keeping one Motorola for himself.

"Thanks, Shalom," Jordan said "Now let's get on with this. We have a long night ahead of us. You're right. You take the guy on the roof and get the hell out of there. We'll get Irit and disappear. Oh, and Shalom, I really appreciate your help. We couldn't do it without you."

Shalom looked embarrassed and managed to stammer, "It's nothing, Jord. My pleasure, man."

"Plan sounds good to me," said Ronni as he pulled out onto the road. They approached the hospital to their right and stopped to let Shalom out of the pickup before they reached the entrance. They waited to watch him climb up with surprising agility onto the roof of the one-story building. They checked that he was on the Motorola and drove into the car park.

It was not unusual to see Bedouin coming to the hospital since it was the only medical center in the area. The nearest other hospital was Soroka Hospital in Beer Sheva. Everyone—Arabs, Bedouin, tourists, and, of course, the Jewish population of Eilat—used Yoseftal. Nobody even turned to look at Ronni and Jordan as they entered the hospital.Shalom had told them where Irit was and they walked calmly down the corridor towards her room.

As they approached, Jordan spoke softly into the Motorola, "Do it now!"

Up on the roof Shalom heard the order and crept up quietly in the dark behind the agent on the roof who was seated on the ground with his back to the air conditioning unit. He looked like he was dozing in the warm evening air. He was not expecting anything. Shalom came up quickly and brought down his open hand to the side of the agent's neck. He definitely did not want to kill the guy, just put him out for an hour or two. His well-aimed blow had done the trick nicely. The guy would have a hell of a headache when he woke up. He jumped down off the roof and ran straight over to his car. He got in, started the engine, and was well on his way down to the hotel by the time Jordan and Ronni got to the entrance of Irit's room. He had to be clear away as soon as possible.

Jordan and Ronni pretended to be going past the doorway but as they drew level Jordan swiveled around and took out the unsuspecting agent with a light side-chop to the neck. It was an old pressure point blow he had learned in the agency. The agent went down without even knowing what had happened to him. Jordan caught him as he went down. He opened the door and dragged the unconscious man into the room.

Irit was asleep and had not been disturbed by the noise. Jordan approached the bed and stared at her. She was covered in nasty, painful-looking bruises and cuts. Her oval face was framed by her long full hair that cascaded on the pillow. Her large eyes were closed in sleep. He could not forgive himself; this was his fault and his alone. He bent over and kissed her carefully but fully on the lips.

"Knew this would wake you up, Sleeping Beauty," he said as she woke up with a start, bewildered.

It took her a moment to get her bearings and recognize the pair of them in her room. "Jordan, I knew you would come for me. I have been waiting for you. Shalom told me that they would keep me here until you came. I was so scared that they would get to you. I'm so sorry that I let you down," she said softly.

"It wasn't your fault, Irit," Jordan answered. "It was that idiot at Yotvata, but that's in the past. You did a great job, irresponsible, but a great job of delaying them. How are you feeling? You don't look too good. Think you can make it out of here?"

"Sure I can, Jordan. I feel great except for the broken arm, but that's also okay, I guess, since it is in a cast. Reminds me of the guy that said he would give his right arm to be ambidextrous. I won't move without another kiss, though." Irit winced as she laughed; her eyes alight with the moment.

Jordan and Ronni looked at each other and smiled. Jordan took her face in his hands, looked into her eyes, and said, "No time now for small talk or kisses. Quickly, get into this Jellabiya we brought for you. We have to make tracks, but don't forget to fill out the comment card before you check out." He laughed as he turned to Ronni. "Ronni, please get your ass to the reception. I will tell you when to take out the third guy so we can get the hell out of here."

Ronni left the room and Irit struggled out of the bed. She took off the hospital nightdress. Jordan helped her out of the sleeves and pulled the Bedouin dress over her head. She was dressed in a couple of minutes. She was beat-up, but she still had a hell of a body. No permanent damage. The bruises would fade back into her pretty olive skin soon; the cuts would take a little longer.

She caught him admiring her body as she was taking off her hospital gown. "Don't even begin to think about it, you dirty old man—although it would be great to add the hospital to our locations." She laughed and stole a kiss.

Jordan opened the door and they exited the room quickly after checking that the corridor was clear. He hoped that no doctors were doing their rounds at the moment. There would be too many questions, too many minutes lost. Just before they turned the corner to the reception he told Ronni via the Motorola to divert the agent's attention so that he could get Irit outside and into the car. He saw the hospital director come out of his office and speak with the agent. They turned around and disappeared into the office. Jordan and Irit were almost out of the hospital when the agent came out of the office and spotted them at the entrance.

"Stop immediately or I will shoot!" the agent said nervously, drawing his pistol.

Ronni was quicker than the agent. He came up behind him and brought down the butt of his gun on the agent's head. The agent slumped to the floor. People in the reception area started screaming and hospital security appeared from out of nowhere.

Jordan and Irit were already in the car, aware that their presence was now known. It would not be a long time before the area would be swarming with agents and police. People were starting to flow out of the hospital to look at them. Ronni jumped into the moving vehicle as Jordan gunned the engine and turned right out of the car park toward town. In the mirror he could see a security guard noting something down, probably the numbers on the license plates.

"Why in hell are you going towards town, Jordan?" shouted Irit above the noise of the engine to make herself heard.

"I am not going to town. Just driving to Ahaz Street and then around the back again and up to join the Arava road. Everybody will tell them that we left for town and that will buy us some precious time. Trust me," he answered and concentrated on the road ahead.

Jordan raced down the street and burned rubber turning left into Ahaz Street, ignoring the red lights. He accelerated up the street and hung a left that would take them back to the Uvda road above the hospital. They reached the spot where the Oresh truck was parked. Jordan skidded to a halt. Irit got into the truck while Ronni and Jordan quickly pushed the pickup over the lip of the road and into the ravine. The incline was not steep but the pickup made a hell of a racket as it rolled down the ravine hitting rocks and kicking up clouds of sand and dust as it descended. There was a noise of bending metal and broken glass as it came to rest against a boulder halfway down the ravine. It was good cover for the night. It would not be discovered until daylight when it would not matter anymore.

They had gotten Irit back relatively easily—no shooting, no loss of life, only three agents that would have rather large headaches. He felt a renewed sense of energy and purpose now that he was with Irit again. They could not get to him through her again.

They joined Irit in the truck and pulled out onto the road. The old truck creaked and moaned and billowed black smoke behind them as they merged onto the road.

So far so good, thought Jordan. Turning to the others he asked, "Did I ever tell you about the guy I interviewed once with the T-shirt that had 'My main aim in life is to live forever' printed across the front? The whole interview I didn't get the meaning. It was only after he got up and turned to leave at the

228

end of the interview that I got it. On the back of the shirt it said, 'So far so good!' Funny, huh? Well guys, so far so good with us. Maybe forever is too long, but we can certainly agree on a lot more time, right?"

They all cracked up in the small cabin of the old truck, alleviating the tension.

Now it was Ronni's turn. "In all my years since I came to Eilat, I have not had such good luck since you came along, Jordan," he declared laughing hysterically. "First they blow up my house and possessions and now my pickup is in the ditch—and all that in one day! Still, I've never had so much fun since the army days." The laugh sounded a little too shrill to Jordan, false. Perhaps it was just nervous tension. The stress they were under, that was it.

Jordan did not reply, just nodded and drove on up into the hills and onto the plateau above Eilat. The truck's engine growled and clanked with the effort. He slowed down as they approached the border crossing with Egypt. He pulled over to the side and cut the lights.

Turning to the others, he said, "Now, your people, Ronni, are on the other side waiting for us. The Israelis have no clue as to what is happening. We will approach slowly. Hold on when I do, since it could get rough. I think that we are the only ones that ever have tried to break out of Israel and not the other way around, so we should surprise them. Matter of fact we are probably the first truck ever seen going this way towards the border. They'll think we are mad. Ronni, if we have to start shooting, then only shoot at their legs. Even if they shoot to kill, okay?"

Ronni smiled and nodded in agreement. They pulled back onto the road with full headlights approaching the Israeli side of the crossing. Jordan approached slowly and was thankful that only one of the two border guards came out of the hut to meet them.

The truck pulled to a stop and the guard came around to the driver's side to see what they wanted from him at this time of night. Everyone knew the border was closed.

Jordan lowered the window and the guard found himself looking down the barrel of a gun.

"Don't even think about it," Jordan said as he read the guard's thoughts. "Act completely normal and do us all a favor and raise the barrier. No one will be hurt."

"I must warn you that if you do not I will be forced to hurt you. I do not want to do that but I will if I have to," he added menacingly.

The guard nodded nervously, frightened by the tone of voice. He backed off and went around the truck to raise the barrier. He untied the rope tying the primitive barrier down. It was one of those barriers anchored on one side by a concrete block and that raised itself by weight. Suddenly the guard started to reach for his gun.

"Another bloody hero, Ronni. Please shoot him in the leg," Jordan ordered Ronni who obliged. The bullet caught the guard just behind and under the knee.

He screamed out in agony as he collapsed onto the road holding his knee.

Jordan saw the other guard through the guardhouse window grab his rifle. The guard started out of the hut but Jordan had to wait for a few agonizing moments until the barrier was high enough for the truck to get through.

Ronni was already out of the vehicle, slamming the door closed, and shouting at Jordan to get going towards the Egyptian side.

Jordan took off towards the Egyptian post. The guard came out of the hut firing, but was too nervous to shoot accurately. He seemed only concerned for his friend. He had not noticed Ronni get out of the truck. As he ran past him Ronni stepped out and brought him down roughly with a punch to the stomach. The guard fell onto the road clutching at his belly.

Ronni bent down and said to him, "Sorry we had to do this, but believe me that it was necessary. You should be okay soon, as should the other fellow. I only shot him through the leg, flesh wound."

The guard doubled over and vomited all over the road and his uniform, clutching his ample stomach.

Ronni went into the hut, found some handcuffs, and went over to the wounded man. He was still writhing in agony on the road. He tore off a strip of his Jellabiya and quickly made a tourniquet out of it. He bound the man's leg just above the bullet wound and pulled the tourniquet tight. He could see that it was a clean flesh shot and would not do much damage. He looked around quickly. No other cars had passed by, but that could change any minute. They had to hurry.

He dragged the other guard over to the wounded one and handcuffed them together, back-to-back in a sitting position with the barrier pole between them. He then went over and pulled the door to the hut shut, locking them out. Even if they managed to get out of the cuffs, they would not be able to raise the alarm until their shift was relieved. It was just an added precaution. They could scream all they wanted to—no one would hear them during the night. No one would see them until daylight.

Sure that he was safe now, Ronni turned around and sauntered over to the Egyptian border post. Irit and Jordan sat waiting in the truck.

"Sorry I'm a bit late, but I got slightly delayed by events at the crossing. They didn't want to stamp my passport," he said laughing.

"How did you do this, Ronni?" Jordan asked incredulously. "The Egyptians knew we were coming and welcomed us with strong Turkish coffee."

"It pays to be in with the Bedouin. Maybe you'll want to be one, too, one day. Nothing money cannot buy, my friend. My people came over the hills from Taba and bribed them. They only make about a hundred dollars per month, so two hundred for each of us and we're in without any questions. The Israelis will be upset with them, but we'll break the barrier on this side too. They will tell them we forced our way through. Come, no time to waste. Let's go."

He turned to the guards and spoke with them in fluent Arabic. One of them went over to the small hut and came out with a pair of handcuffs. Ronni cuffed them together. He turned to the barrier and shot away the woodwork that held it together. The whole thing collapsed as if in slow motion as it fell onto the road and splintered.

He turned, thanked the Egyptians, and got into the truck.

"Drive down towards Taba please, Jordan," he requested, "and my people should be a couple of kilometers down the road."

Jordan turned the truck onto the road, amazed by the ease with which they had just entered Egypt. Six hundred dollars and you were a tourist. Unregistered, but a tourist nonetheless. The truck rattled and groaned noisily over the rough terrain. The smell of diesel in the small rusty cabin was almost overpowering. He hoped they'd get to the Bedouin soon, very soon. He couldn't stand much more of this truck.

His thoughts turned to their situation. Three men and a wounded woman against the rest of the world, he thought. He refused to recognize the hopelessness of their plight. Don't forget, he reminded himself, so far so good. Somehow they would make it to Taba, to the Bedouin tent on the Hilton grounds and then see what plan they could come up with. With any luck it would be a long time until the border episode would be discovered. There was hardly much traffic on the road at night, and no traffic through the post. That should give them time to get into Taba and lie low until the evening.

They drove on in silence until they spotted some camels by the side of the road, lit up in the headlights.

"Pull over, Jordan. The rest of the way is by camel limousine, I'm afraid. You guys should have some really sore butts by tonight," Ronni said, grinning.

Jordan pulled the truck over and rolled to a stop by the camels. He switched off the engine which turned over a few times and coughed before going dead. Three Bedouin appeared out of nowhere and ran up to Ronni, hugging him each in turn, obviously happy to see him again. Turning to the others he introduced them by name, but neither Jordan nor Irit could tell them apart anyway. They were all about the same height; all had beards and were wearing the same Bedouin turbans around their heads. In the dark they all looked alike. It was useless to try and remember their names.

They hauled the kit bag out of the van and the Bedouin loaded it onto a camel.

Covering their tracks was useless now, so they abandoned the truck by the side of the road.

Irit mounted her camel and almost fell off as the beast raised its back legs first, getting onto its knees, and then standing awkwardly. Jordan could tell by looking at her that she was enduring no small degree of pain from her injuries. She was taking it bravely.

"Well, what the fuck are you two gawking at? Get on your camels and let's get the hell out of here. Long ways to go, you know." She was laughing at them now.

Soon they were all aboard their camels and the Bedouin led them off on the trek to Taba through the Egyptian hills. It was a beautiful moonlit sky. They could see clearly what looked eerily like a moonscape terrain ahead of them. Here and there a rabbit darted for cover, and they could hear small rodents scurrying around in the underbrush around them.

The trek lasted for almost four hours. It took them over hills and down ravines, and through thick, dry brush. They rode the camels in silence, preferring not to stop at all but rather reach Taba as quickly as travel by camel allowed. That was not too fast in this terrain. As they descended the plateau the camels went down sharp inclines to get to the Red Sea area where Taba was located.

Finally the lead camel halted and the Bedouin rider made it sit down. It sat down awkwardly, first onto its backside and then onto its knees.

The Bedouin coaxed all the camels into the sitting position. Ronni motioned them all to get off and come together silently. Jordan helped Irit gently off her camel.

"We are now almost directly above the Taba Hilton," said Ronni. "So you and I, Jordan, will go over to the edge and spy out the land. The rest of you stay here until we return. Do not make any noise; we are too close now. Please gather up the stuff while we are away. Do it very quietly. We shall make our way down to the tent soon." Ronni finished speaking and motioned for Jordan to follow him to the crest of the hill. He took out two pairs of the night glasses from the equipment bag.

Jordan adjusted the glasses on his head. He could see everything in a sort of green snowy haze, but he could still see much better than with the naked eye.

They lay down side-by-side on the top of the hill and scanned the Taba complex. Strong searchlights flooded the area with bright light. The place was crawling with armed guards concentrated around the main hotel building. Jordan guessed that all the heads of state and dignitaries were well into their nights' sleep, comfortable in their luxury suites. They were looking forward to the next day, the day that they would make history—front page news around the world.

Heavily armed soldiers patrolled the convention center with guard dogs on leashes ready for the first signs of trouble. The news of the Yoseftal Hospital rescue was sure to have been passed on to Einhorn pretty quickly. All security and military personnel in and around Taba were probably alerted to his possible arrival. Ask no questions, shoot to kill.

However, it seemed that the guards at the border crossing had not yet been relieved after the nightshift. There was no unusual activity near the hill above Taba from where they were watching. Had they been alerted to what had gone down at the border, there would surely have been extra patrols all around the perimeter of the complex. It could not be long until the Israelis found their border guards cuffed to the post. The whole area would then be screened with a fine-toothed comb. They had to get in fast.

Jordan signaled to Ronni with his hand and they crawled back out of sight before Jordan spoke: "I think that they have not yet heard about the border crossing. We should get into Taba as soon as possible and hide in the tent. Soon they will be looking for me dressed as a Bedouin and also for you since we took Irit. We were seen at the hospital. We have to get down there and lie low. We have to get the Bedouin and camels as far away as possible from us."

"Agreed," nodded Ronni. "Let's get Irit and go down while we still have the time."

CHAPTER FIFTEEN

CONVENTION DAY, TABA.
SATURDAY, SEPTEMBER 8TH.
EARLY MORNING.

Einhorn could not sleep and it was getting to him. He had never allowed problems to disturb him and had always slept well. Just why he could not sleep tonight he had not figured out yet, but he was uneasy and concerned that something was going to go wrong with the plan. They were right about Kline—real slippery character that one. Where the hell was the bastard? Where had he gone after he had snatched his girlfriend so brazenly from the hospital? He could not have done it without help. Who was helping him? The camel riders fellow had been taken out by the apache strike and must have died in the inferno, or had he? In any case, wasn't the man an agency control, or at least had been? He had forgotten to check these matters out before leaving. Hell, there was only so much a deputy director could remember, he told himself.

A real sense of anxiety was building in him now, though, and he had to make an effort to keep panic from flowing over him. Was he getting too old for the job? He had experienced such setbacks before, he thought, and had always come through and succeeded in the end. But this was different—this was Kline, not dumb Arabs. This was one of the best agents that Israel had ever trained. He felt stabs of fear reach up from his chest and constrict his breathing. He drew in a long fresh breath of the cool air. He had never felt this way before. He had always won, come out on top. That was why he was the deputy director for God's sake. But he still could not keep the thought of Kline out of his mind. It stuck there like an involuntary and annoying twitch on his face. He reassured himself nervously that his arrangements would be fine, that his agents would come through in the end. This peace madness had to be eradicated. He was the deputy director. The cards must be in his favor.

He had been present at the Uvda Air Force base when the Air Force One had touched down in the evening. Everything had gone very smoothly. He had supervised the limousines on the tarmac, lined up according to state and international protocol.

The only limousine not provided by Israel's government was the bullet-proof Cadillac that the Americans had driven down from Tel Aviv. It belonged to the United States ambassador. All the others were the usual black Volvos that were also supplied to cabinet ministers. Each one flew the national flag of that particular president or head of state. Following the American car were the cars flying the Egyptian, Jordanian, and Palestinian flags. The Israeli Prime Minister's car brought up the rear of the convoy. Behind and in front of the convoy were the security Suburbans.

There had been no press conference planned at Uvda, and the dignitaries had all exited the airplane together. They came down the aircraft steps and got straight into their limousines.

The road from the airbase to Eilat had been closed earlier. The long convoy had wound its way down to Eilat under the tightest security ever in place in the area. Soldiers lined the road and snipers had been positioned on the high ground. Israel Air Force Apache helicopters followed the convoy from above. It had gone very well, and within minutes of their arrival at the Hilton they were all settled into their suites. They had arrived just before the Shabbat set in.

He glanced at his watch and saw that it was three in the morning. They had to get through the day now and wait for the signing ceremony after Shabbat ended. The lunch scheduled was just a Shabbat lunch, nothing formal that would break the Jewish Saturday.

Einhorn felt acute anxiety come over him. He couldn't stay in his room any longer.

 Climbing out of bed, he decided to take a walk around the grounds of the hotel and slipped into a tracksuit. As he opened the door to his room he remembered his gun, and went back to get it. He opened the small room safe with his card and took out his gun. He slipped it into the waistband of his pants as he closed the door to his room behind him.

He rode the elevator down to the ground floor and went out into the cool early morning breeze coming off the Red Sea.

TABA.
SATURDAY, SEPTEMBER 8TH.
CONVENTION DAY.
THREE A.M.

Ronni and Jordan silently unloaded the arms they had packed on the camels. Ronni motioned to the Bedouin and they disappeared into the night as quickly and as quietly as they had come.

The three of them were soon at the edge of the hill overlooking the Hilton. For a fleeting moment Jordan wished he had not become embroiled in this plot. He felt a flash of fear in the pit of his stomach, but pushed it away quickly.

His thoughts were cut off by Ronni. "Jordan, I think we should skirt to the south of the hotel and get down to the beach towards the bay and Raffi Nelson's village. From there we should be able to make it along the shoreline and bluff our way into my tent as Bedouin. In any case I asked my guys to be by the entrance to the Hilton from the village side in case we came through this way. I guessed that we might have to, since the front entrance is not where we would be welcomed very warmly, to say the least. Hopefully the guards are not yet aware of the border event. We shall try and blend in with my people. Once the border stuff is found out, there will be no way in or out of Taba at all."

"I guess that's as good a plan as any that I can think of right now," Jordan replied nodding.

It was going to be a problem getting down to the tents from where they were. The night was clear with the moon lighting up the whole area. It was also very quiet. Any break in the silence of the night would bring attention and capture. The sides of the hill were rocky and strewn with small rocks and stones. It would not take too much to dislodge one that would clatter down the side of the hill and bring guards to check on the noise.

Jordan motioned for them to crawl back a few yards so that they would not be seen standing. In a few minutes they had distributed the small arms amongst each other for the walk southwards and had started off along the hilltop. Even though the terrain was rough with many stones, they could see their way clearly in the strong moonlight. They were soon at a respectable distance from the hotel and grounds. Irit found the going very rough and had to be helped by Jordan as every step sent more searing pain through her bruised and wounded body.

Jordan sensed Irit's discomfort. "Are you okay, Irit?" he asked.

"I'll survive, Jord," she whispered back.

Suddenly Jordan held up his palm and motioned for them to stop and crouch. They had just lowered themselves to the ground when a pack of wild dogs came running into view. Jordan put a forefinger to his lips and motioned for them to maintain absolute silence. The pack came to a stop not far from them, eyeing them suspiciously. The dogs seemed unsure of whether to attack. Jordan knew that he could not use his pistol should they decide to attack. He quietly pulled his large flashlight from his belt and switched it on. He scanned the dogs and chose the one he thought was the pack leader. He brought up the flashlight and aimed it at the dog. The animal was blinded by the strong beam of light. It pulled back its mouth in a sneer. It growled loudly with teeth bared and saliva dripping. The leader was disoriented by the flashlight. The rest of the pack also snarled, their eyes reflecting red in the flashlight's beam, waiting for the reaction from their leader.

Jordan prayed that they would turn away. It was up to the leader, but he was showing no sign of backing down. It was a large animal. The dog's right ear was torn and there were scars from the fights it had been in on the way to proving his pack leadership. The hair stood up on its back. It lowered its head as if to rush them. The pack followed suit.

The pack must have stood there for about a full minute, waiting to see what the leader would decide. They were waiting for the sign to attack.

The attack never came. Slowly the leader turned around, still keeping his eye on the three humans. He was still growling menacingly as he led the pack back into the darkness from which they had appeared. It was over in a flash, but they would have to watch for any signs that they might return.

Jordan blew a sigh of relief, "Phew that was a very close call."

"Certainly was," echoed Ronni. "I think your blinding him turned the trick."

They got up, Jordan helping Irit. They dusted themselves off before contemplating the way down to the seashore. As it happened they were in luck, since Jordan could now make out a well-worn track down to the sea a few meters from where they stood. He cupped one hand to the side of the flashlight and followed the beam down the side of the incline. It seemed smooth and almost rubble-free. As far as he could make out it led almost all of the way down. It certainly ran down until the flat land at the bottom. It was perfect. They had come up just above the Nelson village. Jordan could make out the shapes of the bungalows at the back and towards the southernmost part of the village.

Jordan motioned for them to follow him and for Ronni to follow Irit at the back. They had to be ready should she fall or lose her balance on the way down. They inched down slowly, making sure that each step was on flat land and that no rubble was sent tumbling down that could give them away. If they were seen now there would be no cover. They were totally exposed on the side of the hill. Fifteen long minutes later they were down on the flat land not too far from the shore, shielded by the wall of a bungalow. He hoped that the bungalow was not occupied. If it was he hoped that the occupants were the kind that slept very soundly.

They separated themselves from the bungalow by a good few meters and then took off their backpacks. They carefully emptied the arms on the ground quietly. Jordan gave Ronni and Irit a pistol each, making sure that they were loaded, the silencers fitted. He showed Irit how to unlock the pistol, but she nodded and told him in a whisper that she had done some small arms firing in basic training in the army. Jordan gave Ronni one of the stun guns and a couple of canisters of the tear gas and packed the rest under his belt. He turned around and started off for the entrance to Taba.

They walked as quietly as they could between the small one-room bungalows and soon made out the back entrance checkpoint to the Taba complex. They could see three of Ronni's Bedouin staff on the other side not far from the entrance. Jordan could see that two were males and one female.

"You think of everything, Ronni. You're good, almost agency good," Jordan said in a whisper, and smiled at the Dust Rider.

"I'm not bad, actually," agreed Ronni. " I told them to make like they are taking a swim and to meet us on this side. What the hell are they waiting for? They should be here by now."

He had not finished speaking when the gate opened and the three Bedouin walked out of the complex and towards them. They saw Ronni who motioned them to do as they had planned and take a swim. They went down to the water's edge by the bay below the village, stripped down to their underwear, and waded into the cool waters.

After a couple of minutes they came out of the water. They picked up their clothes and approached the bungalow where Ronni, Jordan, and Irit were waiting.

Ronni hugged them quickly when they met. He then took their clothes from them. He handed the woman's set to Irit and gave one of the men's clothes to Jordan.

He turned to Irit and Jordan. "It is imperative that we be as identical as possible, so put on these clothes. We shall then re-enter Taba after our 'swim' in the bay."

They took off their own clothes and handed them over to the Bedouin. They then dressed in the clothes that the Bedouin had given them. After Ronni checked them over and gave them an approving nod, they turned around and approached the gates.

"Ahalan wah sahalan," Ronni greeted the Egyptian border guards who opened the gates without more than a glance in their direction. They were a lazy bunch, Ronni could tell, and not prone to too much work. In any case, these three had just gone over to the bay for a usual night swim. It was their habit, the guards would be thinking. They were always doing that in the hot summer months.

"Shoukroon," Ronni said, "thank you" in Arabic, as they passed the open gate and walked into the complex.

Ronni knew that the three Bedouin would go down the seashore and walk until they came to one of the myriad of Bedouin tents that lined the Sinai shores. They would hole up with their friends for a few days. They would disappear into Sinai, he thought, and no one would know any better.

The three of them looked at each other. They had passed the first test. They were in the Taba complex.

TABA.
SATURDAY, SEPTEMBER 8TH.
CONVENTION DAY.

They walked quickly from the gate in the direction of Ronni's tent. It was situated on the shoreline below the hotel complex. Since the patrolling guards had seen them go past earlier, they passed without challenge. Some of the soldiers even greeted them warmly in passing. They did not answer and continued on towards the tent.

It seemed almost as if time stood still as they approached the entrance flap to the tent. They walked on, expecting at any minute to be stopped, to be challenged by the soldiers. The tent came towards them in slow motion. It was nerve-wracking. Every step that brought them closer was an agonizing one. It seemed to them that all eyes in the complex were on them. At any time the searchlights would be swung around and onto them and the guards would surround them.

Then they were inside stepping into the warm coziness of the carpets and multi-colored cushions piled everywhere. The ever-present teapot sat on the glowing coals, the welcoming smell of Bedouin tea filling the air. They were greeted mutely by the others, who had been warned not to make a fuss when Ronni and the other two entered.

They quickly put the arms and night vision glasses in the kit-bag and hid it in the corner under a mountain of small prayer carpets. They sank down gratefully into the deep cushions around the warming pot.

They huddled around the glowing fire while they sipped on glasses of the welcome tea that Ronni poured for them. The brew brought on drowsiness. Jordan looked at his watch. They had to get a few hours of sleep. He turned to Ronni.

"So, we are here, great. Now, how do we get some sleep in order to be as ready as we can when we decide to act?" Jordan asked.

"Yes, you and Irit should take a nap. Irit needs the rest badly. Cover yourselves in cushions and blankets as near the flaps of the tent that you can. Even if they come and check they will not see you."

Jordan took Irit by the hand and helped her towards the corner of the tent, not far from the pile of rugs and the hidden kitbag. He knew that he was tired, but felt slightly dizzy as they approached the corner. He could not focus properly. It was a strange feeling. Even on the harshest of missions with lack of sleep he had never felt this out of it. He put it down to extreme fatigue. He lay down quickly beside her in the soft cushions. Settled in among the warmth of all the cushions he could feel himself slowly drifting into a welcome sleep.

CHAPTER SIXTEEN

TABA.
SATURDAY, SEPTEMBER 8TH.

Jordan was not sure how long he had been asleep when he was rudely shaken awake. It took him a while to get his bearings and remembered that he and Irit had fallen asleep in the Bedouin tent in Taba. His head throbbed, his vision blurred. It was unusual for him to fall asleep so quickly. It seemed to him as if he were climbing to the surface from a great depth, swimming upwards towards the light, towards consciousness.

What the hell was the matter with him? He usually woke quickly and alert. Life in the agency had taught him that. Why this feeling now?

Jordan rubbed his eyes and looked up. He was looking straight up the barrel of a pistol. The man holding it was Ariel Einhorn, Deputy Director of the Mossad. He was smiling.

"I trust that you had a good rest, Jordan Kline. I am sure that the small amount of drug in your tea will have allowed for total relaxation, yes?" he asked politely. "Now, I do hope that Ronni over here has been good to you and hosted you both well on the trip through Egypt to Taba, yes?"

The realization washed over Jordan like a huge wave. "No way. Ronni! Not you!" Jordan cried out loud. Anger and shock flooded over him. "Why, in God's name, why? Why did you do it, why, in God's name? I thought we were together in this thing."

Einhorn interjected, cutting him short, "Now why don't you allow me to answer this, Ronni? I believe that Jordan and his girl will be well satisfied with my explanation. I am sure of it."

"It is like this, Kline. You see, you were becoming a real nuisance to our plans, getting in the way all over the place. Not only getting in the way, but also, mind you, getting some fine citizens killed. Especially the lady in Eilat. Your secretary, I believe? You swapped cars and she gets killed. It's your fault entirely, you stinking bastard. The blame can be laid squarely on your shoulders, not mine. In any case, Ronni here has been a control in the agency for a long time now. He minds the early warning station at his Dust Riders place."

"Now, we tried the first option of stopping you by force. We did not really succeed at all except in causing a bloodbath or two. Again, your fault entirely. When you turned up at Ronni's place, he decided to join you and host you all the way down to Taba. What could be better than to escort you right into our hands? That way you would also behave reasonably on the way, would you not, yes? Actually we have been looking for you everywhere, and then Ronni does the right thing and guides you right into our hands, yes?"

Einhorn's explanation was like a punch to the face and Jordan caught it squarely on the jaw. The deaths he had caused came back to haunt him. Linda, Alex. He felt a wave of helplessness envelop him. They had died in vain. He felt helpless.

"But Ronni," Jordan said looking at him, incredulously, "what about the trip to Jerusalem, the Apache that wiped out your place, shooting the soldier at the border, Yoseftal and all the rest—" He trailed off. His mind raced with all the unanswered questions.

"I had to be good to get by you, Jordan. You had to believe in me, in my intentions. You were one of the best the Mossad ever had. Nothing but normal behavior that you would expect from me would do. I have been a control since not long after you left the agency, but you would not know that. I am no less a Zionist than you are, and I follow orders. I knew something was up when I read the press, and I must say the trip to Jerusalem enlightened me somewhat. That is why I drove up—my curiosity was piqued. The Apache wipe-out was planned with me, since in any case we planned to rebuild the outpost with new technology. No worries there. The equipment, camels and dogs were evacuated prior to the missile attack."

"Helping get Irit back? That was no problem at all, either, my pleasure. We didn't really kill anyone doing it, just gave a few guards a headache. I am sorry I had to shoot the poor soldier at the border, but again, I needed to keep to the timetable. He didn't know of our mission. Besides, the real shooting just proved again that I was for real. I still am. The Deputy Director here has filled me in on the details."

"I must say that I do approve of this plan to get rid of these idiots that plan for peace. There can be no peace; there must be no peace. The Arabs understand nothing of peace, only terror. Any agreement will only allow them to get closer, to re-arm and to be able to sow more terror with greater ease. So you see to guide you along the way, to escort you into Taba was the best way to avoid any further bloodshed. That is why I decided to do this when you turned up at my place. It was my decision alone." Ronni seemed exhausted by his speech.

Einhorn motioned with his gun for Jordan to get up and kicked Irit in the ribs hard. She woke up with a start and screamed. A look of complete resignation washed over her face when she realized that she and Jordan were now captives in Taba. She nursed her ribs and Jordan saw her eyes, her angry eyes and waited for the outburst.

"I do not know who you are, but I will kill you for that kick, you bastard," she said to Einhorn, "and that is if Jordan does not get you first." She got to her feet, holding her side and stood alongside Jordan defiantly, her eyes blazing anger.

"Well we shall see about that later. Right now I do not think that you are in a position to decide anything at all my dear. Irit, isn't it?" Einhorn continued, "Last time I checked only you, Kline, were on the invitation list for our party. I shall now gladly add the lady, since we would not want either of you to miss the signing ceremony. I must add that I am sure that the agreement will blow up in their faces." He laughed at his sick joke. "In any case, we shall kill you after the explosion, since by then there will be a veritable mountain of bodies. Your execution will not be noticed amidst the bloodbath. Yes, before you die you will witness the power of our group. You will witness the genius of our plans that not even the powerful Americans could envisage, yes?" One more of those yeses and Jordan could care less if he were killed trying to get Einhorn.

"What shall we do with them, Deputy Director?" asked Ronni.

"Please cuff them together and take them to the Marhaba restaurant. It is not open tonight and is the ideal place to hold them. Keep a close guard. We know what Mr. Kline can get up to, don't we?" Einhorn looked at Jordan and Irit. "Now, I have important business to attend to. Have you not heard, there is a peace signing convention taking place just after the Shabbat ends? We can't miss that, can we?" He pulled the flap aside and exited the tent.

Before they were cuffed together, Jordan managed to jam the on button on one of the Motorola's that he had kept in his pocket that Shalom had given them. He knew that they would go for Shalom now. They would try and kill him quickly and quietly. Ronni would already have told them about Shalom. He hoped to God that Shalom would hear the Motorola. He knew that the distance was good since the Motorola's were designed for up to forty kilometers' reception. No harm in trying.

"Get a fucking move on," shouted Ronni. "I don't want to kill you two before you enjoy the signing. You must get the chance to see the most powerful man in the world die, not to mention the others."

He pushed them violently towards the exit. Jordan and Irit were led unceremoniously out of the tent and towards the Marhaba restaurant.

THE SANDS HOTEL, EILAT.
SATURDAY, SEPTEMBER 8TH.
CONVENTION DAY.

Shalom had dressed in his suit and was almost ready to exit the hotel on his way to the ceremony. He sat in his office having a smoke and contemplating what lay in store for them in Taba that evening.

The phone rang on his desk, breaking the silence.

He picked it up and barked quickly, "Yes, Shalom here. Who is this?"

"Rachel here from the switchboard. Thought you might like to know that an Agent Cohen has just asked if you were at the hotel. He does not look like a nice person. I told him no, I did not think so. He obviously didn't believe me and I can see him now on my security monitors. He is going down the corridor outside your offices. He'll be there pretty soon, Shalom. Just thought you should know."

Shalom did not even answer her but put the receiver down. He threw the cigarette onto the carpet and stepped on it. He crossed the office quickly and went into the outer office. He took out his handgun and slid in behind the door at the entrance to the offices. He left the light on in his office and the radio on. The communication channel with the security guards in the hotel was also on. The lights in the outer office were switched off, and the door to his office was slightly ajar. It was impossible to make out if there was someone in there unless the door was opened a little more.

Shalom heard the footsteps approaching outside. He saw the shadow under the door as the agent stopped at security. He held his breath. The door opened slowly, and the agent entered. Shalom saw a gun with a silencer in the agent's outstretched hand. He was oblivious to Shalom behind him. There was no question that this time Agent Cohen was looking to take him out permanently.

"Looking for me, Mr. Cohen?" Shalom asked quietly from behind.

The agent was surprised. He did his best to swing around quickly to get a shot in. There was a sharp crack as the pistol fired. The bullet embedded itself in Shalom's desk. Shalom brought down the butt of his gun on the agent's head. Agent Cohen went down like a sack of potatoes onto the office floor.

Shalom dragged the limp body into his office. He picked up his Motorola and locked the office on his way out. The agent would be unconscious for more than the necessary time. The ceremony could not be more than a couple of hours away. He knew that he had to plan differently now. He couldn't just waltz in as a guest. There was bound to be an APB on him. He doubted, however, that everyone was on the lookout for him. It would be just the agents involved in the final plot, the ones that were on site at Taba. Still, he knew that he could not go as an invited guest. The people that had sent agent Cohen to kill him would not make a second mistake.

He went down the service corridor and rode the elevator to the lobby. Exiting left, he strode the few steps into the hairdresser's shop situated just off the main lobby.

A few customers sat reading the dog-eared magazines while waiting their turn. Shalom strode over to an empty barber's chair and sat down. He turned to the hairdresser.

"Ronen," he spoke, his booming voice more an order than anything friendly, "shave my head completely. Do it now!"

Ronen the hairdresser had rented the space since the opening of the Sands. He had built up quite a respectful business that came as much from the citizens of Eilat as from the tourists and visitors. He raised his hand and quieted the waiting crowd. He picked up the electric shaver and walked over to Shalom.

"My, my, we are in a mood today, aren't we?" Everyone in the hotel really liked Ronen. Most gave him their business, especially since he gave them a good discount. That he was a good hairdresser also helped. He did not add any more to his sentence, just quickly and efficiently shaved Shalom's head until it was white and gleaming in the neon lights of the salon. When it was complete, Shalom thanked Ronen, told him to put it on his tab, and exited the salon. He went back down to his office and picked up his wetsuit gear and his goggles. The agent was still out on the floor. He took an undersea harpoon and took his gun from the safe. He had a plan. He relocked the door on his way out.

He went to his car and threw the gear in the trunk. He opened the driver's door and slumped into the driver's seat. It was as clear as crystal that something had gone terribly wrong. Someone had fingered him. Someone had sent Agent Cohen to take him out. What the fuck had gone wrong? Where was Jordan? The plan had seemed to be going well.

He heard a crackle on the Motorola in his pocket. Fishing it out quickly, he turned the volume up as high as it could go and listened. What he heard made his blood turn cold.

He heard Ronni's voice clearly now. "Get a fucking move on. I don't want to kill you two before you enjoy the signing. You must get the chance to see the most powerful man in the world die, not to mention the others."

Bloody hell, thought Shalom, his mind racing, his heart pumping. It was Ronni that had turned on them. He must have been very good for Jordan not to have seen through him. Like lambs to the fucking slaughter he thought. They had been led like lambs right into the trap. Ronni must have planned the whole thing, the bastard. He had led them right into the trap, and they had followed. Shalom hoped he would get the chance to meet Ronni again, to get even. He hoped the chance would come soon. Anger boiled up inside of him.

He turned the ignition switch, shifted the gear stick, and drove out of the delivery ramp and onto the street. As he drove around the lagoon he noticed that no one was following him as far as he could make out. He guessed that they had counted on Agent Cohen taking him out cleanly. He would have if Rachel from the switchboard had not warned him just in time. That had been a stroke of luck. He must remember to thank her and give her a big kiss if he lived through this.

He glanced at his watch. It showed three p.m. He pushed the accelerator down just enough to keep within the sixty-kilometer speed limit. He did not need any cops stopping him for speeding now. He did not want anything holding him up. He had to get to Taba as soon as possible. He had to find out about Jordan and Irit. He must try and free them. First he had to find out where they were. He figured that they would not be killed until after the ceremony was over and the dignitaries had been assassinated in the fireball. Actually, knowing the type of people that had set up this plot, they would keep him very much alive. They would keep him where he would be able to see the ceremony and the ensuing carnage that they would unleash. They would definitely enjoy having Jordan around to appreciate their genius. Like small kids, they needed acknowledgement. But where would they hold them, where would their prison be until their execution?

Shalom turned left at the New Tourist Center intersection and headed towards the Dolphin Beach.

TABA.
SATURDAY, SEPTEMBER 8TH.
CONVENTION DAY.

Cuffed together, Jordan and Irit were pushed brutally into the Marhaba restaurant.

"Which table shall we take, Irit? You choose, my love. We have the run of the place tonight. How about that romantic booth over there, maybe add that to our locations, too?" asked Jordan.

Irit laughed.

The guard behind them shoved his rifle into the small of Jordan's back, "Shut the fuck up. You heard the orders. No talking."

They were shoved into a far booth at the back well away from the entrance to the restaurant. Jordan took a look around. He could see both the new convention center beyond the entrance as well as the beach just below. There were still some bathers taking in the afternoon sun. He guessed that they were part of the considerable entourages that accompany the heads of state on their travels. On an occasion such as this it was very probable that many wives were also accompanying their high-ranking husbands. Protocol not only allowed for this but also demanded it as they lent elegance and color to the ceremonial functions.

When the time came for the signing ceremony, Jordan guessed that he and Irit would be taken up onto the roof of the Marhaba. While at some distance from the actual steps of the convention center, it still had quite a clear and panoramic view of the area.

Ronni turned and spoke to the two guards that Einhorn had ordered to watch the two captives. One of the guards went out of the Marhaba and stood guard at the outer entrance. The other guard took up a position two booths away from Jordan and Irit. He made sure that they could see his gun. It was pointed directly at them.

"Jordan, I now have to go off and run some errands. See where I can help, that sort of thing. Do be good now and we shall meet towards the ceremony time when we shall watch it together from the roof. Oh, do not worry. I will be back with plenty of time to spare. Be bad, and the guard has orders to shoot—and shoot to kill. Now that would be a shame. I am so looking forward to viewing the affair with you two. Be good now," he repeated and with a wave of his hand he was gone.

Jordan looked at the guard who seemed uneasy but threatening.

"I have to go take a leak," he told the guard bluntly.

"No leaks allowed," answered the guard curtly.

"Very well, then I will take a leak right here in the restaurant," answered Jordan. He stood up and started to fold up his Bedouin shirt.

"Okay, okay, but you will just have to go with her. I am not uncuffing you from her," the guard said. Then he added, laughing, "And in any case, you don't have anything she hasn't seen."

The guard followed them the short distance to the toilets and made as if to enter with them.

"You also want to see what I've got, you a fucking faggot?" asked Jordan. "You know there is no way out of the restaurant at the back."

"Very well, but no tricks. I will be right here by the door," the guard threatened.

Jordan let Irit into the toilet first and then followed with his handcuffed hand first. He took a look around. The only thing that could help them was a small window that overlooked the beach area. He wondered where Shalom was, wondered whether they had already taken him out. They had surely sent an agent to eliminate him right there in his office in the hotel. They would not leave anything to chance. With Shalom out of the picture and him and Irit under guard, there was nothing to stop them. Nothing could get in the way of their plans.

If I were with them, he thought, I would not let two captives live until the ceremony. That would be a big mistake. Huge mistake. As long as there is an enemy within, you do not allow him to live but kill him on sight. Rules of the game, but these people didn't live by the rules. Einhorn was vain; he wanted them to witness and appreciate the genius of their plans, the power they wielded. He wanted them to witness the bloodbath that they could make happen. He wanted them to appreciate that they could make it happen even in the most guarded place on earth. Einhorn needed them to witness this, to applaud him on the achievement, to have one of Israel's finest operatives see how good he was. Just as well, thought Jordan, it did not matter what was keeping them alive, just that they were still alive. While alive they still had a chance to spoil the party.

Jordan took off his keffiyah that he was wearing. He stood on the toilet seat and placed it on the ledge of the window against the pane of glass. If anyone were to see it there, they might think it out of place. He tore out a loose door hanger from behind the toilet door, and stretching his hand out of the small opening in the window, scratched a capital "J" as best he could into the plaster of the outside wall. It was a long shot, but still worth the effort. He would have to come up with a plan to get rid of his guards, but right now he needed time to think.

He pushed open the door and brushed past the guard with Irit in tow.

"Slow down, Jord, you're hurting me. The cuffs are cutting into my wrists. I only have one good arm," Irit shouted.

"Sorry, Irit. I forgot for a second that we're attached. Great word 'attached.' I like it. Hey, this is even better than marriage. You can't run from me now," he said. He massaged her wrist with his free hand. He smiled and hoped that he looked cheerful.

They went back and sat down again in their booth. Irit rested her head on his shoulder and whispered into his ear, "Jord, it looks like we are in a hopeless situation here. I see the marriage 'hupa' getting further away all the time. Will we ever get there? It doesn't look good."

"Did I ever let you down, Irit?" Jordan asked in mock amazement. "Where is your faith, girl? When this is over I shall make sure you have the biggest and nicest hupa that a Jewish girl ever had. And take note, I said WHEN this thing is over, not if. You are sitting next to Jordan Kline, and he will make things okay. Always has, always will." He said it more to convince himself than encourage Irit, but it came out okay, and they both smiled.

"No fucking talking. I remind you two," the guard spat out in his heavy Russian accent. He was probably one of the new immigrants that had recently made Aliyah or immigration.

Jordan sat silently and began to take stock of his limited options. He had to admit that they weren't many.

DOLPHIN BEACH, EILAT.
SATURDAY, SEPTEMBER 8TH.
CONVENTION DAY.

Shalom rolled to a stop in a cloud of dust and gravel in the car park of the Dolphin Beach resort. He couldn't help but smile at the recollection that just a day or two ago he was here to save citizens from terror. Now he was the hunted.

He did not have much time if surprise was to be on his side. He had to act quickly. He slammed the car door shut, opened the trunk, took out the bag with his diving gear, and slammed that shut, too. He took the stairs down to the water two at a time.

Menahem, the resort manager, stood chatting with a couple of the lifeguards that were still on duty. He approached him walking awkwardly as his feet sank down into the soft sand.

"How can I help you, sir?" Menahem asked, not recognizing Shalom.

"How can I help you, sir?" mimicked Shalom, and they both started laughing as Menahem finally recognized his friend.

"My God, what happened to your hair?" asked Menahem.

"Long story, no time to tell, but I needed more air to the brain my friend. In any case, Menahem, I need to borrow a water scooter for a couple of hours. I need it pronto. That okay with you?"

"Take it, take it. What are you waiting for? Mi casa, tu casa, amigo," he shouted at Shalom. Shalom entered the men's changing room and got into his diving suit as quickly as he could. He picked up a tank of oxygen on his way out and put the gun and harpoon into a waterproof bag that he had in his kitbag from the anti-terror squad equipment.

Descending quickly down the wooden stairs to the small marina he took the key to one of the water scooters offered him by the supervisor and hopped onto the machine. He attached the key around his wrist with the small length of rope, put it into the ignition, and the motor roared to life. He slowly opened the throttle as he coasted towards the open sea marked by red buoys. As he passed the final buoy he piled on the speed.

Shalom was beginning to really enjoy the scooter ride, the wind in his face, the great view of the shoreline as it rushed past him. Tourists on the shore waved to him with enthusiasm as if they knew him. Soon he was alongside the Princess Hotel. He would arrive opposite the Hilton Taba in a couple of minutes. He slowed the craft and looked around. In the distance he could see the outline of the Hilton. He could also see that at least two sailing ships fully loaded with tourists were anchored offshore at a respectable distance from the hotel.

One looked like the Orionia, a beautiful old sailing ship. It had been refitted at Southampton in England and sailed to Eilat to serve the tourists on short day trips along the Sinai coast. The company marketing the day trips to the tourists was called the Red Sea Sports Club. They did a great job selling everything from day trips on board the sailing ships, to desert safaris in Jeeps, camel rides, diving trips, and other water activities. It was now at anchor offshore allowing the tourists to do some snorkeling in the beautiful clear waters among the tropical fish.

Shalom knew that the security people would not let the boats get too close to shore and the hotel today. In an hour or so they would be told to up-anchor and get back to their moorings in Eilat.

As he got closer he could see that there were quite a few people having a good time on the beach below the hotel. There was a lively game of beach volleyball going on at one end. At the other a crowd sipped what looked like colorful cocktails at the beach bar. Others lay on their sun loungers taking in the sun. He guessed that these were part of the delegations that had come to the convention. They were enjoying something that they did not have at home in such good quantity or quality.

He opened the throttle and approached one of the tourist sailboats. He was careful to keep the ship between himself and the shore. He put in his mouthpiece, opened the oxygen tank, and strapped it to his back. He tied his waterproof bag to his body and slipped under the water quietly, leaving the scooter bobbing on the waves above. He had attached one of his diving weights to the craft and hoped that it would not drift too far in the next few hours. He then turned towards shore and kicked powerfully with his fins.

Shalom knew the Taba beach by heart, he had been there so often. He knew that the water was shallow for about thirty meters out to sea and then dropped dramatically down to a quite a depth, probably about twenty meters he guessed. The shallow part allowed swimmers to stand at the edge of the deep. Many swimmers liked to snorkel up to the edge and look down into the depths. Today Shalom doubted that there would be many swimmers among the delegations, just a sun-thirsty crowd.

He came in below the Hilton beach, just below the edge of the deep drop. He unstrapped the oxygen tank from his back and peeled off his diving suit until he was only in his swimming shorts. He then wrapped the suit and his goggles around the tank and watched as the package sank slowly down to the sea-bed. He followed it with his eyes and saw it kick up a small cloud of mud as it hit the bed and settled.

He swam up the face of the drop and into the shallows near the beach, coming up slowly and breaking water only with his shiny, newly bald head. He scanned the shoreline for security but saw only the lifeguard on duty. Hotel security personnel were stationed at either end of the beach area. He could imagine that the rooftop snipers that he could see would probably be scanning the beach and shoreline through their high-powered sights. They would not be expecting an attack from a simple bather. They would be on the lookout for a possible terror attack, maybe something like the one that had happened in Eilat recently.

He noted that there were some guests sitting at the beach bar, some eating what looked like shuwarma in pita bread. The guests sunning themselves on the loungers were getting a per-fect tan to show during the ceremony. Some looked just a little too pink. He guessed that they would be hurting some come the evening. A group of guests sat in the shallow water very near the shore. Shalom swam in their direction, still careful to keep his body underwater.

Shalom got reasonably close to the group and then again scanned the shoreline. The flags of all the nations in attendance flapped in the wind near the convention center. He could make out the Egyptian, American, and Israeli flags and guessed that the Jordanian and Palestinian flags were right up there along-side the others out of sight. There seemed to be no real threat-ening activity around the hotel. He glanced at his watch. It showed almost four p.m. It was still the Sabbath. Since all the preparations had already been made, everyone was just waiting for the dusk to come and for the convention to begin. It was the calm before the storm.

His eyes followed the steps up from the beach, around the Marhaba restaurant and leading to the back entrance to the hotel. An elevator was located there to take tired guests up to their suites after a day at the beach. He looked at the restaurant. He could see that it was dark inside and guessed that it would be closed until after the convention. It would not be needed. Taking a closer look he picked out something white on the ledge of a small window at the back of the restaurant where he knew that the toilets were situated. It looked like a towel or cloth of some sort, but why would it be there, on a toilet window ledge? If it was a sign from Jordan, it could be that they were being held there. It would be the best location for a temporary prison cell since it was closed. Nobody would disturb the captives or their guardians in the restaurant. It was conveniently far enough away from the convention center and the hotel.

Shalom raised himself out of the water slowly and waded towards the shore. No one took undue notice of him. He strolled casually towards the lifeguard station and helped himself to a white towel to dry himself. This, he knew, would be the natural thing to do. He did not want to arouse suspicion. He wrapped the towel around his waist and started up the steps in the direction of the Marhaba. As he got closer, he could see a rough "J" scratched into the plaster on the outer wall of the restaurant. He realized in an instant beyond all doubt that Jordan and Irit were inside. He had found out where they were being held. It was a good start.

MARHABA RESTAURANT, TABA, EGYPT.
SATURDAY, SEPTEMBER 8TH.
CONVENTION DAY.
FOUR P.M.

Jordan desperately tried to formulate some sort of a plan. He let his eyes wander along the beach and shores of the Red Sea below. Either he was getting old or rusty, but he could not think of any plan of action that might get them out of this situation. In the old days, he thought, I would already be free of this, out of here and planning havoc among the enemy. His mind was blank.

As his eyes scanned the beach, he saw one of the guests in the water stand up in the shallows and approach the shoreline. He didn't recognize the man. He had a bright, white, and shiny bald head, but something about him was familiar. The white bald head did not really suit the rest of the man's body. His body was tanned but his head was white. How could that be? Jordan realized that it was newly shaven. He also knew why.

A surge of joy washed over him. He recognized the swimming shorts. He recognized the kitbag that was so nonchalantly carried over his shoulder. God knows how many times he had carried an identical bag on training with the anti-terror squad. Conscious of the guard watching him, he was careful not to show any emotion.

Jordan followed Shalom with his eyes as Shalom took the towel, dried off, and tied the towel around him as he started up the steps towards Marhaba. He knew that he must have seen the keffiya on the ledge of the toilet window, maybe also the "J" he had scratched hurriedly on the wall; they were trained to see things that did not fit in with the view, with the whole picture. Jordan realized that he had to get back to the window. That would be where Shalom was headed. He leaned over and whispered into Irit's ear, "Irit, you gotta go to the washroom, and you gotta go now. Tell the asshole."

Irit stiffened and said to the guard, "I have to go to the washroom, please."

"No washroom. You guys just went a little while ago. No more washrooms. Nyet washroom," he barked back at her.

"No, you don't understand, it's a ladies thing, and I have to go now," she said bashfully looking straight at him with a hint of a sexy smile.

"Okay, okay. Get up and go with her, Kline," the guard answered, a little embarrassed.

"No choice really. You know how ladies get," said Jordan apologetically as he was yanked along this time by Irit, playing the part perfectly. Once again the guard took up his position outside the washrooms. Once again Jordan and Irit found themselves in the toilets of the Marhaba.

Jordan stepped on his toes to take a look outside just as Shalom's gleaming bald head appeared framed by the window.

"My God it is really good to see you Shalom," whispered Jordan. "A pretty sight for sore eyes and all that shit. I was beginning to think that they had taken you out. Be careful, we have one guard inside and another at the entrance."

"No time to linger, Jordan. Here, take this," he said and pushed the small harpoon gun through the slit in the window. "Great little thing, doesn't make much noise. I will work my way to the front and take care of the other guy there. Give me five minutes, and then take your guy. See ya."he said, and the bald head disappeared as quickly as it had appeared.

Jordan hid the small harpoon gun under his clothes and they went back to their booth in the restaurant and sat down. The guard went back to his usual place two booths away and stood with his gun ready.

Jordan took a look at his watch. It was past four o'clock in the afternoon, and the convention would begin soon. It was scheduled to start at six. He stared at the guard until the guard turned his gaze away. Jordan slowly brought out the harpoon under the table. He kept his gaze on the guard. It was a little difficult getting the harpoon gun lined up since his right hand was cuffed to Irit. He managed take it out silently. Could he fire it accurately when he had to? There was no point in thinking this over, wasting any time on it. There was no other option.

Some minutes went by and there was suddenly a dull thud of someone falling against the entrance door. The guard turned for a split second to try and see what was going on. Jordan took out the harpoon gun, leveled it as best he could at the guard's legs, and fired. The harpoon gun made a whooshing noise as the harpoon took flight like an arrow, unwinding the thin rope attached to the gun. The guard screamed in agony as the harpoon embedded itself in his thigh. He dropped the gun. Jordan tugged on the rope, pulling the guard down and towards the booth where he was sitting.

At that moment Shalom entered the restaurant towing the limp form of the second guard by the heels. When he saw the second guard trying desperately to reach his gun that he had dropped as the harpoon hit him, he ran over and brought the butt of his pistol down on the man's head. The guard lost consciousness and went limp. Shalom located the keys on the guard and quickly unlocked the cuffs. Jordan rubbed his wrists. He placed his leg on the guard's thigh and pulled the harpoon free. He pushed the harpoon in and reloaded it. Blood ran from the guard's open wound. He tore a tablecloth into a long strip and bandaged the wound as best he could. They undressed the guards quickly. They tied them up, dragged them to the back and locked them in the toilets. With napkins stuffed in their mouths it would be very difficult for them to raise the alarm. In any case Jordan figured that they would be out for at least a few hours.

Jordan looked at Shalom.

Shalom answered Jordan before he could ask the question, "Yes, they came for me at the hotel. Rachel from the switchboard saved my life. She warned me about the man on his way down to my office. Same man that came to question me before. She saw him on the security monitors. I was waiting for him. Then I had to change my appearance a little, and Ronen did that quite well, and rather quickly. I think he likes me bald, the sweetie." He laughed. He followed up with the rest of his story about the Dolphin Beach scooter, the underwater swim, that he had seen the keffiyah in the toilet window and the "J" scratched on the wall.

"Lucky we stayed in some kind of practice with the anti-terror training, huh Jord?" he added, looking at Jordan and Irit. "How are you doing Irit?" he asked concerned, turning to her.

"I'll live, but a bit black and blue for a while—that is if they don't shoot us. If they do shoot us, then I will die black and blue," she answered smiling then wincing as she tried to get her arm into a better and more comfortable position.

"Ok," Shalom continued. "I have to get into the guard's clothes and stand guard at the entrance so that everything looks kosher from afar." He quickly put on the army uniform and pulled the cap down on his bald head as far as it could go. Should be okay for the rest of the time we have to wait here, he thought. He glanced at his watch and saw that it was now four-thirty. Good, only one and a half hours to go now.

HILTON CONVENTION CENTER, TABA.
SATURDAY, SEPTEMBER 8TH.
CONVENTION DAY.
5:55 P.M.

The convention center main ballroom was beautifully laid out for the start of the convention. A vast array of cakes, pastries, and small sandwiches was displayed perfectly on two buffets that ran down both sides of the hall. Hilton International had flown their best pastry chefs in from the Hilton Vienna for the occasion. In deference to the Jewish dietary laws, the affair was kosher. All the pastries and sandwiches were made with milk products alone so as not to offend the Israeli delegation. The entire cutlery collection was the best Christofle, the linens of the finest Egyptian cotton, the chinaware Rosenthal, and the champagne flutes Reidel crystal. It was in the hall that they would toast the historic agreement. The very best Dom Perignon champagne was on ice ready to be served.

There were twenty round tables of ten seats each arranged between the buffets for the dignitaries. A podium had been placed on a small stage for the only speaker. The main speeches were to be on the steps outside the hall where they could be broadcast worldwide. This podium, decorated with the seal of the President of Egypt, was for the welcome speech and toast that the president would make before the gathering. He would make the speech that would formally open the convention and invite the heads of state to gather outside on the steps. There he would formally announce that peace had finally come to the Middle East, or at least between the Israelis and the Palestinians. The peace would be in addition to the treaties that were already in place between Israel and Egypt and Israel and Jordan.

All the tables had place names arranged on them, and each of the dignitaries had been informed of the table places allotted to them in the hall. On each table there was a tall silver table number holder visible from all angles to enable the invited guests to find their seats easily.

At precisely five o'clock the guests started to file into the grand ballroom and take their places. Attentive waiters were in attendance and poured coffee as they sat down. Here and there a tea was requested and a beautiful wooden box was presented to the guest with a wide and inviting variety of teas to choose from.

It was not too often that even these guests saw a pastry buffet such as that put on by the Austrian chefs. The guests attacked the displays with gusto. The tall black forest cakes went over wildly, as did the Napoleon slices and the Sachertorte. The egg salad sandwiches went quickly and the ever-popular smoked salmon and cream cheese disappeared fast. As a gesture to the host country the hotel chef had put up a couple of small counters that were giving out small, bite-sized pita breads stuffed with a mini falafel ball and smothered in Tehini sauce. The hungry crowd also wolfed these down. Just as quickly as the trays with the cakes and sandwiches were devoured by the hungry guests they were replaced with new trays prepared beforehand and stored in the pantries just off the main hall. The chefs were taking no chances with this event, better to make a few too many than a few short.

An hour was allocated for the afternoon tea event, and the time flew by quickly. The guests enjoyed the food and excited small talk at their tables. Towards six o'clock the crowd hushed as the President of the Republic of Egypt got up from his table and approached the podium.

Dan Heller, Junior Cabinet Minister, Chairman of the House Security Committee in the Israeli Parliament, watched in faint amusement and in excited anticipation. He looked at his watch and saw the second hand and the minute hand joining each other as the hour struck six.

HILTON TABA GROUNDS.
SATURDAY, SEPTEMBER 8TH.
CONVENTION DAY.

David Hofstein was a little nervous, though one could not tell by looking at him. The tall contractor was taking a satisfied look at his creation, the Taba Hilton Convention Center. He was not among the guests invited to the afternoon event. He was not really connected to the treaty or the negotiations that had led up to the agreement.

He had been invited to the greater event in his capacity as a leading Israeli industrialist and of course as the main builder of the convention and casino project for Hilton. He had absolutely no desire to be among those people in the hall; he despised them. They wanted to go down in history as peacemakers, but what did they understand except the fact that the President of the United States had forced them to come to this agreement. They didn't understand that strength lay only in Eretz Yisrael Shlema, the land of Israel whole, complete. To give back the territories would be a cardinal sin; for this sin they would die.

Hofstein looked up at the position he had chosen from which to watch the proceedings, from where he would send the signal from his mobile phone. He flipped open the phone to take another look at the numbers on the screen—the numbers that would bring sanity back to the Middle East. He flipped the phone shut and kissed it before slipping it into his jacket pocket.

The location he had chosen was just behind the bank of terraced seats that had been constructed specially for the ceremony. It was directly opposite the steps leading up to the entrance to the hall. The seats could accommodate up to four hundred people and were banked to allow for an unobstructed view of the proceedings from each seat. At the top of the construction was a platform to accommodate the television news crews from the channels selected to broadcast the historic event: CNN, IBA Israel broadcasting corporation. Ramatta the Palestinian TV station, Egypt TV Channel One, and Jordanian TV. They each had room for their cameras and a small simultaneous translation booth alongside it. The many clusters of the national flags of the countries flapping in the afternoon breeze added to the carnival atmosphere with bursts of color.

His chosen place allowed him to take cover behind a concrete supporting wall of the casino building, a wall that could easily withstand the force of the blast.

At last, in only a few minutes, all their work, all their careful planning would bear fruit.

TABA CONVENTION CENTER.
SATURDAY, SEPTEMBER 8TH.
CONVENTION DAY.

Ariel Einhorn had every reason to be satisfied. It was just five minutes before the guests would file out from the grand hall to cross the courtyard and take their seats on the grandstand opposite the entrance steps. He guessed that this might take about half an hour. Following this the five heads of state would file out to take their places on the marble steps. They would be accompanied by their deputies, foreign ministers, defense ministers and senior cabinet ministers. There were wingback chairs for the heads of state. The others were allocated standing spots behind them. There were small stickers on the marble with the names of those that were to stand on them during the ceremony to remind them of their places.

Einhorn knew the names and the sticker places by heart, as did Dan Heller. After all, it was they who had decided who stood where, and who would be nearest the blast. Who might live and who might die. It was exciting to play God.

Nothing could stop them now, nothing at all. The only threat to their plan was under close guard in the Marhaba restaurant, and Ronni would be inviting him to watch the ceremony from the rooftop at the restaurant. Then he would take care to extinguish the last remaining leads.

He looked across the ballroom and let his eyes take in all his people stationed every few meters around the hall. Each was wearing the orange tags, each ready to carry out his commands without question. He saw Ronni who now wore an army uniform with an orange tag pinned on his chest. He was on the other side of the room, and Einhorn walked across to him.

"What's up Ronni?" he asked casually.

"Just checking final arrangements. My Bedouin guys did the falafel service in the mini pitas, did you see them? They did a great job, lent an air of authenticity to the event, I thought. Well, I must be off now. I have invited guests to share the signing with me, as you know. Wouldn't want to disappoint them, would we?" Ronni smiled at Einhorn and strode out through the front entrance.

Einhorn followed him out and went over to check once again the spot he had chosen and which he must reach so that he was protected when he sent the wireless signal to the explosives lying and waiting in the pipe under the stairs. He could see that he was going to be protected by a stairwell. It led to the basement under the convention hall from the far side of the building. The blast should go up and outwards according to his calculations. He should be just fine.

MARHABA RESTAURANT, TABA.
SATURDAY, SEPTEMBER 8TH.
CONVENTION DAY.
SIX P.M.

Shalom was beginning to sweat in the guard's rough army uniform that was a little small on him. Beads of sweat ran down his spine under the shirt, and he rubbed his back against the doorframe to alleviate the itching. This only made the shirt stick to his back and made him even more uncomfortable. He could hear the annoying buzz of a mosquito around his head but could not see it. He made a feeble attempt to slap it away. They just loved him. He would probably soon feel the itch of a bite.

He looked at his watch and saw that it was already after six. He knew that the guests would be exiting the hall now to take up their seats. He could hear the distant sound of many voices drifting over the trees. Ronni would be back soon to take Jordan and Irit up to the roof to enjoy the spectacle planned.

God, the flies were really annoying him. He tried to slap them away as they landed on him. He wished he had his repellant cream with him, as more mosquitoes began to swarm around him. It was driving him crazy between the sweat, the flies, and the shrill whine of the mosquitoes. He couldn't take this much longer, he thought. He suddenly felt the cold steel of a gun pressed against his neck.

"So, Shalom," Ronni sneered. "I have been waiting for you, my friend. I figured you would come along for the show if you were still alive, that you would want to join Jordan and Irit. Well I would not have you miss the fun for all the Goddamn

Bedouin tea in China. There will be a time to kill, but now it's time to watch." He turned towards the entrance door, keeping the gun pressed firmly into Shalom's neck, "Hey, you two lovebirds in there," he shouted, and continued "I am coming in with Shalom in front, so no dirty tricks now or Shalom will miss our show. Can't watch the show if you are dead!"

He shoved Shalom into the entrance and advanced slowly into the darkened restaurant behind his captive.

Jordan and Irit sat in the last booth. Jordan looked at him and put his forefinger to his lips. "Shh, you'll wake her up. She needs rest. Don't forget she's kinda bruised right now and does have that broken arm. Let her be, Ronni. Let her sleep a few more moments."

"Okay, five more minutes. Then it will be time to go up on the roof. The ceremony should be starting soon. God, I wish I had the cell number of the bomb and the phone to blow it. It would be so fucking great to go down in history as the guy that blew this." Ronni answered, excitement lighting up his face. He shoved Shalom along the passage between the tables towards Jordan. He wanted them all in his sights, all together.

As he neared their table Ronni gave Shalom one more violent push, enough to set himself off balance slightly as he did so. It was enough. It was what Jordan was waiting for. In one fluid movement Jordan raised the harpoon gun, centered it quickly and fired just as Shalom ducked.

Ronni tried desperately to aim the gun at Jordan but was not yet in a stable position. He pulled the trigger. The bullet went wide and embedded itself in the back wall with a dull thud. The second bullet went over their heads and smashed into one of the pictures on the wall. Glass rained down on them.

The harpoon flew through the air and entered Ronni's body between the ribs. He dropped the gun and looked down incredulously at his wound. Blood started gushing out from around the steel shaft.

He dropped slowly to his knees. He looked down at the harpoon sticking out of his chest and tried feebly to hold it, to pull it out. His blood covered his hands.

Jordan reeled in his catch, pulling on the rope attached to the harpoon. Ronni was drawn slowly along the floor on his knees, smearing the floor with the blood flowing freely from his wound. He opened his mouth but only a steady stream of blood flowed out and down his chin, dripping onto the floor. He was now on his knees face to face with Jordan.

Jordan looked into Ronni's eyes that were beginning to cloud over.

"I hoped it would not come to this, Ronni. I really hoped it would not. In your dying moments please know that we shall stop this plot. Your death is in vain, you fucking traitor. Now die, asshole!" He pushed Ronni backwards with the heel of his shoe onto the floor.

Ronni groaned for a few seconds, kicked his feet once, and was still. One of his bloodied hands still held the harpoon. The blood slowly spread outwards from the wound in his chest across his army shirt and pooled on the floor to one side of his body. His lifeless eyes stared at the Marhaba ceiling, the look of surprise still in them.

THE TABA CONVENTION SIGNING CEREMONY. SATURDAY, SEPTEMBER 8TH.

All the invited guests were now fully settled in their seats on the massive grandstand. Some were peering through opera glasses to get a better view that brought them nearer the action on the stage. Others were reading the program printed especially for the occasion as a souvenir. It listed the order of the speakers. The opening paragraph of the peace agreement was printed on the front cover in embossed gold letters.

The Egyptian army band played in the background while the dignitaries filed out of the hall and walked over to their allotted place for the ceremony.

The television crews were now hard at work following the goings-on at the top of the steps and roaming the crowd for celebrities and wives attending. The major network anchors were running commentary on the procedures and informing the viewers of what to expect next, who was still to appear, and in which order the heads of state would appear. The eyes of millions around the world were tuned in to this historic show. It was a blockbuster event.

A sudden hush fell upon the crowd. The last of the standing dignitaries had taken their places behind the row of wingback chairs, and it was time for the leaders to make their entrance. A well-known Egyptian TV anchor stepped up to the podium and cleared his throat.

"Ladies and gentlemen, brothers and sisters, welcome to this honorable gathering in Taba, Egypt. We are here to witness the historic peace agreement between the State of Israel and our Arab brothers from Palestine. We Egyptians are especially honored that Taba has been chosen as the site for this unprecedented event and are proud to be able to welcome you all here with open arms.

I would now like to invite each leader to come out on these sacred steps and take his seat. As each leader appears he shall be accompanied by the national anthem of his country. I request that you all remain standing in respect for the leaders and their anthems. Following the anthems each leader will make a speech to the assembled and to the world watching. This will be followed by the signing of the copies of the peace agreement that are lying ready on the table over there," he said and pointed dramatically to a table on the other side of the steps that had three chairs behind it. Three leather-bound copies of the agreement lay on the table. Three Mont Blanc fountain pens were carefully placed by each agreement.

The announcer continued in a dramatic, theatrical voice, "When all the leaders have been announced and are seated, I will invite them according to protocol to come up to the podium and address the gathering. May Allah bless us all with peace in our time."

"I would now like to invite his Royal Highness from the Hashemite Kingdom of Jordan, King Ibrahim." He raised his voice as he announced Ibrahim, and the crowd burst into a loud and spontaneous applause as the King came out of the hall and stood before the crowd. The national anthem of Jordan, known as the Al-Salam Al-Malaki Al-Urdoni, "Long Live the King," was played by the army band, following which the King took his seat.

The anchor was quickly back again. "And now, ladies and gentlemen, I announce the leader of the Palestinian fledgling state, our esteemed brother and father of the Palestinian people, Abu Mahmoud." Again the raised voice, again an ecstatic welcome was afforded to Abu Mahmoud. He appeared from behind the speaker, dressed in his legendary khaki army uniform, keffiyah headdress, and the ever-present pistol tucked under his belt. The band struck up the anthem "Biladi", "My Country," the official anthem of the Palestinian National Authority since it had been adopted by the Palestinian Council in 1996. It was also known as the "Anthem of the Palestinian Revolution." The music was actually composed by an Egyptian, Ali Ismael.

Abu Mahmoud waved to the crowd and took his seat after standing to attention during his anthem.

The anchor again appeared behind the podium, and announced, "And now I have the distinct honor of inviting the leader of our esteemed and friendly neighbor, the Prime Minister of the State of Israel, the Honorable Avner Dotan."

The legendary soldier statesman appeared on the steps to a rousing welcome from the crowd. The band started playing the Israeli anthem, the "Hatikva", "The Hope". The music to the Israeli anthem was sad and moving, and the simultaneous translation appeared on an electronic strip on both sides of the steps. The Israelis present sang their anthem with gusto, while the translation lit up "...then our hope, two thousand-year hope will not be lost, to be a free people in our land, the land of Zion and Jerusalem." Dotan, too, took his seat alongside the other leaders.

"And now, ladies and gentlemen, the leader of the free world, the Honorable President of the United States of America, Jonathan Cabon."

The crowd was in frenzy now, loving every minute of the carefully orchestrated event. Hell, they were making history, part of something to proudly tell their children, to be passed down the family generations.

President Cabon covered his heart with his right hand as the band struck up the "Star Spangled Banner." Officially named the anthem in 1931 by congressional resolution, the lyrics had been taken from a poem written in 1814 with the music adopted from a popular British drinking song written for a London social club in 1780. Cabon was already waving to the crowd as the band played the last sentence "O'er the land of the free and the home of the brave." He then approached Dotan, Abu Mahmoud, and King Ibrahim, shook their hands, and took his seat. He took his time doing this; he knew that the television stations were covering every second. It was his time in the world spotlight.

With the next introduction the anchor was nearly in tears. "And now, the host of this glorious gathering of heads of state, our exalted leader and father of the great Egyptian people, the Honorable President Butrus Badawi."

President Badawi stepped onto the platform behind the speaker, went up to him, and shook his hand. The anchor looked as if he were going to keel over. The President had actually shaken his hand.

The crowd was now stamping their feet on the wooden planks, clapping their hands and screaming applause. Badawi acknowledged their adoration with a wave of his hand, and stood to listen to the Egyptian anthem, "Bilady, Bilady, Bilady," "My Country, My Country, My Country," adopted officially in 1979.

When the band had completed the anthem, Badawi went over to the gathered leaders and shook their hands one by one, welcoming each with a few whispered words. He then approached the podium and gestured for all to be seated.

MARHABA RESTAURANT, TABA.
SATURDAY, SEPTEMBER 8TH.
CONVENTION DAY.

Jordan, Irit, and Shalom had heard the introductions and the anthems from inside the Marhaba but were concentrating on trying to plan their next steps.

The Egyptian president was speaking now, and he would be followed by the others. Jordan guessed that first King Ibrahim would be invited to speak, followed by Abu Mahmoud, Dotan, and finally Cabon. Following that Badawi would officially invite Dotan, Cabon, and Abu Mahmoud to the table for the signing ceremony.

They did not have long to come up with a plan, maybe half an hour at the most, and that was if each speaker took the allotted five minutes. It was getting tight.

"What's wrong Jordan?" Irit asked, putting a hand on his shoulder.

"Well, I am just thinking back to what Ronni said when I asked him to leave you be for a while, to let you sleep a few minutes more."

"He certainly didn't say anything spectacular as I recall," answered Shalom pensively.

"Yes, I know, but please tell me what he said exactly as you remember it, either you or Irit. No not you, Irit, I forgot, you were asleep," Jordan said matter-of-factly.

"Well," started Irit, "as I was actually kind of waking up I heard him say that I could sleep for five more minutes and that then he would move us up to the rooftop to watch. Does that help you any?"

"But," Jordan said, "he also said that he wished that he had the cell number for the bomb and the phone with which to blow the convention to hell, right?"

"Okay, that is what he said, but what of it?" asked Shalom, "We need a plan, and we need one now. You're wasting precious time, time we do not have right now. What the hell good would a cell number be to us? Why are you even mentioning it, we are losing time here."

Jordan got up, energized. "I will tell you both just exactly why I mention it. Ronni just gave us the best plan. He didn't even know he was doing it. Not only that, but I also think they gave us access to the equipment that we need to fuck up their plans. At the very least delay the detonation. My God, it has been staring at me in the face all the time we have been here, and I did not think about it at all until good old Ronni reminded me. He was useful after all."

Irit and Shalom got up and confronted Jordan. Shalom asked, "Well Kline, are you going to let us in on the secret or what?"

Jordan went over to the back booth and pried a small plastic box off the wall.

He brought it back and handed it to Shalom. "There's your solution, Shalom, if I am right."

Shalom and Irit looked at the plastic box and both burst into laughter.

"This is the solution, this is what is going to stop the bomb, this small piece of plastic junk is what is going to fuck up their plans, right?" asked Shalom with incredulity.

"Yes, my friends, this is the answer. A few days ago after Josh was killed, I came over for lunch with John Macdonald the GM here at the Hilton. We ate right here in the Marhaba. At some stage I wanted to make a quick call to you, Irit, on my cell phone. Macdonald told me that I couldn't, that all cell transmissions were blocked here by this little box. A radius of about fifty feet he said it covered. He also told me that it covered nearly all cell phones and was updated recently by the company that sells them. Now all we need to do is get close enough to the casino steps and leave it there. Whoever tries to connect with the bomb by using his cell phone will not be able to because our little friend here will block his signal. Again, that is if I am right."

"My God, Jord, what a simple piece of equipment can do, I mean, not a simple piece of equipment but you know what I mean, my love. Thank God you had lunch with Macdonald that day and called me, no, tried to call me. You are a genius, but what now?" Irit was getting excited now, mixing her words and feelings. Jordan had to smile at her accent.

She caught his smile. "I will definitely make you pay for that, Kline!"

Jordan thought aloud, "There will be trained agents operating among the invitees, probably at least a handful I would imagine. Now, they probably do not know what will go down, but they do know to follow orders from Einhorn. They will kill us immediately if given the chance. We have to get in among the crowd so that it will be difficult for them to get a clean shot at us."

"Correct," said Shalom, "and then one of us must get near the steps with the box and try and leave it there. If the bomb is blocked, I think that will flush out the perpetrators of the plot who will probably try personal assassination instead. We need to take that into consideration, too, and warn the leaders to get the hell off the steps and into the hall. They need to get out other side as fast as possible."

"Then I suggest the following," Jordan said and continued. "You, Irit, will write a note to the CNN crew that there is a plot to blow up the convention during the signing ceremony. Write that they should announce this over their PA system immediately. Write that they should evacuate immediately. Shalom, you will create a diversion of some sort, perhaps by giving yourself up in public and making a show of it. That will allow Irit to get to CNN. I will try and get close to the casino entrance and place the box somewhere as hidden as possible."

They were silent for a moment. The strong voice of Prime Minister Dotan came over loud and clear. There was only one speaker left, President Cabon. Following that, President Badawi would invite them to the ceremony table. There was no time to waste now. They had to pray that they could get there in time.

Irit was already writing the note on a waiter's guest check-book that she had found on the service station and had it finished before two minutes were up.

"Right, you two, let's go and do it. By the way, I'll be seeing you all soon, and I count on you both to make damn sure of that," Irit said in a trembling voice.

"Leave one by one. You, Shalom, go via the back of the hotel. Irit, go straight to the bank of seats and try and get to the CNN position without too much fuss. The crowd will be watching and listening to the speeches, and I guess most of the guards will be also. I will get as close to the steps as I can when I hear your diversion, Shalom. Not a great plan, but the best we can do. It is so stupid it might just work. Thank God we didn't use plans like this in the agency during my time. If we had, chances are I would not be sitting with you guys now."

The Dotan speech was just over and they could hear the thundering applause that he received.

"Right, let's get the fuck out of here now. We do not have any more time," Jordan spat out and guided them to the door. "Good luck, and see you soon."

First out was Shalom since he had the most ground to cover. Irit left next followed by Jordan. There was no guard in sight. Everyone was at the event. History was about to be made. No one wanted to miss the chance of witnessing that.

THE TABA CONVENTION SIGNING CEREMONY. SATURDAY, SEPTEMBER 8TH.

President Cabon had just wrapped up his speech and the applause was dying down when the crowd heard a commotion from the manicured lawns to the left of the casino. They all turned as one to look at what might be making the noise.

What greeted their eyes was amazing. A man wearing only his underwear was waving wildly and screaming at them from the grass. He was shouting that he was turning himself in to the police. He was clearly unarmed. How had a madman got into Taba?

All heads turned and followed the guards and policemen who raced across to apprehend the fellow. Soon security from virtually all the nations in attendance had run across and jumped on the screaming man. It was all over within a couple of minutes. The man was shielded from the guests and led away.

Irit and Jordan hurried to their positions while the guards were occupied with the diversion.

Irit climbed the steps past the invited crowds that were preoccupied with Shalom's antics and approached the CNN anchor. She bent down and delivered the handwritten note. She whispered in the man's ear, "Read the fucking note—fast." Then she turned and was gone in a flash. Back the same way she came. No one noticed her come or go.

The anchorman stared in amazement at the note. He held it like he was holding a stick of dynamite, a look of terror on his face. Who was the woman? Where did she come from?

He did not know what to do with it. He was in a panic. Finally he waved at an American marine to come up to the platform.

Jordan heard the commotion that Shalom had caused and also saw Irit climb up to the CNN position. Good girl, he thought. Might even make a good agent one day. She sure was showing her true colors today, he thought, even with the painful arm.

During the uproar Jordan quietly approached the bank of seats and pushed his way in between two important-looking ladies in the second row and sat down. He felt for the little box in his pocket and traced its outline reassuringly with his fingers. He hoped that the batteries were still fresh. He wondered how long the box had been attached to the Marhaba wall.

He looked up but Irit was gone already and he could see the CNN guy staring forlornly at the note. My God, move man, move. Jordan willed the CNN anchor to get moving. Finally after what seemed an eternity the anchor waved for someone to come to him.

Jordan saw that a marine had been called and was climbing up to the TV platform. The marine and the CNN anchor conversed intently and read the note again and again. Jordan willed them to get on the PA system.

Suddenly something hard was pressed into his back from behind the bank of seats, and a familiar voice said menacingly in his ear, "I have just about had it with you, Kline. You are in my face every fucking Goddamn time I turn around." It was Ariel Einhorn, and he was not in a good mood.

Just then, the PA system came on and the marine's voice broadcast on the loudspeakers: "I would please ask that no one panic, but there is a bomb threat. I am an American marine, and I do not speak lightly. I ask that we take this seriously and that all leaders please evacuate through the hall and to the back of the complex. Do it now. Do it fast, but calmly."

"You bungling bastard, Kline. This means that I will blow it now and not wait for the bloody ceremony. Either way we win. The blast will kill them before they can evacuate. Let me show you how to kill the President of the United States!" He took out his cell phone and flipped it open. A row of red numbers lit up on the screen.

"Go ahead, Einhorn, do your stuff. You win," said Jordan in a tired, resigned voice.

"Damn right I win. Take a fucking look," he said as he showed Jordan the screen and punched the call button. The screen immediately showed the call fail sign. Einhorn pressed the call button again. Again the call fail sign lit up.

My God, thought Jordan, my little box of tricks is working after all.

Einhorn called to a guard with an orange tag to come forward. "Take this bastard to the main hotel and hold him there. If he tries to escape, kill him. Now do it. What the hell is wrong with this cell phone? The goddamn thing doesn't work. What the fuck is wrong with it?" he screamed. He punched the call button again and again.

The thickset muscle-bound guard came forward and grabbed Jordan by his left arm in a vice like grip. Jordan felt in his pocket for the box. He had to get it out and drop it somewhere close to the steps before the goon took him out of range. If he got too far away it would not block the signals and they could activate the bomb. He had maybe fifty feet.

He could hear Einhorn on his Motorola talking to Heller and Hofstein, screaming that they needed to carry out Plan B, the assassinations. Shalom had been right. Einhorn threw the cell phone onto the ground in disgust as he moved away from

Jordan. It was useless junk to him now. It rolled over a few times on the grass a short distance away.

Jordan turned to see the steps and the ceremony table and was glad to see that the leaders had all been led away into the hall behind. Most of the standing dignitaries were also off the steps now. There was, of course, still the threat of assassination to cover. He knew that Einhorn could get up close to the leaders. For that matter so could Heller, but he figured that Heller would leave the dirty work to Einhorn and Hofstein.

The announcement had created a stampede and the crowd was running in all directions in a frantic effort to get away from the area. There was total panic.

Jordan grabbed a hold of the box and tried to take it out of his pocket. Fear gripped him as he realized that the box was caught in his trousers by one of the small screws that had stayed in the box after he had pried it loose from the wall. He tried to get the damn screw loose. The screw tore through his trousers and cut his leg. It would not come loose. He tried desperately to think of something as the guard dragged him away from the scene.

He had to delay and keep near the steps for as long as possible to allow for as many people to get away as possible. Hofstein would still be trying to connect to the bomb. He could see Einhorn in desperate conversation with Heller and Hofstein. They had deadly, determined, and desperate looks on their faces. He could see through the scattering crowds that they had taken out their guns and were approaching the steps in pursuit of the leaders. My God, he thought, they were going to get close enough to assassinate them after all.

He turned around and punched the guard right in the stomach. The guard was not expecting the punch but was in great physical shape. He smiled. While it winded him slightly, he recovered quickly and kicked Jordan behind his knees viciously. Jordan sank to the ground on his knees just in time to feel the impact of a back-handed blow to his head that left him dazed on the ground. He tasted sand, grass, and blood in his mouth.

The guard pulled him to his feet roughly with one hand and held him upright. He hit him again, this time in the face. Jordan's vision blurred. He could hardly stand from the force of the blow. He made a mental note to train even harder when he was back into his old life. He was in terrible shape. He saw Einhorn's phone lying in the grass where he had thrown it in disgust. He had to get a hold of it somehow. The guard was holding Jordan and shoving him towards the hotel. Soon the guard would push him past the cell phone. He would have no chance to retrieve it after that. Think, Kline, think. He was trying to focus. His head hurt like hell from the punch.

Jordan made like he was going to throw up. The guard saw this and let him go for a split second apparently not wanting some asshole throwing up on him. Jordan staggered a few feet and then fell to the ground on all fours. He had figured the distance right. He had fallen right over the cell phone.

He pretended to retch, scooping up the phone as he did so. He really did want time to retch, but the guard pulled him up roughly again. Jordan still felt weak from the blows he had received and couldn't fight back. He slipped the phone into his free pocket. This would definitely not have happened in his prime years, Jordan thought. He would have taken the guard out quickly, even if he were the larger man. He tried the box again. This time he felt it come free, loosened when the bastard had hit him so hard and he had fallen. He could feel the pain from the screw embedded in his thigh.

He took the box out of his pocket slowly and wrapped his hand around it, shielding it from the guards' view with his body. The guard had shoved and kicked him halfway to the hotel now. Jordan figured that he had to act now. He pulled the box out of his pocket and spat in the guards' face at the same time. With all his remaining strength he hurled the box as far as he could towards the hotel. The next blow was not long in arriving. It landed on his face. The punch hit him on the side of his head, spinning him around. He was face-down on the soft grass again, the taste of blood more pronounced this time. Maybe a broken nose too, he thought. Jesus, he was getting his ass kicked royally.

He slowly turned over on his back and smiled at the brute looking down at him. He was beginning to swallow blood. He spat some out. It landed on his chest. He laughed at the guard who kicked him viciously in the ribs. Jordan did not feel it; he was beyond pain now.

"One more time and I will kill you, you bastard," the guard said as he picked Jordan up with one hand.

"Okay, okay, I'll be good from now on." Jordan mumbled through a mouthful of blood. Blood dripped down his front now—not a pretty sight but it did not disturb Jordan. He had been there before. He was having trouble concentrating now from the force of the kicks and punches. He shook his head. His vision cleared a little and so too did his mind. He fumbled in his pocket for the cell phone. His hand was throbbing. It was difficult but he managed to flip it open. It was his guess now that signals could actually get through to the bomb under the steps. He hoped that he had thrown the box far enough.

TABA HILTON HOTEL.
SATURDAY, SEPTEMBER 8TH.
CONVENTION DAY.

Irit had gone straight to the hotel after giving CNN the note. She had entered through the front entrance sure that everyone would be at the ceremony and that the hotel would be much less guarded than before. She was right; there were only regular security at the door, with some American marines, Egyptian security service personnel and Israeli security on duty.

She made her way quickly to one of the hidden seating corners at the back of the lobby and settled down to wait and see what would happen. She realized that she was trembling and could not control it. She felt cold and alone. After a while she could see Shalom being brought in under heavy security and could not stifle a laugh. He was dressed only in his underwear and looked ridiculous being guarded by all the uniformed security. God how she wished she had her camera with her; this would make a priceless shot.

She realized that he had undressed so as not to present a threat to the gathering witnessing history. It was clear that he was unarmed. They would not shoot a crazy man in front of all those people. At least that was what he was banking on. He was right. Irit saw that at last they brought him some clothes, and although under heavy guard, they were treating him fairly. He did not look too much the worse for his ordeal out on the grass. What a great guy he was, and not that young any more.

People ran by to get away from the casino area, running as if their life depended on it. They were tripping up over each other in their panic to get away from the scene. She hoped that no one would be trampled to death or injured badly. Good old CNN, she thought, they had come through for her. They had publicly announced the bomb threat. In reality they did not have much choice. Better be safe than really sorry. This was not after all just a common gathering—this was the gathering of the decade.

Her thoughts turned to Jordan. Where was he? What had happened to him? Was he okay? He should have been here by now.

It was clear that the signals had been blocked since there had been no explosion. They had saved countless lives and had possibly saved the peace agreement. That would have to wait. What about Jordan? Was he in danger, was he still alive? A feeling of dread came over her and she sat back trembling into the sofa, tears running down her cheeks.

TABA.
SATURDAY, SEPTEMBER 8TH.
CONVENTION DAY.

The guard punched Jordan between his shoulders from behind sending him stumbling forward in pain. He fell to the ground again, losing his balance while his hand was trapped inside his pocket. He raised his head and looked towards the casino entrance. He could see Einhorn, Heller, and Hofstein crossing the stage and entering the hall through which the leaders had just evacuated. Their guns were in plain view now. He knew what they were going to do and had to stop them.

There was only one way. He felt the open cell phone in his hand, felt along the buttons below the screen. He prayed that he had the right key and pressed hard. God, he hoped he had pressed the right button.

He struggled up and turned away from the casino in time to see the guard coming at him again, clenched fist ready to inflict more damage. Jordan closed his eyes and waited for the inevitable punishment.

The punch never landed. The guard never got to Jordan. The entrance to the casino erupted in a huge explosion as the bomb beneath detonated. A massive fireball reached up into the sky. The whole entrance to the casino disappeared in an instant. Debris was blown upwards into the air. Chunks of marble, wood, metal, and glass started raining down all around.

Jordan saw nothing of this. The shockwave from the blast had picked him up like a limp rag doll and tossed him ten, maybe fifteen meters into the air. He slammed into something really hard and felt stabs of excruciating pain flooding all over his body. He tried to open his eyes but they were covered in blood. He knew he was wounded badly but had no way of knowing how badly. He could not feel his legs, his body. It hurt like hell to breathe. He could vaguely make out the smell of burning flesh and explosives. Was it his burning flesh? He felt cold. Maybe this time he was going to die, maybe it was his turn. He was having difficulty breathing, his mouth full of blood. Then, mercifully, the pain receded, and everything went black as he lost consciousness.

TABA HILTON HOTEL.
SATURDAY, SEPTEMBER 8TH.
CONVENTION DAY.

Irit had figured that it was safe now to approach the lobby bar and get iced water. No one had noticed her sitting in the corner. She got up and was crossing the short distance between the seating area and the bar when the whole building shook violently. The large panoramic windows on both sides of the lobby shattered from the blast and rained a cascade of glass down onto the marble floor. For a brief moment it made the sound of a really heavy downpour, like a monsoon. Pieces of debris flew into the lobby, and Irit ducked down onto the floor instinctively.

In a few seconds it was all over. The explosion was followed by a deathly silence. Then people started screaming, traumatized by the blast.

Irit lay on the floor. Fear and panic welled up inside of her. She knew where Jordan was now. She knew that she had to get to him. She had to go look for him. She had to know that he was all right.

She got up quickly and ran towards the hotel entrance. Shalom saw her approaching and joined her as she exited the hotel. All the security people guarding him had run to the scene of the bombing.

As they rounded the corner and the casino hall came into view they entered a thick, choking cloud of dust and smoke heavy with the smell of burning flesh, plastic, and explosives. Water gushed high into the air from fire hydrants that had disintegrated in the blast. What was left of the hall was on fire.

They ran to the bank of seats opposite the entrance steps but all they encountered was a heap of bent and mangled steel. There were no bodies lying in or around the seating mess. They ran up the broken steps to the hall and saw five charred body pieces lying not far from where they guessed the doorway had been. They saw with relief that none of them looked like it was Jordan. A burned, black decapitated head lay under a door that had been blown off its hinges in the blast. Shalom thought he recognized Hofstein.

Fragments of clothing were still attached to the blackened corpses that had not been ripped off in the blast. The explosion had sent all the tables and chairs flying to the far end of the hall where they lay on top of each other in a heap, splintered and broken. What had been fine china and glassware was reduced to tiny pieces that covered the hall in a fine rain. Forks and knives, blasted into flight by the explosion, lay embedded in the walls. It was a surreal landscape, something out of a Hollywood horror blockbuster.

They ran on. They scanned the hall but could not find Jordan. All of the dignitaries and all the leaders were being guarded outside the far end of the hall. The bomb attempt had failed in its purpose.

But where was Jordan? Was he alive? Irit had to fight to keep total panic from taking over. Shalom held her hand and told her reassuringly that all would be all right, that Jordan would be fine, and that they would find him. They picked their way carefully around slabs of broken concrete, jutting metal, shredded wood, and myriad pieces of debris as they continued their search. They covered the area quickly and methodically but found no trace of Jordan. Strange that nobody had died this side of the blast. They did not see any bodies apart from those lying at entrance to the hall. They were fast running out of places to look for Jordan. Where the hell was he?

After a while Shalom suggested to Irit gently that it would be better if they went back to the hotel and waited for some sign from Jordan. Perhaps, he told Irit, he would just walk in, smiling as always. Another mission accomplished. She knew it was wishful thinking.

They slowly made their way through the smoke and debris and up the incline towards the hotel. Irit was trembling uncontrollably. Shalom held her tight as they continued up the slope. He feared the worst. He had seen soldiers vaporized by direct hits on the battlefield. He pushed the thought out of his mind.

As they came up the slope Shalom thought he could see something lying just on the other side of one of the garden paths that ran below the hotel. The path ran through what had been manicured lawns and beautiful gardens. It looked like someone had left a dirty red rag laying there, perhaps one of the gardeners. A short wall that framed the path and separated it from the gardens shielded the rag. Shalom broke his hold on Irit and approached.

He could see now that it was a bloodied human hand. Oh God no, he prayed, but instinctively knew that he had found Jordan.

Shalom bent down and slowly turned Jordan over. He was a bloody mess. Irit screamed behind him, and he shielded her from the sight of Jordan's broken and bloodied body. He motioned her to back off. He held Jordan's wrist in his hand and felt for a pulse. Nothing. He wiped some blood from the wrist and tried again. Then he stood up quickly and shouted at the top of his voice: "Get a medic here right away. We've got a live one. Get a fucking medic here. Now!"

YOSEFTAL HOSPITAL, EILAT. SEPTEMBER 20TH.

It was ten in the morning. The hot summer months had passed, but the heat towards the end of September in Eilat was still relentless. The wall-mounted air conditioning unit in the room was battling bravely to offset the heat streaming in through the light cotton curtains. A fly buzzed on the window, trapped between the thin curtains and the hot glass.

Outside the hospital the citizens of Eilat were going about their normal lives. The trauma of the Taba Convention was receding. It was becoming part of history in this troubled region, pushed aside by a new wave of suicide terror attacks perpetrated in Tel Aviv and Jerusalem.

In Taba the bulldozers were busy clearing the debris from the explosion that had destroyed the Hilton Casino and Grand Hall. Plans were already underway to rebuild them.

The world leaders, shaken but unhurt, had departed for home soon after the explosion cut short the ill-fated convention. The White House had already announced plans to convene for the signing of the peace treaty. This time it would be in Washington. The date was still to be announced.

Doctors and medics had rushed to the scene where Jordan lay wounded in Taba. After working on him for an hour they had managed to stabilize him enough to be airlifted to Yoseftal hospital by helicopter. He had undergone life-saving surgery in Eilat. There had been no time to transport him to a hospital up north better equipped to handle his injuries. Doctors had been flown to Eilat to operate on him.

Following surgery Jordan had been kept in the intensive care unit in an induced coma to allow his body to better heal from the shock it had taken. On the fifteenth of September he was taken out of the coma. Five days later he was transferred to the orthopedic ward to recuperate. He was making good progress. The doctors were pleased. Irit had not left his side throughout the period, except to shower and change clothes.

She was dozing fitfully when Jordan finally opened his eyes. He felt like he had just gone all thirteen rounds with Muhammad Ali. He could feel that he was heavily bandaged on his lower body and arms. One arm was in plaster, and from the weight of it he knew that one of his legs was, too. He had a hell of a headache. His head felt as if it were about to burst open. This pain couldn't possibly be from the beating at the hands of that guard, he thought.

He turned his head painfully and looked at Irit stretched out uncomfortably on the cheap imitation leather armchair by his bed, her hand still clutching his. He gave her hand a small squeeze.

She opened her large almond-shaped eyes slowly. A victorious and radiant smile crept over her face. A tear coursed down her cheek. For what seemed an eternity they looked at each other, their eyes conversing, no need for words. They knew each other's thoughts.

Eventually she spoke, "Welcome back, Jordan Kline. We've missed you. It's been too long."

"Where in the hell am I? How long have I been out? What date is it?" he asked her, trying painfully to get a little more comfortable.

"Well, where could you be with three broken ribs, a punctured lung, a broken arm, and a broken leg, my love? Not to forget the broken nose also. You were blown away by the bomb, Jordan. You landed up on one of the paths that run through the lawns by the flower beds. Quite a ways from the casino. Shalom found you. You were barely alive. They brought you back from the dead. But that is enough of that. Good news is we're not far from home; bad news is you'll be here for a while. This time it's you who is in Yoseftal, my love, not me." She smiled impishly. "And no, we cannot add this room to our locations, at least not yet. The date today is September the twentieth, and you have been out for twelve days."

He let his eyes wander around the room. It was full of flowers, full of colors. Get well cards had been placed all around on the shelves, the tables, even taped to the wall.

He smiled and then turned serious. "What happened down there? What was the outcome, Irit? Tell me what happened."

"You've been gone for twelve days, Jord, but I've kept the newspapers for you. Both the *Yediot Ahronoth* and *Ma'ariv* issues. You cannot make the effort to read yet but I will recap for you, my love. The international community is blaming various Arab fundamentalist splinter factions for the bombing in Taba. They are being blamed for the attempt to undermine the peace agreement by assassinating the leaders during the convention. We found the cell phone in your pocket. We turned it in to the agency. It was the proof that we needed to implicate Hofstein and the others, along with the plans showing the pipeline. We are clear now, Jordan, no one hunting us—no APB's. Pleasant change. The prime minister would like to see you when you are well enough to travel, but hush hush. Not many know of our involvement, and he wants to keep it that way. So do I."

"The conspirators turned out to be the heroes as far as the world is concerned. Only five poor souls were killed in the carnage. Everyone else managed to get clear before the bomb detonated. The killed were two Israeli guards; David Hofstein, the contractor; Dan Heller, the politician; and Ariel Einhorn, the deputy chief of Mossad. They were apparently killed by the explosion while rushing to help evacuate the hall. One of the guards was found dead on the grass not far from you. Apparently they think that he shielded you from much of the blast with his body; otherwise, things could have been different."

"Dan Heller was given a state funeral. Einhorn was buried with full military honors as befitted his rank. Hofstein was buried in a quiet corner of the Holon cemetery although hundreds accompanied him on his last journey. All buried with the thanks of a grateful nation for their efforts in trying to save innocent lives. Anyway, that's what the papers printed. An interesting account of events, right? It's just so lucky the terrorists blew the place up just a little too late, isn't it my love? Oh, I almost forgot. Shalom will take a while to live down the picture of him rushing in underpants across the Hilton lawns. One of the people attending the convention thoughtfully snapped him as he did his stunt. It was all over the Eilat weekly. He's in hiding but told me to ring when you woke up. He said he'd come out of hiding for that."

"The authorities and CNN are still looking for the mystery woman who delivered the note. I think that just about covers events. It is certainly enough for you now. You must rest. Oh, I almost forgot. The hotel is running smoothly. The staff can't wait to get you back. You must get stronger. Welcome back, Jordan Kline. Welcome back, my love," she said it triumphantly. She smiled and bent down to kiss him on the cheek.

Jordan inhaled the smell of her close to him. He whispered softly into her ear, "Irit, I am going to marry you."

Stephen W. Ayers

Coming soon in The Jordan Kline Series:

THE RIGHTEOUS WITHIN
The Jordan Kline Series Book 2.
2011

THE KHARTA CONSPIRACY
The Jordan Kline Series Book 3.
2012

www.stephenwayers.com

www.stephenwilliamayers.com

Stephen W. Ayers